P9-CFE-746

HOUSE OF PURPLE CEDAR

HOUSE OF PURPLE CEDAR

Tim Tingle

Cinco Puntos Press
EL PASO, TEXAS

7
Tingle

Printed in the United States.

First Edition
10 9 8 7 6 5 4 3 2 1

Library of Congress Cataloging-in-Publication Data

Tingle, Tim.
  House of purple cedar / by Tim Tingle.—First edition.
      pages cm
ISBNs 978-1-935955-69-6 (Cloth : alk. paper); 978-1-935955-24-5 (Paper : alk. paper); 978-1-935955-25-2 (E-Book).
  1. Choctaw Indians—Oklahoma—Fiction. 2. Oklahoma—History—Land Rush, 1893—Fiction. I. Title.

PS3570.I525H68 2014
813'.54—dc23

2013010570

Book and cover design by Anne M. Giangiulio
Hoke, hoke.

To Dr. Geary Hobson, *the quiet leader and patriarch of a generation of North American Indian writers*

A NOTE BEFORE THE RECKONING

Rose • Winter of 1967

The hour has come to speak of troubled times. Though the bodies have long ago returned to dust, too many ghosts still linger in the graveyards. You are old enough. You need to know. It is time we spoke of Skullyville.

I was born and raised in the Choctaw town of Skullyville, where I attended New Hope Academy for Girls—till it burned on New Year's Eve, 1896. My grandmother went there too. She met my grandfather when he was a student at nearby Fort Coffee School for Boys. By the time Oklahoma became a state, all of downtown Skullyville had burned. The stores, the businesses, the stagecoach stop, all burned. We knew Nahullos set the fires. They wanted us gone.

Almost everyone from that time is dead now, their faces blurred, their stories scratched like formal words in old, old letters.

But once we were alive, all of us, and when good people, Choctaw and Nahullo both, step over our Skullyville graves, we sing as best we can, we sing those old hymns and songs, for they were everything to us. Our religion, our joys, even our sins, they all made up the music. We Amen! at the top of our lungs beneath the brush arbors, we sweat and toil in our gardens and fields and brood over our livestock and our babies both.

I am speaking as a dead one now, and soon I will be. No time to waste. This story must be told. To see not only the unfolding of events but the meaning I ascribe to them, you must know of the vision, for the house of this story is built upon my vision.

The dream came sometimes once a week, sometimes not so often, and always in the deepest hour of night, when neither day's end nor dawn cast any light. This vision that I thought was a nightmare began when I was twelve years old. Though many years passed, in the vision I am always twelve, always sitting in the same church pew, always with my family in what at first appears to be a normal Sunday morning.

Pokoni, my grandmother, has not yet entered the church. I am saving her a seat next to me near the window, where we can both stare out at the swaying trees. Brother Willis reads the scripture in that ponderous tone of his, before he lurches into a sermon "likely to raise the dead," as Pokoni always said.

When Pokoni appears, she walks past our row and approaches the altar, ignoring all else and staring at the wooden wall behind the pulpit. Soon everyone is following her gaze. Even after years of witnessing, I am still startled at the strangeness of the sight.

A man, and I thought I might never know who it was, is slumped over and hanging, his clothing nailed to the back of the church. His body is slowly writhing, his head lifts with every breath, and his vacant eyes return our stare. Always when you thought you knew who hung before you, then you saw another.

Brother Willis steps aside and Pokoni continues walking, but she now becomes a panther, black and silky-skinned, and now she is my Pokoni, then the panther once again.

Through all the days of death and suffering, I longed to see the face of this writhing one, nailed to the cedar planks of our church.

FIRE AND ICE

REVEREND WILLIS & THE BOYS

Young Rose • January 1896

I always feared death by ice. Much more than death by fire. Even as a little girl listening to Brother Willis preach about how the world would end, I was never afraid of fire, of burning up. Fire was warm and if it got to be too hot, you just scooted away. The only real problem with fire was starting it in the morning. Everybody else was asleep, and you had to climb out of bed and freeze your fingers fetching firewood so they could stay curled up and comfy.

"Rose, are you up yet?" Momma said every morning, while the moon still shone and the sun hadn't even thought of waking up. The walls in our house were so thin, she never had to shout.

"Is it morning yet?" Daddy asked, and I could hear him roll over. I knew he covered his head with his pillow to block out the coming day.

"It will be soon," Momma always said. "No need to waste it."

No need to waste it meant they could sleep for half an hour longer, but I better get up and start the morning fire. My grandma and grandpa, Amafo and Pokoni, lived with us too. I guess it's better said we lived with them since this used to be their house. Daddy liked to tell about cutting the cedar and sawing the boards, helping Amafo build this house when he was still a boy.

"I was just a neighbor kid, but I knew if I was a good worker, he'd let me court your mother someday," my father used to say. My little brother Jamey always made a secret face when he heard this. But there were no secrets, not from Momma.

"You don't want to be like those lazy Willis boys, do you, Jamey?" she'd say. "They get whippings sometimes. You don't want a whipping, do you?"

Course that never happened to me or Jamey, neither one. We never got a whipping. But the Willis boys did—and always by their momma—never by their preacher daddy. I never liked seeing anybody get whipped, but especially not the Willis boys. I know they gave living Hades to their big sister Roberta Jean, but there was just too many of 'em to expect anything good, and the how many of them there were, that wasn't their fault.

"Even a good man, a preaching man, brings troubles on himself sometimes," Pokoni used to say, shaking her head at the Willis boys.

I remember her saying that very thing one Easter Sunday when the boys stole the baby Jesus from the packed-away Nativity box. They buried him in the graveyard by the church to see if he would rise from the dead during the service. While Brother Willis was telling about how the stone was rolled away, seven-year-old George Willis started hollering.

"Jesus lives!" he shouted. "He's coming outta the ground right now! Everybody come see!"

What those boys saw was a skunk stirring up leaves around the baby Jesus gravesite, but they didn't know it. They all scrambled out the windows yelling louder than their daddy ever did. Blue Ned Willis was five at the time, and he chimed in with, "We're going to meet Juh-eeee-sus!" He said it over and over again, sounding more like his daddy every time.

The older boys saw Jesus first and were able to stop, but not Blue Ned. He plowed right ahead, stepping over the rise of graves, dodging tombstones, till he learned a life lesson he would never forget. One of the world's ugliest sites is the close-up view of a skunk's backside. With the tail raised.

The skunk sprayed young Blue Ned with a cloud that could be seen—and smelled—from all the way inside the church. Blue Ned rolled on the ground, rubbing his eyes and crying. As the skunk disappeared into the woods, his brother George remarked, "Jesus just wants to be left alone, look like to me."

Reverend Willis simply prayed a closing prayer and waited by his wagon, his head bowed and clutching his Bible, while the Bobb brothers and Mrs. Willis handled the situation. Older brother Samuel, sitting on the front pew with his mother, never even turned his head to see what trouble his brothers were causing. He soon joined his father on the buckboard.

We had been married for over forty years, Samuel Willis and I, and were visiting what was left of Skullyville one Sunday afternoon. He told me how later that evening, during one of his night walks, he found a rope and a burlap sack in the woods by the cemetery, the sort of sack one would use to tote a skunk. Someone, out of meanness, had planted that skunk to disrupt our Easter worship service. The memories came flooding back and we shook with laughter, a very hard thing to do, seeing how the woods had reclaimed our once fine community.

"My daddy thought he would never get the congregation back. Every time he spoke the word Jesus…"

"In that booming voice of his…"

"I can hear him now…"

"Wish we could…"

"Someone would start coughing…"

"To cover up their laughing."

"But he did it," Samuel said. "Oh yeah. He did it. He brought us back. I don't know who laughed that final laugh. I was too scared to turn around. I knew how mad he was getting, Sunday after Sunday. My father leaned over the pulpit and told us all, 'Make your choice. Either get up and follow that Hell-bound skunk to the woods or let Jesus return to his church, but don't be stinking up this temple with your laughter when his Holy name is spoken!' Nobody laughed after that."

I thought Samuel was about to break out in tears when we came to the clearing where the church used to stand, where his daddy was buried, but he didn't. Samuel just looked at the well-kept graves for the longest time.

"I never thought they would burn the church," he finally said.

"At least the church was empty," I replied. "The school was full of girls."

FIRST AND FINAL DAYS AT NEW HOPE ACADEMY
Rose • 1896

Yes, I always feared death by ice. But fire was nothing to fear. You could control fire. The sun was fire. Summer was fire. Cooking, that was fire.

Ice was different. It rode the air. It stung everything it touched. Ice killed the corn, stopped the rivers, killed weak animals. On walks in the woods you would find them frozen dead, their mouths open and crying for something to stop this burning ice.

Roberta Jean and I were boarding at New Hope Academy for Girls that year, rooming with twenty other girls. The school was only a few miles from home, but we were young girls. I was eleven and Roberta Jean was twelve. *We would just be better off staying at school during the week,* our parents figured. We were home by supper every Friday and back to New Hope after church and Sunday dinner. While home we gathered whatever we needed for the next week at school—clothes, pencils, knitting thread and needles.

A week before Christmas we moved back home for the holidays. Christmas Eve we all climbed on Amafo's wagon and Daddy drove us to church. For three hours we sang Christmas songs in Choctaw to welcome the baby Jesus. "Away in a Manger" was always my favorite.

Christmas morning Daddy appeared with a wreath he'd carved from cedar branches. "I saw Maggie selling them at the hardware store in Spiro," he said, "but I made this one."

The wreath was decorated with red and green ribbons, and he proudly hung it on the wall. When we opened presents, Daddy untied the ribbons from the wreath.

"Rose," he said, "these ribbons are for you, to wear when you go back to school."

"*Yakoke*, Daddy," I said and gave him a long, sweet hug.

On the last day of December of 1896, the frost was sifting down, heavying the tree limbs with a silvery shine. We arrived back at school in the early afternoon. Tomorrow, New Year's Day, was a grand day of celebration for everyone, girls and teachers too. The boys from Fort Coffee would wander over, those shy and mumbling boys who almost never spoke so you could hear them.

We would share our first meal of the new year, 1897, with the boys. The cooks from New Hope would work all morning, according to Roberta Jean, "dashing and fussing and frying and stewing," while we girls put finishing touches on gifts we had made for our friends. Our boy friends!

I was new to the school and I shook all over with excitement. Since I did not have a *special* friend, Amafo helped me make a pair of stickball bats for some nice young man.

"Some lucky young man's gonna get 'em," my Amafo said, whacking the sticks against each other. "These make good chant sticks come dancing time!"

All the girls talked at the same time, showing everyone what they had made. *Hoke*, not everybody talked. I spotted Lillie, a shy little girl and tiny as a toddler. She was sitting on the edge of her bed, folding and unfolding a blue handkerchief she had made. She didn't talk. She never talked, at least not so anybody could hear her.

Lillie was deaf and talked with her hands. I didn't know her kind of talk, but I was learning. I walked to her bedside and she looked up at me. I pointed to the handkerchief and then to Lillie.

She nodded quick and a bright new smile crawled across her face. I reached out my palms and she handed it to me. I held it to my face and made a big but soundless word with my lips.

"*Achukma*, good," I said. Lillie nodded and her hands made a sign.

"Thank you," they said. I knew that word.

Besides Roberta Jean, Lillie was my favorite friend at New Hope. She was like my little sister, my sweet and precious Choctaw sister.

Dark came early that night.

"Everybody to bed," Miss Palmer shouted. "We have a long day tomorrow." The frost snuck up on us that New Year's Eve. We were caught without any warm blankets. All we had were the school blankets of thin green wool, worn almost threadbare by years of use.

I don't know how long I had been asleep when Roberta Jean woke me up crawling under the covers.

"Too cold to sleep alone," she said, and her breath floated in the air.

She brought her blanket with her and snuggled up close, but she was freezing cold from being out of bed for just a minute. She rolled over, facing away from me. The soles of her feet touched my calves. They were so cold I shivered, but I kept my mouth shut and rode out this little sliver of cold, knowing that in a few minutes her body warmth would feel good and we could sleep like the Choctaw sisters we were.

I soon drifted off to dreaming, dreaming about the most beautiful Sunday of my life. I was maybe five years old. The snow fell overnight in fat, light flakes, twisting and dancing outside my window when the moon peeped through. I pulled up the quilts, propped myself up and watched for hours, moving my palms in a snowfall hand-dance, all to the rhythm of the snow.

I heard my grandfather creak down the stairs to light the fire. I leapt out of bed, wrapped the lightest quilt around me, and went to visit with him, just me and him. We could have a good talk.

"Rose, baby. What you doing up so early?"

"Just come to see you, Amafo."

"Well, ain't that nice. You come set your blanket on the floor here by the stove." Amafo was stoking the fire and, sure enough, he found live embers where nobody else would even think of looking. He pushed and poked 'em to burning, then turned to fetch more wood from the dog-run.

"I'll have it warm 'fore you know it," he said. I curled up on the floor and fell asleep till he returned with two armloads of stovecut logs. I struggled to my knees to help, but Amafo said, "You just lay on back. I can do this."

When the fire was cracking and warming through the metal, he said, "Now, what we need to talk about, my Rosebud?"

"Ummmm." I stretched and yawned, smiling at him calling me Rosebud. "You think we'll go to church today?"

"Well, I think we will. Let's take a look outside." He scooped me up, blanket and all, and carried me to the front window. We could hear Daddy and Momma stirring in their room, but Amafo just looked their way without saying anything. This was our time. He held me over his belly with his left arm and pulled the curtain back with his right.

"Oh! Amafo, look!" The snow made hills and valleys in the front yard, swoops and dips of purest white, halfway up the tree trunks of the nearby evergreens. To the west the moon still hung yellow, but the sun was coming up. It colored the snow banks, pink and pretty as a puppy's tongue. The pine limbs hung heavy with icicles, sparkling and dripping.

"Yes, Rosebud, I believe we going to church. Snow's gonna melt by noon, be mostly gone when church gets out. Be a purty good ride getting there, don't you think?"

"I think so, Amafo," I said. "Yes, I think you probly right. Looks like we'll be going to church. We better tell Daddy when he gets up. Maybe you can tell him?"

"I 'spect I better," said Amafo, carrying me to a nice warm spot by the stove. "Now, you take a little nap while I make the coffee. How 'bout that, hon?"

"Okay," I said, and in less than a minute I was sleeping sound.

THE BURNING OF NEW HOPE

In my dream I was curled up on the cedar floor, next to Amafo. The icy chill of morning was gone and my cheeks now felt the sweet bath of fire. I pulled my quilt down. The fire lapped hot.

"Wake up, hon," Amafo called, shaking me hard.

I did, but I was not at home anymore. I was at school, at New Hope.

"I musta been dreaming," I said, stretching and yawning.

"Wake up! Get up, hurry!" Roberta Jean leaned over me hollering. Smoke swirled about her head. "Fire! Everything's on fire!"

I was on my feet and we started running, our blankets wrapped around us. We shouldered down the stairs with the other girls. The teachers pushed us aside and ran upstairs against the flow.

"Is everybody out? Is everybody safe?" They said it over and over, but no one answered. We all just ran.

Once outside, I stood clinging to Roberta Jean, shivering and watching the skeleton of our schoolhouse crack and fall, bone by bone. It finally heaved a shuddering breath and fell into itself. A flock of small flaming boards flew in our direction. We dashed to the woods, brushing embers from our blankets.

This was not the fire I knew. There was nothing warm and calming in those yellow and blue flames. I was watching ice, cold bitter ice, come to life, rising from the frozen flames to claim our school.

We were driven by fire to freeze in the ice.

"Lillie! Lillie! Lillie!" The calls rang out through the mad darkness and fiery light. "Lillie!"

"Why does that lady keep screaming Lillie's name?" I asked, covering my ears. "Make her stop."

"It's her mother," said Roberta Jean.

"Then she knows Lillie can't hear her."

Those words floated back at me and I heard them for the first time. I stared at my own breath. Beyond my breath I saw the flames, like flicking and mocking tongues.

Lillie Chukma, good Lillie, was deaf.

She could not hear her mother.

She could not hear the calls to leave the building.

She slept like the seven-year-old baby that she was.

So watchful and eager to please—so very, very deaf.

I dropped my jaw and my face quivered. I tried to scream. Tears flew down my cheeks, tears that will never stop flowing till I see her at Judgment Day and wrap my arms around her. I will tell her how sweet she was and is and how much I loved seeing her every morning, how much I loved kneeling by her bed for prayers each night.

"Lillie," I finally sputtered when I had the breath to sob.

Roberta held me closer and we pulled the blankets over our heads. Our knees shook and buckled and we drifted to the ground to sit in the melting snow, a dark green cone of wool and skin and bones and life while all around us swirled children and teachers and Nahullos and Choctaws and Cherokees and Christians all. But their running meant nothing.

Death by fire had claimed Lillie Chukma.

It was the Bobb brothers, Efram and Ben, who lifted the rafters from our fallen, smoking room and found Lillie's body. Efram raised the roof while Ben kicked aside the still-burning boards to find her charred and fetal-tiny body. They gave it over to the Reverend Henry Willis and he carried Lillie Chukma to her mother.

Roberta Jean tugged me after her and we shuffle-stepped to stand behind Mrs. Chukma. She took her daughter, Lillie Chukma, took her in her outstretched arms, all the while staring at Reverend Willis. Finally her gaze settled on her baby. When she spoke, her words spoke the night.

"A mother should not have to bury a child."

This tiny scene was played out for only a few of us. The rest were running to render aid, only to feel the biting flames that claimed our school. My chest hurt and my lungs ached. I knew that something truly was breaking apart as I stood and watched, wounded by the biggest loss of my life, the loss of New Hope Academy for Girls.

We turned our backs on all of this and walked as the unseen dead might walk. Through smoky fog we walked, Roberta Jean and I, floating against the stream of urgent runners, drawn to their own drowning vision of hope. We wrapped our arms around each other's waists, muted by our grief.

We returned to our small encampment and wrapped the blankets over our heads. We fell to the moist ground and went to grabbing and clutching at each other, first our hair, yanking and pulling, angry pulling, on whatever gave good holding place, arm or foot or ear or skin of thigh. We clinched our fists and flailed away, crying loud and biting even, all the while knowing we did so in the name of love, the only love still granted us in this the most perverse of bleeding worlds.

THE FUNERAL AND EFRAM BOBB

January 1897

Efram Bobb was a stonemason. He was trained by his father, who was himself a master mason. From his early teens Efram displayed, to the immense delight of Mister Bobb, a feel for stone that is impossible to teach. He matched stones for the sheer beauty of their porous skin.

"Every stone," Efram said, "has its own way of speaking to a man who'll listen."

The first time Mister Bobb heard Efram speak of *listening to a stone*, he stood up and stared at the back of his son's head. Efram closed his eyes and ran his fingers over the grainy calluses of rock, the slick, unbroken whisperings of stone. Mister Bobb shook his head in wonder. His eyes filled with tears and he whispered a prayer of thanks for having such a son.

As Efram grew, he matured in every way but height. Five feet five inches tall, he moved with the ease and grace of a small man, though his girth was anything but small. The daily pounding of his mallet chiseled Efram's torso into a gaudy specimen of muscle, a tree stump with a belt and britches. His hands hung well below his knees.

Mister Bobb was so proud of Efram, he often flung his arms around his son to show his joy. The two sometimes boxed, slamming their fists against each other's hardened stomachs. Seeing this, a way so counter to the tribal norm, kinfolks and friends would quietly laugh and mock the two.

Efram was seventeen years old when Taloa was born to his father's sister.

"She'll be as pretty as her mother," his father said, standing over her cradle and smiling big and broad. She was not named Taloa on her birthing day. That name would come soon enough.

The Saturday following Taloa's birthday, Efram and his brother Ben accompanied their father on a buying trip to the hardware store in nearby Spiro, a Nahullo town. They bought cattle feed and a new mule harness. While Ben spoke to loud-laughing Maggie, who ran the store's affairs, Efram and his father stood on the sidewalk.

"Son," his father said, "we need to talk about something." When Efram turned to face him, his father swung a hard left fist and struck him squarely in the navel. "I can still kick your butt!" he said. "That's what we need to talk about."

It was the last thing his father ever said to him. As Efram doubled over, his father spotted a spike in the middle of Main Street.

"Somebody gonna get hurt," he muttered, stepping from the sidewalk. He paused to let a mule-driven wagon pass. The lead mule stepped on the spike and lurched, loosening the strap from a hundred-pound barrel of flour. Efram stood helpless on the sidewalk and watched the barrel roll from the wagon and strike his father in the head before slamming into his chest.

From twenty feet away he heard the sharp and brittle crack of ribs beneath the crushing weight. Efram leapt to his father, lifted his broken body, and laid him on the sidewalk. A jagged piece of rib had pierced his father's lungs and he drowned in his own blood.

The next morning Efram carved the tombstone for his father. Little Taloa, barely a week old, cried and cried with the grieving women at Mister Bobb's funeral. Thus they named her Singing One—*Taloa* in Choctaw.

Following the burning of New Hope, Efram was asked to carve the gravestones for the twenty girls who died. The morning of the burial ceremony, he visited with grieving parents and family members, many of whom had traveled several days to attend the service. Beneath a shady grove by the gravesite they gathered, huddled in blankets from the cold.

As he stood to speak, Efram's eyes settled on the dark clumps of earth rising from the ground, and the bundled bodies in the twenty wooden coffins. Steamy fog hovered over the fresh-dug holes.

"All respect will be given in the cutting of the stone," Efram said. Mothers and fathers nodded and cried softly, surrounded by their living children. They looked to Efram, who stood with his head bowed, holding his broad-brimmed hat in both hands and rocking slightly. Fat tears rolled down his cheeks and he made no move to hide them. Efram's ten year-old cousin Taloa, they knew, was among those who died.

చ్•ఈ

Rose

As we neared the graveyard in the early morning dark, we passed under the arms of fat-trunked sycamore trees. Through the gray branches we could see the shapes of wailing women, their long black dresses, their heads covered with black scarves that hid their faces. My father pulled our wagon to the roadside and eased to a slow halt. Whiteface stomped the ground and munched on brittle sycamore leaves. We sat for a long while before descending into the world of grief.

My father took off his hat and closed his eyes. The old women howled and fell to the ground. When they rose again, their singing cut the day in half. There were two days, the day we lived in, ate in, slept in, smiled and cried in—then there was this day of grief, a day I never knew before.

Nothing was like before, nor would it ever be.

Unlike most funerals, with the wailers grieving for us all, many of the wailers on this day had lost a grandchild in the flames. Their cries took on a purple undertow of deeper grief. Mothers of the dead joined the older women, as they had never done.

"Minti! Minti!" a mother called. "Come, my baby, come!"

The sun came into view to the east and her cries took on an urgent air, as if her baby girl was lost and wandering in the woods. The mother grew more desperate as the sun threatened to rise and devour her baby, just as the fire had done.

My father stepped from the wagon and lifted Jamey and me to the ground, then helped my mother, then Pokoni, and Amafo. By the time we stepped through the trees, the sun was casting yellow rays on the graves of my newly dead girlfriends. A swell of anger took hold of me and shook my body till I could barely stand.

Pokoni reached from behind me and held me by the waist. She laid her head on my shoulder and there we stood, leaning one upon the other. I parted my lips and breathed in the gardenia fragrance, as much a part of Pokoni as her thick black hair.

Brother Willis always stood so strong, but on this day his whole body sagged, from the skin of his wrinkled cheeks to the knees of his britches, still muddy from his night of kneeling and praying in his garden. But when he lifted his eyes to the Choctaw gathering, the coming light took hold. He pulled a hymnbook from behind his back and became the man we knew.

If ever I have had—in the course of all that I have witnessed in my eighty-four years—reason to doubt the presence of the good and living God, I only need turn to the doings of Brother Willis on this sacred day of mourning to restore my faith in the Everlasting.

"We will sing a hymn before we hear the word of the Lord," he said. "Oh, Come Let Us Adore Him," he sang, and how could we not but join him?

> *Oh, come let us adore him,*
> *Oh, come let us adore him,*
> *Oh, come let us adore him,*
> *Christ the Lord.*
> *For he alone is worthy,*
> *For he alone is worthy,*
> *For he alone is worthy,*
> *Christ the Lord.*

He sang a Christmas song of adoration of the child, and how could we not but join him? Standing all together, the living and the dead, how could we not but join him?

> *Am enchil ahleha oklat holitoblit,*
> *Talowh chitoli ka ho haklo*
> *Klolia, klolia, ekselsis Teo.*
> *Oh im aiala momat, oh im aiala momat,*
> *Oh im aiala momat, ho tushpa.*

I marveled at Brother Willis and how he took us from this world. Then the song was over.

He stumbled in his words and before he could announce another page number, Amelia Chukma cried *Oooooo*, and everyone stood shaking and crying. The crying was deep and good. We wailed and looked into each other's eyes and sobbed out loud. I never felt so free to shout my grief and many others did the same.

As if called to join us, our gone-before Choctaw kinfolk covered the graveyard. Through my watery eyes, I saw people standing by their own graves, holding tight to their families. I saw a thousand Choctaws, dead and buried long ago, and all of us were weeping.

Brother Willis let us cry. He stood with his head bowed and his cheeks shone with tears. We stood for what must have been the better part of an hour, and then his voice boomed with the scripture reading.

Following the singing of funeral hymns, we carried our baskets of food from the wagon. Grape dumplings, roasted corn, beans and onions, *banaha* bread, and two large kettles of pashofa. Other families brought chicken and strips of pork, fried and boiled.

Mister Folsom backed his wagon up the dirt roadway and pans of food were placed at the wagon's rear. Pokoni put her arm around me and led me to a cluster of women gathering to begin the serving. Elder women came first, then men and boys, and young women and girls. The usual feasting talk gave way to quiet sobs.

I saw Samuel Willis, even Samuel, lift a finger to his cheekbone and trace the path of a fresh tear. Samuel was distant as the dark he wandered through, but on this day the rolling bones of his face were home to shiny tears. I sighed and wished my fingers too could touch his face.

I turned to Pokoni and she wrapped her thin, strong arms around me. Later, after her death, I found myself thinking that she caught my looking at Samuel that burying day. She felt my sighing, and more than that, she saw the home we would someday make together, Samuel and I. My gift of seeing came from Pokoni, of this I have no doubt.

After everyone was served, we sat in family groupings, without the usual mingling and talking. Long before sunset the last wagonload of grievers, led by two lazy mules, pulled away from New Hope Cemetery.

During the grieving, Efram leaned against the pine tree shading his family. He longed to be about his task of cutting and carving. When his mother appeared at his side with a plate of pork and dumplings, he slid down the trunk of the tree and buried himself in the food, though—in his thinking—this feasting time denied him his work.

While his brother Ben helped their mother to the wagon, Efram untied his horse from the rear of it, nodded his goodbyes and headed to the quarry. An hour later he dismounted twenty feet from the granite quarry's edge, where he had already cut and dragged three of the needed twenty stones. Removing his mallet and carving chisel from his saddlebag, he lifted the first stone to the slab of rock that served as his carving table.

Efram had decided, seeing his family so deep in grief, to carve Taloa's stone first and present it to her mother and father—his aunt and uncle. He stood over the dull slab and gripped the chisel with his left hand to lightly chip the faint outline of letters.

He tapped the chisel barely enough to stir dust from the stone, and his father entered his thoughts. Efram loved his cousin as he did his father. With the birth of the one so soon followed by the death of the other, he saw the events as connected, as did many Choctaws. Taloa, they knew, was sent to take and hold the spirit of the elder.

Now both were gone. Efram whispered her name, then gripped the chisel tight and swung hard, cutting deep the leg of a "T."

"Taloa," he said louder, and swung again, harder still, sending the blade into the groove.

"Taloa." With every swing he called her name louder, with every shout he buried his cut deeper.

"Taloa!" he shouted, till the stone split and Efram slumped to the ground, sweating and panting.

With only a sliver of moon to light his way, Efram lifted the two pieces of stone and stumbled to the edge of the quarry. He held the granite high over his head, swayed back and forth, and flung the stones to the bottom of the pit. As the stones shattered, he fell backwards, stubbornly refusing to break his fall and landing hard on his back.

He struggled to his feet and watched as shadows danced over the shards of twinkling, shattered granite. His anger seemed out of place as he beheld the spectacle of light rising from the dark hole. He mounted his horse and returned to New Hope Cemetery.

Across the road from the burial grounds, trees had been cleared for farming. The five-acre plot still held its stones intact. Limestone chunks of every size and shape decorated the field. Efram glanced at the graves, twenty mounds of dark dirt, then turned to the stones.

He approached a round stone three feet high and rocked it back and forth, loosening the dirt. With a slow and steady tug, Efram lifted the stone from the earth. He rolled it across the uneven road and onto the burial ground, settling it at the head of a grave.

Efram worked till dawn, digging stones from the field till his hands bled and his fingernails were chipped and broken. On stone number seven a buried sliver of limestone cut deep into his left palm. By the time Efram realized he was bleeding, his britches, shirt, and face were covered in blood, and his hair was a thick mass of sopping red.

Just after sunrise Lavester McKesson arrived at the cemetery with a wagonload of fresh-picked flower bundles to set among the graves. He was surprised to see twenty white stones sitting by the graves. Some were tall and cylindrical, some flat to the ground, others were round or oblong, but all shared one unforgettable bond. Blood. They were, each and every one of them, spotted with handprints of blood.

Efram slept at the base of a tree.

"What a sight to see," Lavester later said. "Me carrying sweet-smelling flowers for the little dead girls, and there those stones were. Grave stones, no doubt. That's what they were. But no date or name. Just twenty white stones covered in blood."

"Mon up, son," Lavester said, lifting Efram by the armpits. "Lemme hep you. You not hurt bad, are you?"

"Huh? No, I'm not hurt," Efram said, seeing the blood covering his shirt and britches. "Just a cut on the hand is all."

"Well, let's get you home. I done tied your horse to my wagon. He'll follow along behind. Been a long day for everybody." Efram rose and followed Lavester to his wagon, where two old mules raised their heads in welcome. One sniffed and snorted and the other stomped the ground at the sight of him.

While Lavester pulled away from New Hope Cemetery, a growing number of late-arriving relatives, out-of-towners, approached the gravesite. Climbing from wagons and sliding off horses, they moved without speaking to the fresh piles of dirt over the twenty graves. As on the burial day, they carried blankets and baskets of food and settled onto the grounds for a daylong grieving.

As the day settled to a close, the mourners trudged their way to the waiting wagons. In the hovering light of sunset, the stones glowed a soft farewell.

Chipisa lachi, they seemed to say. See you in the future.

SPIRO TOWN

AMAFO'S SPIDERWEB EYE

Rose • April 1897

One early Saturday morning in April, two weeks before Easter, Amafo quietly slipped into our bedroom. He nudged me in the ribs and grabbed Jamey's left foot, the one always hanging off the bed. Amafo was already dressed, but not in his usual clothes—a white shirt and worn-out blue coveralls. No, he was dressed in his reddish-brown Sunday-only suit.

"Get on up outta bed now," Amafo said. My sleepy eyes stared at his green tie with the big white circles on it, too tight around his neck. I knew that Pokoni was part of the day's design. Amafo never tied his own tie, but liked to fuss and squirm till Pokoni pinched his nose and made him stop.

"Don't be laying around all day!" Amafo said. "Somebody come last night and did all the chores. Nothing fer us to do today but go to town. Figure we kin watch the trains come in at the depot."

We were out of our beds like a house afire. We made our beds quick too, folding back the sheets and covers and fluffing up the pillows, just in case Momma thought about overruling Amafo on the chore-doing business. We put on our going-to-town clothes and tiptoed downstairs to the kitchen.

Momma heated up last night's cornbread and we dipped it in buttermilk for breakfast. Jamey and I didn't say a word at breakfast, 'cept for when Jamey said, "Sure is good cornbread. Yes ma'am."

I shot him a look to say, *That's enough, now. Don't push our luck.*

After breakfast I cleared the table and was just about to fetch pump water for washing, when Momma stopped me in my tracks.

"That's all right, hon. You go on with Amafo. I can do the cleaning."

"*Yakoke*," I whispered, then gave her a good long *thank you* look, the one I knew she felt right through her skin.

Amafo already had Whiteface hitched up and pulled around front, ready to go. Jamey and I climbed onto the back bed of the wagon and off we went. We were so excited we lay on our backs and stared at the treetops, barely speaking all the way to Spiro.

The trains came in late evenings every night of the week, but they were mostly delivering goods and mail, with very few passengers. But on Saturday sometimes as many as five trains would unload passengers—passengers dressed up and coming from Little Rock or Memphis or even as far away as New Orleans.

It was just past nine when we arrived at the train station. Amafo nestled our wagon to a spot behind the depot. He stepped down and around to the tying rail to secure Whiteface, all the time stroking her neck and ears and talking that soft cooing talk that only Whiteface and Amafo understood.

I climbed down on my own and Amafo helped Jamey to the ground. We ambled along at Amafo's pace. I did my best to walk slow and respectful, seeing as how our excitement grew at the noise of the oncoming train. It was bigger than I ever remembered, seeing it so close-up like we were.

The brakes screeched and the train came to a stop near enough for us to smell the grinding metal and feel the hot air rising from the steam engine. We stood and stared gap-mouthed at the train and the people waiting. We climbed the platform steps and Amafo found an empty outside table tucked up against the depot wall. He bought us a bag of roasted peanuts to share, so salty you had to lick your fingers after eating, and a tall glass of lemonade apiece.

Folks crowded to the edge of the tracks as passengers unloaded. A quarter hour passed and an easy calm settled in. Passengers waiting for a connecting train found tables inside the depot and a dozen or so men strolled up and down the platform, smoking pipes and mopping their brows.

Long after everyone else had come and gone, a tall gentleman dressed in a black suit appeared at the door to the final car. A Negro porter rushed to help him from the train. The gentleman was followed by two porters carrying his luggage—three large brown-leather suitcases.

"That's the new Indian agent," we heard someone whisper when he walked by. The agent seemed not to notice that everyone was staring at him. He pulled out his pocket watch and shook his head as he looked up and down the platform. He spoke to a porter and soon a wagon appeared. The agent climbed into the passenger seat as his luggage was loaded in the wagon bed and off they rode.

Less than five minutes after the agent left, the town marshal, Marshal Hardwicke, came driving a wagon pulled by two fidgety black horses, sleek and sweating. He leapt to the platform from his wagon, pushed open the depot doors, and strode to the ticket counter. After speaking to the ticket agent, he slammed his fist on the counter and stormed outside to the platform.

"Did anyone see the new Indian agent?" he said, turning his head from side to side as he spoke. "Was the train early?" Marshal Hardwicke shouted, but no one spoke to him. The marshal was a big man with powerful arms and a mustached face that grew more and more puffy-cheeked and red. Everyone on the platform moved to give him a path, but no one spoke.

A tall, thin lady in a shiny blue dress, the final passenger, stepped from the train. Her face was soft, but her eyes were outlined in black and her cheeks were pink circles of face powder. She craned her goose neck up and down the platform before turning and struggling to drag two large suitcases behind her.

"Hold on, ma'am," a young porter called out, skip-stepping through the depot door. Judging from his size and bright, innocent eyes, he looked to be maybe sixteen years old. "I'm here fer ya."

The porter gave a wide berth around the marshal, but not wide enough. Marshal Hardwicke grabbed his collar from behind and jerked the young man backwards and off his feet. He slammed him against the wall and slid his hand up the porter's neck and under his chin.

"You, boy. You seen the new agent get offa this train?"

The porter nodded as best he could, being pinned up against the wall by his throat. The marshal relaxed his grip and the porter steadied himself, saying, "He left just a minute or two ago. Called hisself a wagon. Probly be at the hotel by now."

Marshal Hardwicke staggered for a moment, as if trying to decide what to do next. That's when I realized he was drunk. I had seen plenty of drunk men before, Choctaws and Nahullos both, but never at this hour in the morning. Drinking was something men did after dark, and mostly in quiet places away from women and children. The marshal cursed at the porter and told him, "Get on away from here if you know what's good for you!"

From where he sat, Amafo kept his back turned to the marshal. When the shouting grew louder he kept his head down. I could tell he did not want the marshal or anybody else to notice us.

Marshal Hardwicke turned to the door, slamming it so hard a piece of cedar door facing, four feet long at least, popped loose and fell to the platform.

"Time we go," Amafo said, thinking the marshal had entered the stationhouse. He rose and stepped around the table to help me with my chair. At that moment the marshal whirled and knocked Amafo against the table. Though violent in its result, I am convinced this was an accidental act. But something about bumping against another man, a weaker man, seemed to breathe new life into the marshal.

He glared at Amafo. His eyebrows wrinkled and his mouth drew tight. He slowly stooped and picked up the door facing with both hands. Amafo huddled with the two of us behind him, holding us back with his arms.

As the marshal stood up, he swung the board in a loop, catching my grandfather on the side of his head and knocking him to the ground. Amafo's eyeglasses scooted almost to the edge of the platform. The marshal drew back the board and slapped it hard against the building, shattering the wood and showering Jamey and me with splinters.

The marshal stood glaring over Amafo. His face was red and his eyes were bloodshot. His fists were clenched tight and shaking. I had heard Pokoni speak of the devil taking hold of somebody, and I think I was seeing the devil come alive in front of me. I looked around for help.

The platform was full of people now. The stationhouse had emptied.

Men and women circled us, but no one moved to help. I cried out and the marshal looked at us, Jamey and me, trembling and cowering against the wall of the building. His face suddenly changed, as if he was seeing us for the first time. His eyes slowly moved to Amafo, who was struggling to stand up.

"Ooohh," the marshal moaned, dropping the board to the platform. The ticket master hurried through the crowd and picked it up.

"It's sharp as a butcher knife. He could kill somebody with this," he whispered, shaking his head.

Amafo was too dizzy to make it to his feet. He fell back to the platform and lay on his side, breathing hard and squinting his eyes. The marshal reached for my grandfather as if he were about to help him, but he stopped himself. In that moment something unspeakable settled on the railroad platform, some new level of meanness. I was afraid, but not too afraid to look squarely at what was occurring.

The marshal stood straight up, slowly and deliberately, dusted the splinters from his shirt and turned to face the gathering crowd. For the first time in my life I saw the power that evil and fear exercise over people. The marshal stared at the crowd. Better said, he stared at each and every person there, every man and every woman, challenging anybody to say a word, to move a muscle. Everyone in their turn took a step back.

When he was satisfied no one dared confront him, the marshal tipped his hat, turned smartly and walked to his wagon.

I knelt over Amafo and realized how old and helpless he was. He looked like a stranger, a tired and fallen stranger.

"My glasses," he said. "Please, where are my glasses?"

I turned to the platform's edge where I had last seen his glasses. A short young man in a tan suit, an out-of-town traveler, stepped from the crowd. He took his hat off as he approached me, in a sign of respect.

"Here you are, young lady." He handed me the glasses. The right lens was shattered, but still snug and tight in the frame. The glass was broken in the shape of a spiderweb, with a small circle in the center surrounded by jagged lines.

"*Yakoke,*" I said. He looked at me strangely. "I am sorry. I meant to say thank you." The man smiled with good humor and nodded to my grandfather.

"Is he—the old man—is he alright? Will he be okay?"

"Yes, I think so. He is my grandfather, my Amafo. We need to go. Can you help me lift him?" The man nodded as Amafo tried to stand.

"Give me my glasses," Amafo said.

I had never looked at Amafo's glasses before. They were part of his face, nothing more. I lifted the glasses high. The frames were much heavier than I had imagined. I watched the sunlight flash against the broken lens and was suddenly overcome with the desire to see through my grandfather's eyes.

The time to be afraid was over and I knew it. Now was the time to see, to truly see what had happened. I turned to the crowd and held the glasses in front of my eyes. Everyone appeared normal through the left lens, blurred and slightly misshapen, but normal to look at.

Through the right lens, the shattered spiderweb lens, everyone was distorted. Legs and arms were broken and people seemed ugly and freakish. I turned to look at the young man who chose to help us, expecting him to appear like the others.

At first glance he did. But then he smiled and I saw through the spiderweb lens that this was a good man. I lowered the glasses from my face and the man nodded to me, as if we shared a secret.

"Are you sure you want to help us?" I asked.

"Yes. Give the glasses to your grandfather and let's get him to his feet."

Each of us took an arm. We counted to three and huffed and puffed and lifted my grandfather to a standing position. Jamey appeared like a rabbit from his hiding place, brushing the dirt and dust from his britches.

"I can see you home," the man said.

"You have a train to catch."

"There will be other trains. Will you be safe?"

"Oh yes," I heard myself saying. "No one would touch us now. No one wants to be part of this."

"You have a wagon?"

"Yes. And I can drive it." I was lying, of course. I had never driven a wagon before. But I knew that in an hour I would know how to drive it, if we were to make it home.

The man tipped his hat once more. I saw respect in his eyes. He turned away and joined the throng of people crowding around the doors of the departing train. I now had the task of getting Amafo to the wagon.

"Here, Jamey," I told him, "come over here by Amafo. Don't get in his way, just walk next to him. He's gonna rest his hand on your shoulder." I positioned Amafo's right hand on Jamey's shoulder, squeezing it soft to let him know I loved him, then I stepped in front of my grandfather in case he fell forward.

The three of us rambled across the platform. Excepting for the shameless and unspeakable horror of what had just happened, we might have been a medicine show act, a horse with a make-believe head and tail and two funny men under a blanket trying to walk in step.

I walked directly in front of Amafo and he rested his left hand on my shoulder. With every few steps I could feel the pressure grow lighter. I knew Amafo was beginning to move under his own power.

"Ho," he said as we stepped to the street. His head slumped and we eased him against the side of the stationhouse. He held his head and wrinkled his face and I knew he was still dizzy.

Amafo looked haggard and ancient, leaning against the white boards of the building. The whiteness seemed to drown him, looming twenty feet above us. His red-brown suit, so crisp and churchly only a few minutes earlier, was now wrinkled and dirty. Two large circles of dust decorated his pants legs, marks of his fall. His broken glasses nestled halfway down his nose.

We lifted Amafo onto the wagon and began the long trip home.

I was only a young lady of eleven years, but I was old enough to know that our Choctaw world was changing. Maybe this day turned out to be one of the best days of my life after all. I learned to see as Amafo saw. I learned to see through Amafo's spiderweb eye.

NIGHT GATHERING

By the time I eased the wagon into the barn and unhitched Whiteface,
I think every Choctaw within fifty miles of Skullyville knew about
Marshal Hardwicke striking Amafo. That evening more people crowded
into our living room than ever before, some families who had not visited
our home in years. The McCurtains, the Folsoms, folks who held high
positions going all the way back to Choctaw days in Mississippi.

Brother Willis and his family were there, of course, with his oldest
son Samuel, and several used-to-be shopkeepers, who always seemed to
be talking about rebuilding their stores. They never recovered after the
burnings. Many families had also lost their barns to nighttime fires.

"It's not the work that keeps everybody from rebuilding," Pokoni
often said. "It's hard to find the will to start up again after you've lost
everything."

"And the fear," I once heard Amafo say.

Pokoni was dashing to and from the kitchen, trying her best to
keep everyone's cups and bowls filled with hot coffee and steaming
pashofa corn soup. Amafo found himself a spot on a step halfway up the
stairs to the second floor. He barely moved a muscle, holding his coffee

cup with both hands and softly blowing. His hat was pulled low over his eyes, discouraging anyone who might try to draw him into a conversation.

To some, he might seem to be sleeping, but not a word escaped Amafo's attention. The stakes were high. We were all Skullyville Choctaws, and our lives were threatened by what had occurred.

I learned much by watching Amafo that night. To the hotheaded young men he was as meaningless as a tree stump—an old man whose youth and usefulness were a thing of the past. I saw Amafo bide his time, allowing one argument after another to fizzle and die.

He already knows what he's going to do, I realized. *He will wait all night if he has to, till everyone else has burned themselves out, before he tells us what he's thinking.* For the first time, I saw a Choctaw elder at work. And I understood—for the first time—why our way is a powerful way. It is a way of waiting and watching, and Amafo was as wise in the ways of survival as a great black cat of the woods.

I was determined to stay up and see what Amafo would do. I set about helping Pokoni. We washed empty cups, of coffee and pashofa both, refilled them and returned them to our guests before they knew they were gone. All this we did without a word between us.

The hours dragged on. It was approaching midnight when I heard Mister Yeager cough, like he always did when he had something to say. He had spent his younger days chasing bootleggers with the Lighthorsemen, our Choctaw posse. "Sure we are peaceable folks," he said. "We're churchgoers, all of us, and we gonna do the Lord's will, best we know it."

He nodded in the direction of Brother Willis, with a tone of embarrassed humility. Brother Willis appeared not to respond. But if you watched him after everybody else had looked away, you saw him take a deep breath and look into his coffee cup with sad eyes.

I was carrying a tray of coffee cups from the living room to the kitchen, where Pokoni was washing with a fury. When Mister Yeager spoke, she dried her soapwater hands on her apron and moved to the doorway to listen.

"I'm just saying we ought to keep our guns near our bedsides," he said. "We got to protect ourselves from the Nahullos, all of 'em. We can't let our guard down."

I sat the tray on the kitchen counter and asked Pokoni, "Why would they want to hurt us? It was a Nahullo that hit Amafo."

She leaned towards me and whispered, "Hon, listen good to what I'm telling you. People who are bullies are driven to punishing those they have harmed the most. And the bullying will usually get worse.

"Look around you. These Choctaw families are gathered together at our house for safety. By the time the marshal and his friends spread their talk about what happened at the train station, every Nahullo in Spiro will be fussing and fuming. More than likely they gonna blame us, hon. But the real thing we got to worry about is this. Choctaw hotheads, that's where the real danger is. All Choctaws are not like your grandfather."

She stepped to the sink, saying, "Now. I'll wash, you dry, and let's make up for lost time."

Ten minutes later my nineteen year-old cousin Wilbur burst through the front door. "We know where the marshal lives," he shouted. "Let's see how *he* likes a board upside the head."

Everybody grew nervous thinking about Wilbur taking a board to the marshal. They knew the marshal would kill him and go unpunished.

My grandmother looked at me.

"If we're going to town, we better bring guns," said Wilbur's little brother Zeke, who had just celebrated his fourteenth birthday. I saw my grandparents trade glances to hear Zeke talk so brave.

The older folks just let the young ones go on with their blustery talk. Even when they called for guns and warring, Amafo kept his hat low and sipped his coffee. Their words, he knew, would fall like hot embers on a coldwater lake. But other words, spoken by elders, caught Amafo's attention—and Pokoni's as well.

Mister Pope, a neighbor and a good man for shoeing horses, said, "Maybe we all should stay here, camp out here. We'd be here to protect your family. They wouldn't dare try anything if we was all here."

"I've got nothing to do that cain't wait. I'll be glad to," someone said.

"We'll all be here if any trouble comes," Mister Pope said. "I'll drive into town tomorrow and buy enough ammunition for us all. Shells, gunpowder. We'll divey it up and reckon the money later. I'll keep good account of everything."

Hearing this, Amafo lifted his hat and looked at Pokoni. Pokoni filled a coffee cup to overflowing and crossed the room to hand it to Mister Pope.

"Here's a fresh cup for you," she said. Mister Pope took the cup without looking at it and promptly spilled it on himself.

"Yow," he hollered, dropping the cup and splashing hot coffee all over his britches. His wife ran to his aid. In the laughter that followed, everyone seemed to forget his idea of a makeshift army, an invitation to trouble. Truth was, our yard was already overrun with an army, the army of Colonel Tobias Mingo.

COLONEL MINGO

Forty-eight children, Colonel Mingo's Army, gathered in the woods east of the house. A highly-respected veteran, Colonel Mingo had fought with a Confederate calvary brigade during the Civil War. The day following a fierce battle, he had lost his left arm to a Yankee sharpshooter as he crouched over a pan of frying ham.

He spent several months after the amputation recuperating from typhoid fever at the Veterans Hospital in Talahina. Colonel Mingo's left sleeve now hung limp at his side. It flopped when he moved, like happy laundry bobbing on a clothesline.

During Choctaw gatherings, Mingo's assigned duty was to keep the children safe. Though soft-hearted, he served his duty with a military bearing that appealed to the older children. Overlooking a few hundred lost teeth, a dozen broken arms and legs, two snakebites and fifty bee stings—he was moderately successful.

Knowing this night was likely to stretch into morning, Colonel Mingo supervised the building of a small campfire. He began by settling himself against the trunk of a two-hundred-year-old oak. *My talking tree,* he called it.

He then appointed seven of the older children—never the same children, but always seven—to be his officers. Colonel Mingo not only built the fire following this chain of command, he conducted the entire evening's affairs through these seven officers.

"Let's begin by getting us some wood. Will, Mary, Ken, Arch, you folks get enough kindling and small branches to get it started. Nita, Boyd, Samuel, you folks start gathering logs, 'bout two, three-foot long logs."

"Yessir, Colonel Mingo!" the officers yelled, scattering into the woods. Colonel Mingo pulled out his pipe and tobacco pouch, filling the bowl and pressing the tobacco down lightly with his thumb. Cupping his hand over the bowl, he struck a match on the sole of his boot and lit his pipe. Soft puffs of sweet, aromatic tobacco smoke filled the clearing. His officers soon returned with the wood.

"Small wood over there, logs over here," he said, waving his right hand in one direction and pointing in the other. "Keep the center clear for now. Good job, officers. Keep it up. Gonna need a lot more wood than that. Let's get going, everybody but Samuel and Will."

"Yessir, Colonel Mingo!" the remaining five yelled on their way to the woods.

"Will, scratch out a circle on the ground with your boot heel, right there in the center of the clearing. Make it 'bout big around as a washtub."

"Yessir!" said Will.

"Samuel, find us some stones. You and Will are gonna build us a fire circle, one we can use every time we come to this clearing. So build it good."

"Yessir, Colonel Mingo!" they said in unison.

"If you want to pick you out some helpers, some of these other children might be big enough to help out. But you got to keep a watch out for 'em. Make sure they don't step on a snake or get covered all over with ants."

Soon most of the children were involved, gathering stones or firewood.

"Girls," Colonel Mingo said, "you'll find buckets on the wall of the chicken coop. Fill 'em up with red clay from the creek bed. That clay will be the mortar for our stone fire circle."

"Yessir," sang the young ladies, dashing to the chicken coop.

In less than an hour, the fire circle was built and enough wood for a week of winters was stacked at the edge of the clearing. Soon everyone found their own listening spot, where they would spend the next several hours till they drifted off to sleep.

"Samuel," Colonel Mingo said, "I want you to take this match and light the fire. Notice which way the wind is blowing. Put your back to it soes it don't blow out the flame. Git your kindling just how you want it, and git real close to the fire 'fore you strike that match, 'cause you only got one."

Samuel was tall like his father—Brother Willis—and thin like his mother. He almost never smiled. Samuel listened intently to Colonel Mingo, then nodded and furrowed his brow to let everyone know he realized the seriousness of the situation.

He picked up a handful of dried leaves and tossed them in the air, watching which way the wind carried them. Then he stacked dried kindling at the base of the logs. He struck a match and held it to the kindling. The sticks burst into flame, but Samuel stayed with the fire till a small log caught fire.

Seeing the firelight fill the clearing, a tiny three-year-old started clapping, but the seven officers *shooshed* her. Colonel Mingo turned his slow gaze to the children. He waited till the embers were popping lazy-like and the flames burned low—yellow and blue hypnotizing flickers.

Some children sat cross-legged, some leaned against a nearby hackberry stump. A few rolled fat logs close to the fire to use as pillows, folding their hands behind their heads. Everyone drew close, for Colonel Mingo always told his stories in a barely heard sleep-if-you-want-to voice.

And they drew close for another reason. Safety in numbers, for Colonel Mingo always began his stories with the same warning.

"Now you children know there's no reason to be scaired 'bout anything I tell you. None of these creatures is still living. And if they are still living, they aren't living in these woods. And if they are still living in these woods, they're probably asleep by now anyway. But just in case they're not asleep, we outta be reeeeel quiet, 'specially if you hear something in the woods, something maybe prowling around attracted by the fire. In fact, maybe we should put the fire out."

"No!" screamed a dozen voices.

"Well, now," Colonel Mingo said, "if anything was asleep in the woods, I 'spect it's awake by now."

Colonel Mingo paused to puff on his pipe. A pink glow rose from the pipe bowl and tiny clouds of smoke floated around his face. With every eye watching him, Colonel Mingo set his pipe against a stone, sipped his coffee, and waited for the night sounds to take over. They floated down from the trees, fluttering sounds of winged creatures taking flight and the soft whistling of pine trees tilting with the wind. The distant croaking of frogs washed up from the creek.

Colonel Mingo lifted his eyebrows. His eyes grew wide and he turned his head slowly, ever so slowly, as if he'd heard something but didn't want *it* to know he was there.

"I'm scared," came a wee voice from behind the hackberry stump.

"Well, I was just trying to tell you children why there's no reason to be afraid," Colonel Mingo continued.

For half an hour, he entertained the young children with tales of friendly alligators and silly rabbits. He told them of tiny men called Bohpoli, who teach the herbal cures. Twice he paused and sent Samuel to the house, once for a refill on his coffee and again to borrow a bowl of pipe tobacco from *your daddy, the reverend.*

When the younger children were mostly asleep, he leaned close to the fire. "You know it's wrong, real wrong, to hit somebody," he whispered. "You all know better than to do that. I'm gonna tell you 'bout a girl that knew better but did it anyway."

JEZEBEL JEZZY

"Don't ever go to striking another person, not with a stick, not with your hand, not with nothing," he said. "There was once an old Negro man who was married to an old Indian woman," he began. "They children was grown and done left home. Then one day the old woman told her husband she was gonna have another child. 'I been thinking we wuz too old for that,' her husband told her.

"Well, the old woman was thinking the same thing, but sure 'nuff, in the usual time come a baby girl born to this sweet old man and woman. The girl was very beautiful. She had the shiny black hair of her father, but it hung in long curls, like her mother's. Her skin was a little bit of both, dark brown and red. She grew to be long-legged and walked real graceful-like. All the boys would stop and stare at her when she walked by. Her mother didn't seem to notice much, but her father did not like it one bit, the way those boys looked at his daughter.

"And how you think the daughter took to all this attention? Well, she liked it just fine, though she never let on. She was shy and wouldn't look at the boys, like a girl 'spossed to be, when she was a young'un. But 'bout the time she come to being a teenager, that all changed.

"They called her Jezzy, from her Bible name Jezebel, and why a daddy gonna let his baby girl be named Jezebel, I'll never understand. Soon as she turned teenager, she started living up to her no-good name.

"The trouble really started when Jezzy took a liking to a boy named Cecil. Cecil was long and lanky too, and he kept his hands in his pockets and hardly ever talked to anybody. But 'bout the third time he followed Jezzy home, like a lonesome puppy dog, she realized she had a fish on the line.

"Jezzy finally took to passing by *his* house whenever she had a chance. Now Jezzy's momma made baskets, river cane baskets, and she was good at it. Since she was old, she'd sit in the doorway when she worked, hardly moving at all. Jezzy brought her water and some little something to eat when she asked for it. Now this old woman sold every basket she made 'fore she made it, 'cause she'd color her baskets any way anybody wanted. She never had to leave her doorstep to make all the money she needed.

"One day the woman saw Cecil hanging around the house, just leaning up against a tree over yonder nearby. That night she told Jezzy's father, and next time Cecil come 'round, Jezzy's daddy had a talk with him, told him to go away and not come back.

"Jezzy was getting old enough to talk to boys, but her parents were too old to know it. So maybe Jezzy had a right to be upset. But when it's your parents, being upset and doing something about it, they two different things. You still got to show respect. And that's what Jezzy didn't have. She had the good looks, but she didn't have no respect, not for her parents.

"One night Cecil come 'round her window real late, and Jezzy and him took off to the lake. They stayed for way too late. Next day her daddy, who was old but he wadn't no fool, he saw the foot tracks by Jezzy's window. He was waiting for 'em that night, till Jezzy was crawling out the window and Cecil was helping her.

"When they turned to go, there stood Jezzy's daddy. 'Son,' he said, 'you come anywhere near this house or Jezzy, you gonna get a whipping you'll never forget.' And the old man waved a cane in Cecil's face.

"Jezzy tried to talk, but her old momma pulled her towards the house. Jezzy jerked away. 'Take your hands off me!' she shouted. When her mother reached for her again, Jezzy reared back and slapped her mother right on the face.

"But when Jezzy tried to take her hand away, she couldn't do it. Her hand was stuck to her mother's face and she couldn't pull it away. Her daddy and Cecil, they all just stood there and couldn't believe what was happening. Jezzy's hand grew into her momma's cheek till the two were joined.

"Nothing they could do about it. Jezzy slept next to her momma's bed that night. When morning came they called the medicine man.

"Medicine man said he'd never seen nothing like this. He tried with his medicine, but he couldn't do no good. After a day or two, Jezzy's momma went back to making her baskets, sitting in the doorway, with Jezzy trying to hide just inside the house. But everybody heard what had happened and they come by to see. 'Cut my hand off!' Jezzy finally said. 'I can't live this way.'

"And that's what they did. A doctor come by one day and real careful-like cut Jezzy's hand off, 'bout wrist high. It bled something awful. He wrapped a bandage around it, even tried burning the stump, but nothing would stop the bleeding.

"Jezzy died that night, bled to death in her own bed. With all the attention going Jezzy's way, nobody noticed, up to now, what was happening with her mother. Jezzy's hand still clung to her face, like Jezzy's fingers were part of her momma's skin.

"As the months passed, Jezzy's hand shrank till it looked like a dried hand of some little animal, like a dead raccoon.

"Her momma still made her baskets. She sat in the doorway, facing her good cheek to the outside and hiding Jezzy's hand. Sometimes when she first woke up, she'd forget about it. But when she washed her face, she'd feel her daughter still hanging on.

"Cecil moved to the other side of the lake, all by himself. But finally come 'round the anniversary of when all this happened.

"The moon was full and so was Cecil's heart, full of memories. He rowed a canoe to the center of the lake and just sat there, with the waves washing gentle. He laid back and stared at the moon, round and pretty yellow. He was almost asleep when the waves started rocking the boat. Cecil sat up.

"Rising out of the water, not twenty feet from him, come Jezzy, the ghost of Jezzy. She floated over next to him and held out both her arms, just to let him see her wrist was whole, now that she was dead. And every year after that, long as Cecil was alive, he'd row that canoe to the center of the lake to see his Jezzy.

"And long as they were alive, Jezzy's momma and daddy never forgot their daughter. They remembered how nice she was as a little girl, how pretty she grew to be. But mostly, they remembered the day Jezzy did what it's even hard to talk about—the day she struck her momma.

"Some things you just never 'sposed to do, and striking a innocent person, somebody weaker, is one of 'em, 'specially not if they be your own momma."

All but the oldest children had fallen asleep sometime during the Colonel's story. They listened like it was all a dream, drifting in and out, but when Jezzy struck her mother, everybody sat up. Colonel Mingo had their attention when he wanted it.

"Don't never," he repeated, "go striking a innocent person. That's when real trouble gonna start."

MINGO AND HARDWICKE'S MEN

Samuel Willis waited till everybody else was asleep before he rose, carried a bucket to the creek and drowned the fire, sending a smokey sizzle over the clearing. Younger children snuggled close to older ones.

Even Colonel Mingo napped and woke up off and on, till Samuel touched his shoulder, saying, "Colonel. Wake up, sir, please."

"What? Samuel. I am awake."

"Some men, four of 'em, rode up not long ago. They been watching us, just out of firelight. There." He pointed to a clump of trees in the direction of the house. Mingo eased quietly to his feet and said, "Sam, you stay here and keep a close eye on these babies. Don't let any of 'em know about these strangers. No need scaring the children."

"Yes. I'll watch 'em, Colonel."

"Good, son. I know I can trust you." Samuel saw his hand move to his hip, to the carved antler handle of his Bowie knife. Mingo moved through the woods away from the men, as if he were going to the corn patch to relieve himself. Samuel shook his head at the savvy ways of his friend and teacher and turned to his promised watch over the children.

Once out of eyesight, Colonel Mingo double-backed on himself and made a wide circle around the woods, creeping low among the surrounding bushes and trees. Lying close to the ground, he studied the men. Four men, just as Samuel had said. He watched their mannerisms, their tense and ready way of crouching, saw the gear lying beside their ponies.

Small ponies for quick getaways, he noted. He waited till the sound of laughter from the house caught the men's attention, then crept close enough to hear them speak.

"If Hardwicke was here, we'd already be on our way home," said a short stout man. "He'd start with the barn, I'm telling you. He'd torch it from all sides, then nail the door shut soes they couldn't follow us. Them horses would die from the smoke."

"Ain't no way we could get to the barn without them seeing us," said another.

"Besides," said a third, "the marshal said to just let him know if they're planning anything. He didn't say nothing about no burning. Not tonight, at least, not till he knows which way the new Indian agent is gonna see things."

"Yeah, Hardwicke talks about keeping a watch out. But if he was here, he'd figure out a way to put a torch to that barn. Knowing him, he'd set fire to the old man's house too. Maybe kill some Indians, get 'em on the run. You all know that's what he'd be doing."

Colonel Mingo slipped back to his campsite, his heart pounding with every step. He carried with him a terrible secret. Mingo knew who set the fire that burned New Hope. He also knew that if he shared the secret, many of his friends would die.

He found Samuel pacing back and forth in the shadows, watching.

"Samuel," he said, "these men were sent by Marshal Hardwicke. I don't think they want any trouble, but one of 'em is talking about setting a fire to the barn, so we have to keep an eye on 'em."

"I can stay awake and let you know if they cause any trouble."

"That's a good idea, Samuel. I'll stay with the children and you keep an eye on Hardwicke's men. We don't want any bloodshed."

"I understand," said Samuel. "I'll report to you every few hours till morning."

"Be careful," Mingo said. Samuel nodded and disappeared into the shadows.

GOODE KITCHEN AND STRONG WOMEN

Rose

Twenty women—wives and kinfolks to the men in the living room—crowded around the kitchen table. While Pokoni and I washed dishes and served the men, they kept us going. They cut corn from the cob, chopped chicken for pashofa, and refilled coffee water boiling on the stove. Their talk circled the affair at the train station, viewing it in a corner-of-the-eye way of talking. Though armed with butcher knives and long-handled spoons, their real weapons were words, and they knew how to use them.

"There's no telling what Uncle Lester would have done if he was still alive. Mercy, did he have a temper."

"I believe the marshal's wife would be shopping for a black dress, Lester have anything to do with it."

"He was not afraid of nothing or nobody."

"Uh-huh. He remind me of that Wilson boy, what was his name? 'Member, the one went in the army. Took after a officer with a pickaxe. Man made him work in the kitchen and he hit him with a pickaxe."

"Nothing good came of that."

"I 'spec he still in jail."

"Somewhere back east."

"Nord Caylina, I believe."

"How's the water looking?"

"Need refilling, look like to me."

"Gonna need another chicken 'fore long."

"With all the noise coming from in there, you'd think they wouldn't have time to eat."

"They men. They gonna find time to eat."

"You know that's true."

"Un-huh."

"They gonna get to the table."

"I believe that."

"Last time my man went to battle, it was over a drumstick."

"Tell me about it."

"Here come the soup pot. Look like somebody done licked the bottom of it."

"Must be my husband."

"Could be mine."

"Yessir. They men. They gonna find time to eat."

"You know that's true."

With the children nestled around Colonel Mingo's campfire, the men going at it in the front room, and the younger ladies helping Pokoni in the kitchen, the older women roosted comfortably on the back porch, bathed in the blue light of the waning moon.

The sounds amongst these women were creaking sounds, the creaks of a rocking chair, the soft creaks of porch planks as tired bodies shifted and settled. Every gust of wind carried earthy smells, of hay and chickens, sometimes the perfume of gardenias.

These older women seemed to float in a different world, a place of whispery music and faded colors. It was a place not between life and death, but rather above life and death, above it all. The calls to action and urgings from the living room, they had no place here. They were fires from a distant hillside. When these women spoke of the men in the house, they spoke of them as if they were children.

"The marshal will pay. He will suffer—and his kind, they will all suffer," a deep voice boomed from the living room.

"That sounds like Bobby Harris, little Bobby Harris," said Mrs. McVann, puckering her lips in soft laughter. "I still remember him begging me for a piece of blackberry pie. He saw it sitting on the kitchen table and went to almost crying, chubby little Bobby Harris."

"Wasn't he a whiney boy?" said Mrs. Mangum.

"He will suffer," another man repeated.

The word *suffer* unsettled the women. The lid of a memory box rattled open and threads of hymns came pouring out. The women started singing to themselves, till one single voice stood out. It was cracked and wavering. The other women fell silent and the eldest woman sang.

Hatak yoshoba chia ma!
Achukmut haponaklo;
Chisus chi okchalinchi ut
Auet chi hohoyoshke;
Chisus okut
Auet chi hohoyoshke.

Hark the voice of love and mercy,
Sounds aloud from Calvary.
See it rends the rocks asunder
Shakes the earth and veils the sky.
"It is finished, it is finished,"
Hear the dying Saviour cry.

Somebody picked up a turtle shell rattle I'd left lying on the porch and started shaking it. The sound was so soft. Those little stones shifting around in the turtle's home made everything around it glow in the color of holy. It was a yellow and blue color, like peeking through rainclouds at a tree-shaded lake shining in the sky.

Holy, holy, holy.

Seeing those old women sitting on the porch.

Holy, holy, holy.

Those old women made it so. Everything was holy. The creaking boards, the wind tilting the tops of the pine trees, the smell of gardenias, the cold silver stars, everything was holy.

Around one o'clock in the morning, the conversation wound down to a light sprinkling. I could hear the loud clicking of our grandfather clock. It sat by the staircase wall of the living room and its quiet noise always filled the house after everyone went to bed.

This was farming country and Saturday had been a working day like any other. Droopy eyes blinked and tired heads went to nodding. Snoring came from every corner.

At one-thirty, Pokoni moved slowly to the living room and settled back in her usual chair facing the empty fireplace. She closed her eyes and when Amafo rose to heat milk for her cocoa, she merely tilted her head in his direction. In a few minutes the sweet smell of scalding milk drifted from the kitchen. Amafo appeared carrying grandmother's cocoa cup, stirring the chocolate to life as he walked. She opened her eyes and accepted the steamy drink.

Amafo moved to the center of the room and stood before the fireplace. The snoring ceased and slumping men sat up. The front door eased open and several men entered, heads down and tip-toeing. The kitchen emptied and women stood side-by-side with their husbands. The vigil, they knew, would soon be over.

"I need your help," my Amafo said, and a room full of anxious eyes turned his way. "You have every one of you been very nice to offer to help me and my family. I accept your offer."

"You say the word, we're ready," said Cousin Wilbur. Mister Pope scooted behind him, leaned over and placed one large hand on Wilbur's shoulder, letting the young man know it was time to listen.

"Marshal Hardwicke expects me to stay far away from town. And if I did, this would all be forgotten. But I will never forget this day and my grandchildren will never forget this day."

Amafo took his glasses off and held them up for all to see.

"It is the day my glasses were broken. But maybe it will be a day of blessings after all. Maybe now the people of Spiro can see, as we have seen for years, the man who is their marshal."

Amafo was tiring now, fading rapidly. His face sagged and he sat down on the ledge of the fireplace. Pokoni reached out and touched him on the knee, and a new breath of energy seemed to fill him. He lifted his head and gazed open-eyed around the room.

"We must all agree to do this, all of us. I need your help," he said. "Many of you work for Nahullos. They gonna try to talk to you about today.

Don't fall into that trap. They gonna ask about the marshal, what you think of the marshal, what he did to that old Choctaw man at the railroad."

Amafo stood up real slow and pulled the hat from his head like he was wiping his brow. The right side of his face, where the board struck him, was deep purple. Even from where I stood I could see broken blood vessels snaking off from the main wound. His eye was swelled shut. A line of dried blood as thick as a bacon slab ran down his cheek.

I gasped and a hot breath of air flew from my chest. Murmurs floated around the room and several husbands and wives moved closer to touch and hold one another. Pokoni blinked several times and thrust her chin up, making sure she held her head high. I knew she was fighting back the tears.

This was Amafo's moment and tears would do him no good.

"When they try to talk to you 'bout it, just walk away," Amafo said. "If you got to say anything, tell 'em how tough you think the marshal is. Tell 'em how you'd never want to cross him. Tell 'em he is a big, strong man. Then walk away.

"They will talk after you leave. They will tell stories about today. More people than the railroad platform could hold will claim to have seen it all. Everyone will talk about Marshal Hardwicke. And when the talk dies down, I will always be there, wearing my spiderweb glasses.

"They will see a lot of me in town. I will cross the street to speak friendly words to the marshal. I will do this. Over and over I will do this, every day I will do this, speak friendly words to him and tip my hat to him, till one day he will turn away from me and they will see who is afraid. That is how we will win. Our enemies will be defeated by our goodness."

"Now, this day is over and the Lord's Day is upon us," he said, replacing his hat. "You are all welcome to stay. Goodnight and God bless you. *Yakoke.* You are my friends."

Amafo helped my grandmother from her chair and the two of them made a slow procession up the stairs. Lamps were blown out throughout the house, women brought blankets and pillows in from the wagons, and within ten minutes an entire household of Choctaws nuzzled in the warm clutches of sleep.

SUNDAY MORNING

Rose

The road to the church was the color of a roan horse, lined with tall pines, deep green and sweet to smell. It seemed every Sunday a breeze caught the tops of the pines just as we rounded the last curve in the road, just before the church appeared in the clearing up ahead. Those green pine trees bowed and waved to everybody passing below.

"God's welcome to His children," Pokoni always said.

Every Sunday morning two hundred Choctaws drove their wagons down that dirt road on their way to the First Christian Church of Skullyville. On the Sunday following my grandfather's hurtful injury, it was twice that many at least. The church was nestled in a clearing surrounded by a tight cluster of pines, elms, oaks and sagging sycamores. The trees to the east of the church were trimmed back and the undergrowth cleared, owing to their closeness to the graveyard. To the south and west, smaller redbuds, flame-leafed sumacs, and thorny wild roses grew unchecked.

After what happened at the train station, the Amafo I thought I knew would have stayed far away from people for at least a month. But this new Amafo, the Amafo born at the station and brought to life at our home last night, insisted that our family be the first to arrive. As we passed beneath the final clump of pines, Amafo took off his glasses, cleaned the lens, and squinted at the sky.

"Take some getting used to," said Pokoni. I expected Amafo to nod or speak in any of a hundred ways to agree, something like "Umm," or "uh-huh," something oldmanish.

Amafo said nothing. He stared at the back of Pokoni's neck till she reached behind herself and took his hand. *Take some getting used to* passed as everyday talk, but Pokoni was not talking about the broken glasses. She was talking about the broken world we were now slipping into.

As we neared the church, I saw a recently formed grouping of families, old to our congregation, but new in their ways. The social order of the church had changed since the New Hope burning. We now had in our midst a family of people who had all lost children in the fire.

This gathering grew every week, as grievers gave way to their grieving. They had settled on a roosting place, a comfortable spot in the shade of the elms near the graveyard. To an outsider, the grieving ones might look like a family of real kin, hovering around the graveyard for the anniversary of somebody's death. But for those of us who knew them, their usual selves, we stared to see the changes.

No one laughed, not anymore. No one looked at anyone when they spoke. No one grabbed a friend by the waist. People touched, but not like before. Women and girls quietly stroked each other's hair. Among the grieving men and boys, brothers and fathers to the dead girls, talking gave way to shoulder squeezing and lengthy handshakes.

My father reined Whiteface to a slow walking halt in the shade of two old oaks. Morning service was still an hour and a half away.

Amafo gripped the side rail of the wagon and swung himself to the ground. Whiteface whinnied and neighed. As Dad tied the reins to a tree, Amafo pulled his hat low and stepped into the woods. Moments later he reappeared in the midst of the grieving ones. Pokoni gripped my hand and we both watched him move among his new brethren. Slow and slower still, he lost himself among them.

My eyes teared up to see him stooped and hollowed through with sadness, but Pokoni only smiled and said, "Sweet child, you 'bout to see why I love your 'mafo so. Stop your tears and watch."

Amafo soon stood before Amelia Chukma, Lillie's mother. He took her hands, both hands, and held them for the longest time. Though she had not been at our last night's gathering, Mrs. Chukma knew the all of it. Her mouth dropped to see the bruises on my Amafo's face. She shook her head and smiled a sweet and tender smile.

Her hand seemed to lift apart from her will, as if awakening from a dull, numb sleep. Her fingers softly sketched the purple lines and swollen flesh of my grandfather. She gently moved her fingertips across Amafo's face.

I watched a leaf fall, swaying back and forth. In one movement, Amafo lifted his palm to Amelia's head and guided her to his shoulder. In the thin arms of Amafo, Mrs. Chukma started slow, as if feeling her way at it, then she shook and sobbed—deep, long wailing sobs.

At first the fellow mourners ignored this loud intrusion, but soon they turned to look. One by one they moved to comfort, some to Amelia, some to their own wives, some to quiet the fears of their still-living children. The wailing cry we needed came bursting forth. A graveyard cry was not enough, not for this scorching act.

This was the final day the mourners gathered by themselves.

SERPENT OF BRASS

Rose

Brother Willis arrived soon with his wife and seven children. Out of respect, Amafo waited till the preacher spotted him and nodded, then he moved to help with the horses. Jamey dashed to the dirt play yard by the church, where the Willis children were already ignoring their mother.

"Stay near the wagon and don't get your clothes dirty before church!"

The Willis children were pelting one another with dirt clods in the usual order. The oldest was clobbering the next oldest and so on, as mischief slid down the branches of the Willis family tree till the three-year-old sat in the mud making the baby eat dirt against his will.

"Church just would not be the same without those Willis children," Pokoni once said. "Reverend Willis could rant and rave all day about the demons of Hell and nobody would listen. But take one look at those children of his and you will never again doubt that demons are real. Yes, the Lord works in mysterious ways His wonders to perform."

Samuel had more sense than all the others put together. He knew not to involve Roberta Jean in their mischief making. Respect for her standing in the community as a young lady had little to do with Samuel's thinking.

Samuel avoided Roberta Jean because of the big black rock she carried in her purse. She had discovered the rock in the lava beds of the Kiamichi Mountains during a summer church campout with other girls her age. She hid it deep in her purse before anyone saw her. That night she explained her theft to the Lord.

"Dear Lord, please forgive me for taking that rock from the lava beds even after we had all promised Miss Stella we would not take anything. I don't think you'll ever understand why I took it seeing as how you don't have any mean little brothers. So I am not asking for your blessing, just your forgiveness.

"I don't plan on ever having to use this rock. Somehow I think just having it handy will be enough to protect me. Amen."

Samuel knew of the rock, had even tried to steal it a few times, sneaking into Roberta Jean's room when she was away. But Roberta Jean never, ever left home without the rock. Barely did she ever leave her room without it. Thus, from his early years, Samuel granted his big sister Roberta Jean her place in the family. She had a weapon and he was convinced she would use it if threatened.

The younger members of the Willis gang were far less bothered. I fully expected one of them to be clobbered by the black rock. In fact, the promise of such a clobbering was one of the main attractions of the First Christian Church of Skullyville, and one reason not to miss a single Sunday service.

On this Sunday, when middle child Blue Ned Willis came skulking from the blackjack oak shadows towards Roberta Jean, she at first pretended not to notice him. Blue Ned lifted his arm and took aim with a glob of hard round mud. Roberta Jean casually reached into her purse and lifted the black rock, holding it high and flashing its sharp edges in the sunlight.

Even a dumb-as-the-dirt-clod-he-held child like Blue Ned Willis understood this message. He shrugged as if to say, *Why waste a good mud clod on you anyway?* —and ran in search of other victims.

Momma and I walked up the three wooden steps and entered the church. A single aisle ran down the center of the building. We found our place two rows from the front and to the right of the aisle, near the window. All the women sat to the right, the men to the left.

The windows were open and the curtains moved with the soft life of an old man napping. I sat on the end of the bench, where it touched the wall, and felt the sunlight warm my cheeks. More than anything, I liked these minutes of settling in, of smoothing my dress just so and lifting or lowering the window to suit the needs of rain or heat or bitter chill. I eased my shoulder against the pine planks of the wall and closed my eyes.

Since Reverend Willis occupied the pulpit, the Willis boys were guarded at either end of their pew by the Bobb brothers, Efram and Ben. They were strong-armed and stiff-lipped and no Willis boy would dare disturb their divine Sunday peace. They always wore identical black suits with knee-length coats and sleeves as thick as trees.

"God has a way of evening things out," Pokoni always said. "He gave those Bobb boys all that arm muscle to make up for not giving them any necks."

Beneath her gentle ribbing was a profound respect for the Bobbs, shared by all in the community. After their father died, Efram and Ben had given up schooling and courting to work alongside their mother on the family farm. The Bobb brothers were hard-working men and worthy of respect.

They kept their arms folded throughout the service, nodding and pointing with their lips while others shouted "Amen" and "Glory Be." They joined in the hymn singing with voices straight from the caves, deep as the dark and awesome as an echo.

Three hundred people were in attendance that morning, squeezed into a church built for a hundred and fifty. Brother Willis moved to the altar, saying simply, "Hymn number 48."

We sang *"Amazing Grace."*

Shilombish Holitopa ma!
Ish minti pulla cha,
Hattak ilbusha pia ha
Ish pi yukpalashke.

Pi chukush nusi atukma
Ant ish okchulashke,
Ish pi yohbiechikbano;
E chim aiahnishke.

Shilombish Holitopa ma!
Pim anukfila hut
Okhlilit kunai hoka,
Ish pi on tomashke.

Pi chukush nukhaklo yoka
Ant pi hopohluchi:
Il aiashucheka yoka
Ish pi kashoffashke.

Brother Willis always knew. The singing was so soft and sweet at first, the words so tender to hear. Every Choctaw could choose to cry or smile, the words let us choose. Soon, with all those new voices, the singing was loud and every word clung to the air till the next one wriggled free. We sang our own stories, sang them to the listening Lord above.

Before Reverend Willis began his sermon, the wind picked up and the pine trees swayed, filling the church with a soft murmuring of whispers. He took more time than usual flipping through the pages of his Bible. He was aware that his words would be repeated over and over in the coming months, at supper tables and all manner of Choctaw gatherings. They would be seen as our response to the attack upon Amafo. Our earthly response had been announced by Amafo, but the all-important Divine interpretation of these affairs fell to the Reverend Willis.

Before announcing the chosen scripture, Reverend Willis adjusted his reading glasses. His eyes took in the entire congregation and when he spoke his booming voice stilled the wind.

"We turn now to the Old Testament, to the Book of Numbers, chapter twenty-one, verse five.

And the people spake against God, and against Moses, Wherefore have ye brought us up out of Egypt to die in the wilderness? For there is no bread, neither is there any water; and our soul loatheth this light bread.

And the Lord sent fiery serpents among the people, and they bit the people; and much people of Israel died.

Therefore the people came to Moses, and said, We have sinned, for we have spoken against the Lord, and against thee; pray unto the Lord, that he take away the serpents from us. And Moses prayed for the people.

And the Lord said unto Moses, Make thee a fiery serpent, and set it upon a pole: and it shall come to pass, that every one that is bitten, when he looketh upon it, shall live.

And Moses made a serpent of brass and put it upon a pole, and it came to pass, that if a serpent had bitten any man, when he beheld the serpent of brass, he lived.

Reverend Willis closed his Bible. He slowly removed his glasses and lay them on the pulpit. He lifted his head and his eyes roamed the church, till every one of us felt he was staring straight into our own souls.

"The serpents are loose among us. We have felt the sting of their bite and the poison of their venom. We have been left to die."

He paused and a nervous shifting crept among the congregation. Quiet *hmmms* and *ohhhs* rose from bowed heads. The reverend waited. When he stepped from behind the pulpit and lifted his arms high, his palms to the sky, all heads rose.

"God will never leave his people!" the reverend shouted.

A deep and whispered *Amen* from Efram Bobb. His mother gripped his arm.

"God has given us a brass rod, made in the image of the serpent. Look upon this rod and life is yours. Forever, my brethren. We have been granted the rod of our faith, our everlasting faith that God is good and we are strong in the face of our tormentors.

"The fiery serpents have been loosed and we have felt their venom. But they are weak and we are strong. We are bonded by our love. Our love for our families, our love for our gathered brethren, our love for this good earth we walk upon, and most of all, our abiding and never-ending love for the good God that put us here."

We stood as one to hear his words. Reverend Willis turned to the pulpit and took his Bible. He held it high and the *Amens* grew louder as we watched. He lowered the Bible and pointed to the door behind us. We turned, half-expecting Christ himself to enter. He then pointed the Bible to our left and to our right, all with slow deliberation, to the bright green leaves of spring and the graves nestled among the trees.

The image of what happened next will stay with me forever.

Reverend Willis lifted the Bible in an arc, like the sun moving from morning to the evening purple sunset. We followed, mouths open and eyes pleading, as he moved the Bible high over his head, then lowered it to point behind himself, at the painting of the crucified Jesus on the cedar backwall of our church.

"He is risen and walks among us," he said.

STATIONMASTER JOHN

The Monday following, Pokoni and Amafo woke up long before sunrise. Pokoni filled a small pan with water while Amafo stoked the fire in the woodstove. When the water was bubbling near to overflowing, Pokoni spread two tablespoons of coffee over the boiling liquid.

The smell of strong coffee soon filled the house. Amafo leaned over the cookstove, tilted his head back, and drew in a deep breath. When the grounds settled to the bottom of the pan, Pokoni carefully poured two cups and placed them on a wooden table between them. As Amafo took a slow sip, she spoke the first words of the morning.

"Where will you go?"

"Maybe buy you something, Hester."

"Nothing I really need. Maybe some thread. Blue, dark green. Don't spend too much."

"Mostly I'll be spending time."

"William, please stay away from the marshal," said Pokoni.

"I can't do that, Hester. I can't show fear. You know that."

"Then be careful. You can do that."

"I'll be careful. I have some new friends picked out. Hope they have time for an old Choctaw."

"I 'spec they will. You purty good at picking your friends."

"You know Maggie Johnston?" Amafo asked.

"One-legged Maggie?"

"Uh-huh."

"Well, I hear she knows how to handle Hiram Blackstone," said Pokoni. "I am thinking she's a good one to have on your side."

"That's what I'm thinking too," said Amafo. Ten minutes later, while Pokoni gathered breakfast eggs, Amafo saddled and readied Whiteface for the three-mile trip to Spiro.

Awakened by the sounds in the henhouse, the yard rooster stretched his neck and turned his eye to the colors of the coming dawn. He scratched the ground, flapped his wings a dozen times, threw out his chest, and commenced his crowing.

"Guess you and me both got something to say," said Amafo, nodding to the rooster.

"Just be careful how you say it," said Pokoni. "Maybe don't be so bold as that rooster." With the coming daylight, she could see that Amafo's cuts and bruises had turned the right side of his face into a swollen mass of blue and black flesh. His nose was purple and a dark spot of blood covered one eyeball.

"Let me make you some eggs. Just take a minute."

"No," said Amafo. "No need to put off going. I better get on with it." He mounted Whiteface and patted her on the rear.

Pokoni walked beside him for the first quarter mile, then squeezed his arm to say good-bye. She stood in the road and watched till Whiteface disappeared in a wispy cloud of fog. The last thing she saw was Amafo reaching into his pocket and slipping on his eyeglasses.

"He didn't want me to see his broken glasses," she said aloud. "He thinks he looks fine except for his glasses. Please Lord, don't let him know what he looks like. Don't let him see himself in a shop window. He would die on the spot. Let me do the seeing for both of us, please Lord."

On the walk home, Pokoni carried on a running conversation with herself, Amafo, and Please Lord.

"I hope you know what you are doing, you shy little man, you," she said to Amafo. "You gonna be the talk of Spiro tonight."

"Don't let him go and get himself killed," she said to Please Lord.

"Yessir, they will talk about my sweet William at the supper table tonight. Wonder how the talk will go at the Hardwicke household?" she said to herself.

"You go doing something foolish and I'll bruise you on the other end," she said to Amafo.

As Pokoni approached the house, she turned and faced the pink clouds to the east and offered her morning prayer. "Please Lord, if it be Thy will, get him home to me tonight. I'll do anything you say. Bring him home safe."

The sun had barely yellowed the tops of the pine trees when Amafo dismounted on a hillside overlooking the town. Still hidden from view, he stood in the shadows of a thicket. Spiro greeted him with a cool blue aura, somewhere between foreboding and friendly.

"This day can go either way," he said aloud. "I 'spec I better keep a sharp eye out for flying boards. Not like last time." Amafo laughed to himself.

Daylight soon replaced the long shadows of buildings. Sharp sunlight flashed upon brass doorknobs, glass windowpanes, weathervanes, silver hair combs, golden watch chains, knife blades, and gun barrels.

Hypnotized by the symphony of light playing out in the valley before him, he leaned against the bark of the oldest elm in the grove. He was more exhausted than he knew. His knees gave way and he slid down the tree till his bottom settled in the leafy mulch of the forest floor.

Amafo welcomed the sleep that fell over him, a brief quieting of the mind in preparation for his return to Spiro.

Monday morning was in full swing when Amafo mounted Whiteface, patted her rump, and descended the gentle slope. He gave a soft tug to the reins and steered Whiteface in the direction of the train station.

"Might as well start at the beginning," he said aloud. He lightly touched his cheek and laughed a nervous laugh. As he neared Spiro he heard the morning sounds, the cranking and rising of a store-front awning, the whish and whomp of a silver-haired woman beating dust from a floor rug.

Nahullos, thought Amafo. *Some good, some bad, like Choctaws.*

At the train station, Amafo tied Whiteface to the hitching post and stepped onto the platform. He walked past the tables and chairs lined up against the wall. When he came to the second table nearest the door, he stopped.

Two feet from the floor he saw traces of his own blood. Someone had scrubbed the wall where he had brushed up against it, but streaks of blood still shone from grooves in the wood.

He peered through the window and saw the clerk and a waiter sitting at a table, drinking coffee and reading the newspaper. Amafo sat in the same chair he had occupied only two days earlier, with his back turned to the stationhouse. Ten minutes later the clerk glanced up and spotted him. He spoke to the waiter and the younger man strode through the door.

"Excuse me, I didn't see you. What can I get for you?"

When Amafo turned and the waiter saw his face, he stepped back. "Oh. I'm sorry. I mean…I didn't see you were hurt. May I help you?"

He stared at Amafo till a look of recognition crossed his face. "You were here Saturday with those children. That was you, wasn't it?"

Amafo nodded.

"I'll get you coffee." The waiter touched his own face without realizing it, then retreated inside. A large bearded man soon appeared, holding two cups of coffee.

"I am John Burleson. I'm the stationmaster. May I sit with you?"

Amafo gestured to the empty seat in front of him. Burleson set the cups down and settled his bulky frame into the chair facing Amafo. Everything about him was massive, his hands, his prominent forehead, his large ears.

"We are sorry about what happened Saturday."

"Thank you. For the coffee too. Thank you."

"What is your name?"

"William Goode. Folks call me Amafo. It means grandfather in Choctaw talk, so you can call me Amafo."

"Well, Amafo, you can have coffee here anytime. I mean that. I'll tell my waiter that when you come to the station, you don't pay for your coffee."

"I appreciate that, Mr. Burleson."

"John, please call me John. I was in my upstairs office when the trouble started Saturday. By the time I came down, everyone had cleared out. I see the marshal broke your glasses."

"They're still good to see through," said Amafo.

"You know the marshal is likely to spot you if you stay in town long."

"I'm not afraid of the marshal," said Amafo.

Burleson leaned back from the table in surprise. "Maybe you should be. I hope you're not considering standing up to him. You ought to know better than anybody how crazy he gets."

"I don't mean to fight him," said Amafo. "There are other ways to stand up to a man. I mean to be friendly to him."

"Why would you want to do that?"

"I need to let him know I am not afraid of him. I need that."

"What will you do if he comes at you again?" asked Burleson.

"I 'spec I'd pray you'd be nearby," said Amafo. Burleson laughed a long and friendly laugh. He sipped his coffee and studied this strange old Indian man.

"Well, I'm not really sure what you're up to, my friend," he finally said. "But I like your spirit." He stood and gripped Amafo's hand. "I wish you well and hope to see you often."

The first passengers of the day were already lining up at the ticket window. As they passed Amafo, several people pointed to his face and spoke about him as if he were not there.

"Look at that old man."

"Somebody sure beat him up."

"You get a little too close to the tracks, Indian?" a young man said, turning to his two men companions and laughing.

Burleson moved between Amafo and the onlookers, letting them know with a quick glance to leave the old man alone.

"You gonna get those glasses fixed?" asked Burleson.

"Don't think so, not just yet," said Amafo.

"Hmmm. I think I know why you came back to town. Sort of a reminder to the good people of Spiro about their marshal. A different way of standing up to him, like you said."

Amafo said nothing. Burleson picked his cup up and emptied it.

"You have a friend in John Burleson," he said, then turned to go.

The sun shone hot on Spiro when Amafo returned to Whiteface.

"Well, sorry to keep you waitin', little lady, but I did alright. I had good coffee and made a new friend," he told her. "Yessir, things went a little better than Saturday."

Amafo was encouraged by John Burleson, but the cloud of dread that accompanied him was as dark as ever. With every passing minute his encounter with Marshal Hardwicke drew closer.

LEGGY MAGGIE AND FRIENDS

HOW THINGS CAME TO BE

For twenty years, Maggie Johnston had suffered under the most despotic boss in Spiro—Hiram Blackstone, owner of the Spiro Drygoods Store. Hiram saw himself as a man in total control of his operation. Though he allowed Maggie to make small decisions, he reserved the large decisions for himself.

Maggie went along with this arrangement. She was simply waiting, after twenty years, for any large decisions to come along. So far none had.

Maggie was a stout woman, never married and in her mid-forties. According to the social customs of the day, this meant she was unlikely ever to be married. But more than one middle-aged gentleman in Spiro realized that a woman such as Maggie—smart, energetic, and earning a living wage—could prove to be a fine companion.

Magggie had other ideas. She had no desire to be anybody's companion. She wanted a man who knew how to say "yes ma'am," or at least a man like Hiram, who knew how to stay out of her way.

Maggie had one superficial flaw, her right leg. From just above the knee down, her right leg was wooden.

When Maggie was thirteen years old, she stepped on a thorny

catclaw bush while drying off after a dip in the swimming hole. The small puncture wound grew into an ugly infestation. Her leg turned black, gangrene set in, and in an endless night of screams and tears, Maggie Johnston lost her leg.

But Maggie's will was stronger than ever after the incident. To the surprise of dozens of lady well-wishers who flooded the Johnston house after hearing of her loss, she fought their pity with a vengeance.

"You eat their little coffee cakes!" she shouted at her mother. "I'm having grits and biscuits."

The next day, at Maggie's request, the best trim carpenter in Spiro fashioned her a make-do leg till the real one arrived from the Sears and Roebuck's catalog. Less than forty-eight hours after her Uncle Samuel buried his favorite niece's leg in his back pasture, only to have Billy Lawton dig it up and feed it to his hogs, Maggie strapped the leather harness to her thigh, strode out the back door, and dug fence post holes with her grandfather till suppertime.

Or so the story goes.

While it was true that Hiram Blackstone could be a bullheaded and cantankerous boss, it was also true that Maggie gave as much as she took. Maggie was self-assured. Hiram was indecisive. She was also bigger, stronger, and more quick-witted than poor Hiram, whose only real advantage lay in the fact that he *was* the boss.

Maggie's eyes were green and bright and her face was full. She was round-figured and mounds of auburn hair fell about her face and shoulders.

Hiram's face was thin and his hair was graying and sparse. Though he combed long strands of it from his left ear to his right, patches of scabby yellow scalp shone through. His blue eyes darted about so fast even regular customers found it difficult to trust him. His high-pitched voice often wavered and trailed away, as if he expected the customer to complete his thoughts.

Several times a month, Maggie talked Hiram into a sale. She had a ready-made sign, announcing SALE TODAY in bright blue letters. She placed the sign in the display window even before prices had been determined. She relished these mini-events and would dash throughout the store marking down prices on overstocked items, generating a flurry of customers and buying.

For the duration of the sale Hiram would loom over customers, muttering, "You better buy that cloth now. She's marked it too cheap and any minute I'm very likely to change my mind about this sale."

Hiram had a favorite annoying line he used on inquisitive customers, whether it applied to the situation or not. "Some do. Some don't."

That was it.

"Will these hinges work with those doors?"

"Some do. Some don't."

"Do your sewing machines come with a guarantee?"

"Some do. Some don't."

"Will these nails rust?"

"Some do. Some don't."

"Will this rope hold a horse for breaking?"

"Some do. Some don't."

Hiram rarely listened to customers and viewed them as a nuisance he would much rather do without. Truth was, without Maggie Johnston, the Spiro Drygoods Store would have struggled to survive even though Hiram Blackstone had no competition in Spiro.

The Monday morning of Amafo's ride to town, Maggie cajoled

Hiram into throwing "the first sale of the month!" Hiram was sitting at his desk, contentedly counting his money. Without warning, he heard the familiar thumping of stump against hardwood floor.

"Mr. Blackstone," Maggie declared, bursting into the office, "we are running out of shelf space for all these children's clothes. It is time to put some cash in the register. You know a sale always brings in the customers."

"Some do. Some don't," said Hiram, and that was all the approval Maggie needed. She thumped her way to the front window, separated the curtains, and with her sign already in hand, announced to mingling sidewalk browsers that the sale was on.

From his viewing point above town, Amafo noticed the commotion at the drygoods store. Like all shy folks, he realized that the easiest place to remain inconspicuous was in the midst of a crowd. He left Whiteface tied to the tree and joined throngs of townspeople on their way to the store.

Customers gathered on the sidewalk, watching the spectacle unfolding in the front window. Maggie plopped herself backwards, then rolled over and stood up in the display window. With pen in hand, she crossed out current prices and replaced them with lesser ones. Most items—children's pants and shirts and dresses—were reduced by more than half of the original price.

"Maggie Johnston, you get down from that window this minute!" hollered Hiram in his squeakiest voice.

"I'll come down when I'm finished," said Maggie.

Hiram resorted to a hissing whisper. "Maggie, you are creating a sale with no profit. We will starve. You will be out on the streets by tomorrow."

"Maybe that will be a blessing," said Maggie. "I'm sure the good people of Spiro would never let a girl go hungry. My wooden leg doesn't eat that much."

The crowd howled with laughter with each exchange. But Hiram was not laughing. He was turning beet red. Seizing the opportunity, a skinny grandmother fought her way through the door and said to Maggie, "Dear, would you mind handing me that cute little boy's blue suit as soon as you finish changing the price to something affordable?"

Maggie made the requested change and handed her the outfit.

"Bless you, my child," the woman said.

Hiram grabbed a sleeve of the coat and gave it a good tug. The woman was as strong-armed as she was strong-willed. She fought back. The tug-of-war lasted less than a minute. A loud *rippppp*p cut the silence, froze the crowd temporarily, and left Hiram holding a tiny blue sleeve torn at the seam.

He looked as if he might cry. Maggie leapt from the window and wrapped her arms around Hiram to steady herself, since her wooden leg couldn't bend at the joint like a regular one.

"It's a good thing I know how to sew," she said, taking the sleeve from Hiram. She then turned to the customer, who stood holding the remainder of the suit.

"We will knock an additional ten percent off this item, ma'am, for the inconvenience and the rudeness you had to bear."

To the crowd she said, "Let's all come inside. I'll make coffee for everyone and we can enjoy the new prices." Hiram fumed.

"Don't mind Hiram," said Maggie. Amafo entered the store with this second wave of customers. When everyone else had filed past Hiram, Amafo stood beside him in a quiet show of support.

"Are you alright?" Amafo asked.

"Yes," Hiram said, spitting out the words. "Leave me alone."

Hiram turned to glare at this new intruder, but when he saw Amafo a change came over him. "*That bruised face, those broken glasses,*" Hiram thought. His mind connected the man before him with stories floating around about Marshal Hardwicke and an elderly Choctaw at the train station.

"Thank you for asking. I am fine," Hiram said. Amafo nodded and strolled to the invisible safety of a rack of men's suits.

After a brief disappearance to the stockroom, Maggie returned, thumping her wooden leg in double time. She dashed to a cluster of ladies fingering spools of thread.

"Pick out the thread you like," she said. "I'll come around and mark it down soon's I get to it."

Hiking her skirt and lifting her Sears and Roebuck's leg, Maggie tapped a short older gentleman on the shoulder and asked him, "Sir, would you mind pulling this shoe from my wooden leg. Other than muffling the thumping when I walk, it's totally useless and it slows me down. I need all the speed I can get today."

The man knelt before her and lifted her leg as if it were a religious relic. Maggie saw for the first time the dark blue skin of his swollen face—and at that moment a shift in time occurred, a noticeable shift that struck Maggie in a way she would later describe as *like Saul on the road to Damascus.*

She gasped and lifted her palms to cover her face and eyes.

"You I know," she said. "I dreamed about you last night." She paused and breathed into her hands. "How did you find me?"

"I know about you, Maggie Johnston."

"What is your name?"

"Amafo. I am Amafo. It means grandfather in Choctaw, and that's what most folks call me. Amafo Goode."

"Will you…lift your head…so I can see you?" Amafo tilted back his hat and lifted his face to Maggie. She touched his bruised face as only Pokoni would, soft and tender, running her fingertips across his cuts.

Maggie lowered her leg to the floor and straightened her dress.

"Please stay right here. Don't go. Don't move. Wait for me. Please."

"I'll wait for you," said Amafo.

Maggie strode to the front of the store where Hiram still stood.

"Hiram," she said, taking off her apron as she spoke, "I have private affairs I must attend to. We have more customers than we've had in a week of Sundays. I brought 'em in, you can take over from here. I will see you in an hour."

"You are not leaving me here alone with these people," whispered Hiram. "I'll fire you, I'm warning you."

"You'll be fine, Hiram. Just smile and take their money."

She returned to Amafo, saying, "Let's go to the stockroom. Hiram will have his hands full out here. He won't bother us."

She led Amafo to a desk where two chairs sat facing each other and gestured for him to sit. In the quiet of the room Maggie studied his face.

"Marshal Hardwicke did this to you?"

"Well," said Amafo, "I 'spec the board had something to do with it."

"Hmmm. Yes, I can see that. I want to ask you something, and please don't say no till you hear me out. Normally I would just tell you what I was going to do, but I don't think you'd put up with that."

Amafo smiled and said, "I just might surprise you. I'm really just a pitiful old Indian. I'm not nearly as strong as I look."

Seeing how thin Amafo was, how his shoulders slumped, how his skin hung loose on his battered face, Maggie had to smile. "You are strong enough to still have a sense of humor. I'm not sure I could be that strong."

Amafo's eyes sparkled.

"I have a friend, an older man, a good man," said Maggie. "He's a doctor. Please let me bring him here. I want him to look at you. Please let me do this. I will never stop worrying unless you do."

Amafo sighed and rose as if to go. He opened the back door and stood looking down the alley. When Maggie did nothing, he said, "You would just let me go, without trying to stop me?" Maggie saw the smile on his face.

"I'll be back in ten minutes. You'll be fine, just stay out of Hiram's way. He's a nice man, really. He just forgets his manners sometimes."

Amafo returned to his chair as Maggie thump-sped past him. He closed his eyes and said a silent prayer of thanks. Amafo knew that whatever happened from this day forward, Maggie Johnston would be his friend.

"What a team we make," he said to himself. "A beat-up old Choctaw and a wooden-legged woman. Yessir," he laughed, "Marshal Hardwicke won't know what hit him."

Maggie returned in less than a quarter of an hour. A tall elderly gentleman carrying a black bag followed her into the room. He was wearing smart brown pants and a suit coat. He removed his hat, showing a thick head of white hair, and nodded at Amafo, waiting to be introduced.

"This is Dr. McGilleon," Maggie said. "Doctor, this is Amafo Goode, the Choctaw man I told you about."

"Pleased to meet you," said McGilleon, extending his hand. Amafo returned the handshake. "Now, let me take a look at those cuts," said the doctor, settling himself on a chair and gently removing Amafo's glasses.

Thirty minutes later, Dr. McGilleon took one final look at Amafo's wounds. "They should be healed in a few days," he said, rising from his chair. "It is a pleasure to meet you, Mr. Goode."

After thanking the departing doctor, Amafo gingerly patted his cheek and wondered aloud what Pokoni would have to say. "My wife'll have to pull them bandages off and go lookin' around, just to make sure he did it right."

"I'd do the same," said Maggie.

"I should be going. I've come to Spiro to have a friendly chat with the marshal."

"You are a funny man," Maggie said, shaking her head.

Amafo stared at the floor and said nothing.

"You are serious," said Maggie.

"Yes, I am. I mean to show him I am not afraid of him."

"Amafo, you have had a long day already. Please wait till morning. Come see me first and we can talk about it. Will you promise me that?"

Amafo closed his eyes, nodded, and rose to go. He made the slow climb uphill to the elm grove where Whiteface waited. Before turning home, Amafo knelt to pray.

"*Yakoke*, Lord, for all the good people you lead me to today. Let your blessings fall on all these Nahullos. Thy will be done."

TERRANCE LOWELL

The day after meeting Amafo, Maggie woke up laughing. She'd been dreaming of one of her life's finest moments, a day in her thirteenth year when tragedy turned to triumph. It happened thus, two weeks after Maggie's leg was amputated.

"You know you must be more careful now that you've lost your leg," her mother told her over breakfast.

"I did not lose my leg!" insisted Maggie. "When you lose something, you don't know where it is. I know where my leg is. It's buried in Uncle Samuel's pasture, that's where it is. It isn't lost."

Actually, Maggie's leg *was* lost. Unknown to her, no-good Billy Lawton had already dug her leg up and fed it to his hogs, so in point of fact her leg was lost.

"Maggie, dear, you must think of this as a blessing," her mother said.

"Mother, puleeeeze do not say that anymore."

"Now Maggie, you'll be able to do things that no one else can do. It *is* a blessing."

Maggie retreated to her room, slamming the door behind her. Ten minutes later she said, in her best sing-song imitation of her mother's voice, "Mother dear. Come see what I can do that nobody else can do."

When her mother entered the room, Maggie sat on the side of her bed with a sweet smile on her face. She held a small-toothed hacksaw in her right hand, while her left hand held a handkerchief, a lavender silk handkerchief Mrs. Grisham had given her just yesterday. "To help you in your time of loss," Mrs. Grisham had said.

At the precise moment her mother realized she was about to witness something truly sardonic, Maggie lifted the lavender kerchief, revealing a missing four-inch chunk from her leg. She had sawed a wooden plug from her handmade leg.

"Maggie, what have you done?"

"Now, Mother, don't get upset. I've just lost my leg—or part of my leg. Can you help me find it?"

" Oh, Maggie!"

"But Mother, wait. You were right. I can do things with my leg no one else can do. I can saw my leg. Anytime I want, I can just saw away. What a popular girl I'll be at campouts. No need to bring firewood. Just bring Maggie!"

Her mother ran from the room crying, but the idea that maybe she *could* do things with her wooden leg that normal legs would not accomplish intrigued Maggie.

If nothing else, she thought, *I now carry a near-lethal weapon, a club with which to bludgeon any boys who tease me.*

Thirty-one years later, Maggie's wooden weapon did save a life, Hiram Blackstone's, from the dull blade of a butter knife. Maggie actually saved three lives—her own, Hiram's, and a stranger named Terrance Lowell. But Terrance's problems began long before he met Maggie.

Terrance Lowell was misunderstood. Anybody could see that.

His first-year school teacher never recognized his talent. One morning Terrance put his teacher's new straw hat on the back of his pet turtle.

"Come see the magic hat!" he shouted. As the unseen turtle slid the hat across the schoolroom floor, the teacher grew angry. While she fussed at Terrance, the turtle enjoyed his breakfast.

How was Terrance to know turtles eat straw?

One mishap after another plagued young Terrance, till he met Miss Palmer. She was the fourth in a series of teachers who did their best with Terrance. Miss Palmer was actually making progress. Under her tutelage, Terrance came to school twice a week. This was progress.

By mid-October, Miss Palmer, having realized she had a truly sad little boy on her hands, determined to make a difference. One morning, while the other children were busy with a reading assignment, she approached his desk.

"Terrance."

"Yes," he said, staring at his untied shoestrings, sprawled in random squiggles on the wooden schoolhouse floor.

"You have nice eyes."

Terrance waited for her to continue, waited to be rebuked, for his shoestrings, maybe his laziness. Miss Palmer also waited, till Terrance lifted his eyes. When he saw her smiling, he quickly looked to the floor.

Miss Palmer touched his shoulder and said, "They are fine eyes, Terrance. I call their color hazel. Look at them in the mirror sometime."

That very evening, Terrance did as she suggested. He looked at his eyes in a mirror, a broken piece of a mirror. His father had hung the jagged glass on the rear wall of the barn. Terrance scooted a chair to the crowded corner where his father kept a small basin, a razor, the feared razor strap, and the broken mirror, held in place by three rusty nails.

Climbing on the chair, Terrance settled himself into a remarkable private moment. He first tried sneaking up on his own reflection, looking quickly then glancing away. Finally satisfied that his own eyes held no mockery, unlike the eyes of others, he stared and stared, bewildered by the beauty of their coloring. He saw sunbursts of soft yellows and greens.

"They are my eyes," he said. "Mine eyes." He took a long, soft breath and whispered, "I have nice eyes."

He leaned so close to the mirror a white cloud, borne of his breath, covered his reflection. Lightly touching the mirror's slick surface with three fingertips, he discovered that his very own fingers could wipe away clouds of blindness. So he moved closer, drawn by the miracle unfolding before him, his own eyes filling with light-rippling tears.

The next day, just before the lunchtime break, Miss Palmer said his name. "Terrance."

Terrance raised his hazel eyes to her. "Yes?" he asked.

"I made a special pecan bread for the students. Will you help me carry the box from my wagon?"

On the way to the wagon she said, "Your shoes look nice today."

Terrance glanced at his feet and realized he had tied his shoes without even thinking about it. Miss Palmer saw it too, and her response would change his life.

"From now on, you and I will be friends," she said, patting his head. "And you will learn to read."

Terrance tossed and turned in his bunk that night. He didn't go to school for a month. Those words circled like swamp mosquitoes around his head, day and night.

"It just ain't fitting. My daddy cain't read. My momma cain't read. Maybe if I wuz gonna be one of them college goers or sumptin, but I ain't never gonna be. I am who I is, and who I is is Terrance, son of my daddy and my momma's best friend!"

In a rare moment that night, as he blew his nose on his pillow, Terrance made a decision. "I still love her and forgive her her transdressings, but I got to leave a teacher woman who wants me to read. That's just how it's got to be!"

The next morning he packed his dirty pillowcase with everything that mattered, waited till the sun was hovering between rising and noonday, and trudged to school for the final time. He stared at her through the schoolhouse window till the students pointed and laughed. When Miss Palmer smiled at him, he gave her a small wave and turned to face the world.

With all hope of marrying Miss Palmer gone, Terrance Lowell entered a dark period of his life. With every passing year, Terrance strove desperately to be bad. He wanted more than life itself to be a true outlaw, a wanted man, a desperado waiting for a train, with his very own wanted poster, proudly displaying his unshaven face and unbrushed teeth.

Terrance lived like a locust-eating hermit in the scriptural desert of rundown saloons, determined to carve his place forever on the tree trunk of the West, a man everyone would recognize and fear—Terrance Lowell, badman.

In his dreams.

Terrance first tried gambling. He hung out at saloons with killers and robbers. He started by dealing cards from the bottom of the deck, a ploy which immediately caught the attention of every player at his table. Known killers leaned forward and eyed Terrance with suspicion. Hands flew to expectant holsters as outlaws readied themselves to riddle Terrance with bullet holes. He had visions of lying blood-splattered and breathing his last breath on the whiskey-sotted floor of a cowtown barroom.

"Tell Miss Palmer I still love her, but I ain't learnin' ta read," his raspy voice would utter these, his last words. And somewhere Miss Palmer would feel a tear flow down her cheek as she thought of him, truly her favorite student ever—poor misunderstood Terrance.

Terrance never suffered this fate, however. He was so inept at cards, he lost anyway, badly, in spite of his cheating. He moved from bottom-dealing to hiding cards. He hid cards in his boots, under his hat, up his sleeves. Nothing helped.

Terrance became a well-known gambler, not famous like Doc Holliday, but renowned on a regional level. He was welcomed at card tables across Oklahoma and Texas. Barroom clients bought him drinks. Dancing girls—not the younger, prettier ones, but the older ones with bulging thighs and bright red mouths—they'd surround the card table whenever Terrance Lowell sat down to play, just to watch him pull cards from everywhere and still lose.

In his sober moments, Terrance admitted to himself that, other than his unsatisfied ambition to be a badman, he was living a comfortable life. Local businessmen knew that no real money would change hands when Terrance appeared. He didn't have any. And where else could very low stakes poker attract such attention?

Ahh, the girls, the notoriety, the infamy of sitting at a table and playing cards with Terrance Lowell himself! And this once-in-a-lifetime opportunity only cost a businessman a few drinks and sometimes a few dollars for staking Terrance for a hand or two.

But Terrance Lowell's life of glory was short-lived.

The beginning of the end came when Terrance decided he needed a gun, if even just for show. People, after all, asked questions.

"How many people you killed, Terrance, uh, Mr. Lowell?"

Terrance saw quickly that a shy muttering of, "Aww, not all that many," left onlookers disappointed, bored, and likely to wander off to more colorful conversation.

With a gun he could pull back his coat, grip his pistol handle, glare at the questioner and growl, "You could count the notches on the barrel of my gun. But then again you might just die trying."

Terrance decided the time for fantasies was over. He needed a real reputation, a real criminal record. He needed a real gun.

There was one place on earth where Terrance knew he was always welcome. Red Oak, Oklahoma. If he was down on his luck, he could count on the local marshal to let him sleep in the city jail. All Terrance had to do was help him drink his whiskey and show him a few card tricks. One evening, before retiring to his cell, Terrance was admiring a Colt .45 pistol hanging on the wall of the jail.

"Your deal, Terrance."

"Nice gun."

"Yeah, it's a pretty one," agreed the marshal. "It belongs to a horse thief we caught last night. Looks like he's gonna be hanged. He's got a nice little wife and four young'uns. It's a real shame, 'cause his wife can't even shoot a gun. Don't know what'll happen to that pistol."

"Real nice gun."

"Yeah, the gun that won the West," said the marshal.

"From what?"

"What you saying, Terrance?"

"Won the West from what?"

"How am I supposed to know? From a bunch of drunk Indians, I guess."

"Some battle."

"Well, you gotta admit, Terrance, cowboys and Indians did get a lotta press."

"Good-looking gun," said Terrance.

"Terrance, why don't you just shut up and take the gun! I'll just say I never saw it. Deal the cards!"

So Terrance Lowell had a gun. Now the only decision was *trains or banks?* Which to rob? Realizing banks were easier to catch, Terrance thought he'd try one of them first.

Spiro First National Bank seemed like a good one. It wasn't too far away and nobody knew him in Spiro. The fact that the Spiro bank was one of the richest in Indian Territory never entered Terrance's mind. He was, after all, on the trail for glory, not mere financial gain.

At the precise moment Maggie Johnston left through the rear door of the Spiro Hardware Store to fetch a doctor for Amafo, Terrance Lowell saddled his horse, patted his hip where his newly acquired gun rested, and turned his sights to Spiro and long-awaited glory.

Like gravy on a well-fired stove, the plot thickened.

SNAKES AND SPIDERS

Rose

"Amafo is coming!" Jamey hollered. "He's almost here." Jamey dashed in the kitchen to tell Pokoni the news. "I saw him riding Whiteface just now, coming over the hill.

"Leave him be," said Pokoni. "He'll be very tired, too tired to talk. You know he don't like to talk much anyway."

"But, Pokoni," Jamey said, "it looks like he's been in a fight. His face is wrapped in bandages."

Pokoni dried her hands and walked to the road to met Amafo. They spoke for a short while and Pokoni touched his face several times, inspecting the bandages. I could see they both were smiling. Amafo led Whiteface to the barn where Daddy was feeding a load of hay to the milk cows.

"Go on inside," he said to Amafo, taking Whiteface by the reins. "I'll see she's fed and watered."

At the supper table, Jamey grabbed the chair next to Amafo. *My* chair. He rubbed and wiggled against Amafo all supper long, staring bug-eyed at him till Daddy picked his plate up and said, "Time for you to get upstairs. Leave Amafo alone, son."

"He will talk when he is ready," Pokoni whispered, and Amafo pretended not to hear. He did not say a single word at the table. He just cleaned his plate and moved to the living room. I knew if I helped Pokoni and my mother clean the kitchen, then sat quietly on the floor by the fireplace, Momma would let me stay up and hear what Amafo had to say.

Once everyone was settled around the fireplace, Amafo appeared to fall asleep. His head dropped to his chest and I saw his shirt move up and down in his napping way. Then I must have fallen asleep, for the next thing I knew my Amafo was standing over me with a cup of hot cocoa.

"I hope you like it a little burnt," he said. "It's the only way I know how to make it." I nodded and took the hot cup from his hands.

"That's what you claim, anyway, funny man," Pokoni said.

Looking around the room, I saw that my mother and father had already gone to bed. Pokoni smiled at me through the rising steam of her cocoa.

"You are learning to sleep anywhere," she said to me, "just like old people." We sipped our hot cocoa, blowing cooling whispers in the dark till the rocking sliver of half moon shone through the window.

"I made two friends today," said Amafo, and he told us about meeting John Burleson and Maggie Johnston.

❧❧

Amafo arose the next morning in the same hushed hour before dawn, somewhat relieved that his night of fitful sleep was over, a night of rolling on his tender cheek and lying awake in dull and throbbing waves of pain. Following a breakfast of bread, coffee, and eggs with runny yellow yolks, he climbed aboard Whiteface and pointed her nose in the direction of Spiro. Pokoni followed him only as far as the gate this morning. Shortly later the white fog enveloped both horse and rider.

Once under the elms, Amafo dismounted, tied Whiteface to a stout branch, and knelt to pray. Ten minutes later he sat at his table at the train station, cupping a mug and breathing in the rising aroma of hot coffee.

"I see you've met Doctor McGilleon," John Burleson said, touching his own face and easing into the chair opposite Amafo.

"Yes," Amafo nodded. "Maggie Johnston made sure of that."

"So you've met Maggie?"

"Ummm."

"Well, she's a one-man army, Maggie is. You are safe in Spiro as soon as word gets 'round you're under Maggie's wing."

A pause followed while both men sipped their coffee and gazed at the empty railroad tracks.

"You seen the marshal yet?"

"No. 'Spec maybe today."

"Folks are talking already, you know."

"I figured they would be by now."

"You still think it's a good idea, you coming to town so soon?"

"You 'member how you learned to ride a horse?" asked Amafo.

Burleson laughed softly and took another sip of coffee. "You mean climb right back on after you've been throwd?"

Amafo nodded.

"That might work. Long as you remember you are dealing with a mean man, a man as mean as a wild boar. And a coward too. If he lifts a hand to you again, you let me know. Hardwicke is married to a lady who seems to bruise awful easy."

Amafo took a long breath.

"I don't believe he's gonna bother me much anymore," Amafo said. "Well, I 'spec you have work to do. Believe I be going. Can I pay for the coffee?"

Burleson put a hand on the old man's shoulder. "Amafo, my friend. We have an agreement about your coffee here, remember? Besides, I owe you something."

"You don't owe me," Amafo said, touching the bandages on his face. "None of this was your business."

"We all owe you. We've been blind to Hardwicke and his ways for too long."

Amafo quietly made his way down the sidewalk to the hardware store. With his hat pulled low, he settled on a pine bench by the front door. Five minutes later Maggie emerged, carrying a broom and eyeing a dusty cobweb in the display window.

"I thought I told you to move on down the road," she said, swinging the broom and splitting the cobweb.

The uprooted spider landed on the floor and crept through Maggie's legs and out the door. Seeing no spider, Maggie began a series of small and comical pirouettes. Using her wooden leg as support, she turned around and around, swatting the floor with the broom as she did so. Amafo laughed out loud and Maggie flashed him a look through the window.

"Oh," she said, stepping outside to join him. "I didn't know you were there, watching me make a fool of myself. Why didn't you say something?"

"I was having too much fun watching you," he said.

"Well, I just hate these spiders. If I thought setting fire to the place would get rid of 'em, I might be tempted to do it."

Amafo raised his eyebrows in mock amazement. "You would burn helpless momma spiders just trying to make a home?"

Maggie leaned her broom against the storefront wall and sat beside Amafo. "No," she said. "Of course not."

The two sat side by side for several minutes, walking the road of thoughts without speaking. Maggie smoothed her dress and laid her hand on Amafo's knee.

"If the truth be told," she said, "I sometimes wonder what it would be like to have a family. Especially since I lost my mother. I've always had somebody to take care of, you know."

"I'm real thankful 'bout you taking care of me," Amafo said. When Maggie patted his knee, he said softly, "Maggie Johnston has a soft spot in her heart. We wouldn't want that to get around town."

Maggie beamed and smiled at him. When he cast his gaze to the floor, she mistook it for shyness. Actually, Amafo had spotted the spider.

He stuck the tip of his boot in the spider's path and she crawled over his boot and up his britches leg. He reached down and took her on his fingertips, then gently placed her in his pocket. The spider settled in a cluster of thread and lint.

"I been visiting with John Burleson down at the railroad depot."

"John is a good man," said Maggie.

"Then I thought I would come up and see how Hiram was getting along, having to put up with you and all."

"You seem to forget, old man, I still have a broom handy," said Maggie. "For all I know, you might be part spider."

"Mag-geeee!" bellowed a voice from behind the counter.

Maggie and Amafo turned to see Hiram, hands on hips and scowling, impatient at Maggie's "loitering on the job," as he was wont to call it. Hiram would die before admitting that Maggie's socializing accounted for the bulk of the store's sales, but Maggie knew it.

"I think I hear my mother calling," whispered Maggie, and the two smiled like mischievous kids. As they nodded their good-byes, Amafo looked across the street and settled his eyes on the true purpose of his visit.

"I'll stop by later," said Amafo, not looking at Maggie. She caught the serious tone in his voice and followed his gaze to Marshal Hardwicke, standing in the doorway of his office. The morning sun caught the eave of the building and cast a shadow across the marshal.

"I'll put coffee on," Maggie said. "Let's go inside." When Amafo didn't move, she gave his arm a gentle squeeze. "Hiram won't mind. We've all had dealings with the marshal. Enjoy your coffee and we'll visit. Best to leave the marshal alone."

"I'm here to pay him a visit," said Amafo. He touched his bruised and tender cheekbone. "This affair is not over yet."

"Amafo, look at me," Maggie said. "I know that man. I have worked across the street from him for twenty years. He is meaner than you can ever know."

When Amafo did not reply, she turned to the marshal. "This is no game to him," she said. "He could kill you in the dark of night, and you would never know what hit you. No one would ever know."

After a long pause, she added, "No one in town would even want to know. They wouldn't care. You are safe. You are well. Leave it alone."

"Seems to me *leave it alone* is what folks have been doing for those twenty years you talk about. It hasn't solved much, don't seem to me like."

Maggie took a deep breath. "Amafo, I don't want to see you get hurt."

"This old man is not gonna get hurt," Amafo said. "You got to trust me on this, Maggie." He rose, put a hand on the wall to steady himself, and turned to the marshal.

When Amafo stepped from the sidewalk, Maggie knew she could do nothing to stop him. She entered the store and walked quickly past Hiram.

"Maggie," he said. "There are shelves to stock and work to do. Your loitering is costing us money."

Maggie stopped and gave him a look he seldom saw.

"That old man is about to get himself killed, Hiram. I will stock the shelves later," she said.

Hiram swallowed twice and lifted his eyebrows in a curl of a question mark. "Oh my." As Hiram watched, Maggie lifted his keys from his desk drawer and made her way to the gun display. She unlocked the cabinet and removed a shotgun.

"What are you doing, Maggie?"

"I'm borrowing a gun." She scrambled through dozens of boxes in the bottom drawer of the cabinet. When she found the matching shells, she began loading the shotgun.

"You can't borrow a shotgun, Maggie. Put it back."

"Then I am buying a shotgun," said Maggie. "Take it out of my pay."

"Maggie!"

"For the last time, Hiram, if Amafo dies because we do nothing, it will hang over our heads for the rest of our lives. We are bigger than that, Hiram. You and I both. We are better people than that. Now let me do what we both know is right."

"Maggie."

"What?"

"You can have the shotgun. Just see that Amafo doesn't get hurt."

"Thank you, Hiram," Maggie said. She quickly made her way to the back of the storeroom and pulled down the ladder to the attic. Hiram steadied it for her as she climbed.

"I'll hand you the gun," he said, reaching up for it. When Maggie hesitated, he said, "Maggie, I will hand you the gun." She gave it to him, then turned to the task of climbing the ladder with her single mobile leg. When she reached the attic, Hiram climbed two rungs and Maggie leaned to take the rifle by the barrel.

At its highest point the ceiling was only five feet tall. Maggie ducked, then fell to her knees and crawled to a small window facing the street.

During her first year of employment, Maggie had sewn bright green curtains for all the windows in the hardware store. The curtains over the attic window were the only ones still remaining. They were sunburned and browned with age. No one had pulled the blinds or parted the curtains for the past twenty years. People forgot the window was there.

When Maggie lifted the blinds, she heard the powdery sound of ripping cobwebs and a cloud of dust filled her nostrils. She coughed and rubbed her nose. She couldn't lift the window, and when she turned to the ladder, Hiram stood on the top rung holding a crowbar.

"Thought you might need this, Maggie," he said, scooting the crowbar across the floor.

"Thank you, Hiram, I do."

"Hurry, Maggie. The marshal has stepped back in his office."

"Did Amafo follow him?"

"Not yet. He's waiting for him on the sidewalk. I think the old man is too smart to go inside."

"Let's hope so," Maggie said.

It took Maggie half a minute to pop open the window, set the crowbar aside, and rest the barrel of the gun on the windowsill. She squinted and eyed the line of the barrel to a spot above Amafo's shoulder, aiming at the empty doorway to the marshal's office.

Amafo stood facing the door with his arms relaxed at his sides, as if waiting for a friend. When he lifted his head and turned his ear to the door, Maggie knew the marshal had spoken to him.

"Do not go through that door," she said aloud. Maggie felt sweat running down the tip of her nose.

Marshal Hardwicke emerged from the shadows and thrust himself to within a few feet of the old man's face. Amafo took half a step back and winced at the stale smell of his breath.

"What do you want?" the marshal asked.

"Nothing. Just saw you across the street and thought I'd speak."

Hardwicke lifted Amafo's hat from his head and leaned forward, looking hard into his eyes.

"You better leave, old man," he said.

Amafo felt a cold shiver roll over him. Short, quick breaths burned inside his chest and his heart pounded. He had seen eyes like these only once.

When he was barely six years old, he saw a large cottonmouth water moccasin near his grandfather's house.

It was stretched out, flat and lifeless across a fallen cypress tree on the banks of a swamp. He broke a thick branch from the tree and poked the snake to be sure it was dead. It was not. The snake rippled his muscles and lifted his head from the log, slowly turning to face his tormentor. His eyes were like none the young boy had ever seen. They shone back at him, dark and empty, and gave no hint of feeling, no clue of intent.

The young Amafo remembered, too late, his grandfather's warning.

"A cottonmouth will sometimes attack a man, and it can outrun a boy. Stay clear of water moccasins."

He knew the snake could strike him at will or slither after him through the swamp. He stood immobilized by fear till the snake moved in slow undulations, writhing from the log and plopping into the algae-covered surface of the swamp.

The boy ran to his grandfather's house and stayed near the old ones that day and the next, till his grandmother finally asked him, "What is the matter with you? Did you see a snake?"

When he looked at the floor without replying, she wrapped both palms around his head and sang prayers over him for a quarter of an hour.

"You stay close to home today," she said. "After that, you be hoke."

"Did you hear me?" Hardwicke said. "You better leave before you get hurt again."

"Good day," said Amafo, touching his hat and turning away.

The marshal watched as Amafo made his slow way to the end of the sidewalk, then stooped his shoulders and entered the millinery shop three buildings away.

Maggie kept the gun on Hardwicke till he re-entered his office. "Maggie," Hiram called from below. "I'll hold the ladder steady. Looks like it's safe to come down now."

"Thank you, Hiram," she said, backing slowly down the ladder. "I am proud of us, Hiram."

"I am afraid for that old man," said Hiram. "This affair is far from over."

"That's what Amafo said," said Maggie.

Later that day Pokoni met Amafo at the gate, raising her hand to shield her face from the blazing colors to the west. Amafo dismounted and led Whiteface by the reins to the barn. Pokoni accompanied them.

"How did the day go?" she asked.

"Hoke. I picked up your thread."

"I wasn't talking about my thread."

"Well, I stopped by the depot and John Burleson bought me a cup of coffee."

"That's never happened before," said Pokoni.

"Not since yesterday," said Amafo. "Then I visited Maggie, then the marshal."

"You saw the marshal?"

"Yes. We bumped into each other."

"You bumped into each other?"

"Yeah. But it was better this time. He didn't have no board. I just told him good day and went on and bought your thread."

"Wait here for a minute," Pokoni said. Amafo stopped and turned to her. She closed her eyes and reached to touch his face. Her fingers were curled with arthritis. Amafo felt his eyes tear up to see the purple spots on her crooked fingers.

"You know how much I love you," he said.

Pokoni nodded a slow, sweet nod. "I do," she said. She removed his hat, ruffled his hair with her hand, and sang *Amazing Grace* in Choctaw over him. *Shilombish Holitopama*.

With the loving couple thus occupied, the forgotten spider crawled from her temporary home in Amafo's pocket. She sought and found a new place to raise babies on a rafter overlooking Whiteface's stall. While the family slept, the spider went to work, crissing and crossing an intricate weave, wrapping her web, like gossamer armor, around the fate of the old man Amafo.

THE FIST OF DARKNESS

HARDWICKE AND THE AGENT

A week after the incident at the train station, a festive reception was
held for the newly appointed Indian agent at the county courthouse. The
invited guests were the business and political leaders of the county. They
came dressed in their finest attire, climbed the courthouse steps and
were ushered inside by the agent's servant, where an introductory line of
a dozen county officials awaited them. Last in the line was Agent Taylor,
who welcomed this opportunity to meet his new friends and business
associates in the community of Spiro.

Marshal Hardwicke waited across the street at the jailhouse,
eyeing the unfolding of the greeting ritual. When he felt assured
the last of the guests had entered the courthouse, he put on his coat
and crossed the street. He entered the building by the side door and
made his way down a back hallway before stepping into the flower-
decorated foyer.

A small orchestra provided the evening's entertainment, an
orchestra consisting of Mrs. Maude Lapham on the piano and her oldest
boy Nathaniel on the violin. Between the third and fourth musical
numbers, Mrs. Lapham smiled and bowed and thanked her audience

for the applause, while she reached behind her and viciously pinched the neck of her son, who had spat on his shoes and was casually wiping them on his britches legs.

Much to the chagrin of Mrs. Lapham, the crowd applauded this move with more gusto than the music, for it seemed to represent their own feelings. Though dressed in their best, the residents of Spiro were cattlemen and farmers and felt no more at ease than did poor Nathaniel.

A bar had been set up in one corner of the courthouse—two long tables covered by a white cotton cloth and manned by an out-of-town bartender hired for the occasion. The whiskey was from Kentucky; it was old and expensive. Guests practiced the art of pleasant conversation as they lined up and waited for their drinks. Spotting the makeshift bar, Marshal Hardwicke pushed his way through the crowd.

Sidestepping the line, he approached the bartender. He took the glass offered him, slung the whiskey down his throat, and held his glass out for another. The bartender eyed him for a long moment.

"I'll make it easy for you," Hardwicke said, grabbing the bottle. He found an unoccupied table in a far corner, away from the crowd. Slamming the bottle on the table, he called to a group of cowboys waiting in line.

"Hey, drinks are on the house, boys. No waiting over here!" He was soon the center of attention, surrounded by a group of barroom acquaintances, men who sometimes served as deputies in pursuit of Hardwicke's brand of justice.

Agent Taylor, still shaking hands and greeting his guests with a quiet charm, witnessed the entire incident from the corner of his eye. He noted that as Hardwicke fell under the spell of his liquor, his followers began drifting away. Hardwicke called for another bottle when the first was emptied. When no one responded, he stood up clumsily and staggered his way to the bar.

The bartender looked to Agent Taylor, who simply nodded. Thinking he had bullied his way to the top of even this echelon, Hardwicke grew bolder.

"Someone bring Agent Taylor a drink," he said. Lifting a glass and spilling whiskey on the bar and himself in an effort to fill it, he stammered, "Here, bring this to the agent."

The room fell silent and all heads turned to Hardwicke. Wives took husbands by the arm and even the marshal's friends shuffled away in groups of twos and threes, till Hardwicke was left alone.

He gripped the bottle by the neck and made his way to the side door from which he had entered. Before leaving, he cast a long look at the agent, who returned his gaze.

DEAD BY THE HAND

The night Ona Mae Hardwicke decided to leave her husband, she spent the early evening hours on the back porch, recovering from a sweltering day of planting her vegetable garden. She settled on the steps and spread her legs apart, lifting her skirt and letting the west wind cool her thighs.

Dark clouds covered the setting sun, broken by jagged flashes of lightning. Ona Mae saw her life now as clearly as if she were reading the *Book of Days* in God's own hand. She saw it in the sky, beginning with the purple bruises stretched across the horizon. She knew this color, the pain of bleeding tenderness, the long weeks of healing. Her twenty-year longing for change was like this lightning—bright and promising and devoid of hope.

Without thinking, she moved her hand to the forehead curl she had twisted since she was twelve, twisted it sometimes to the point of tears. Ona Mae cried now, twisted her hair and cried like a child.

She remembered, sometime in the third year of their marriage, finding a redtail fox in a trap behind the chicken coop. Its leg was snapped and the fox lay in a dying stupor, barely able to lift its head and growl at her as she knelt beside it. She moved closer and closer till her eyes were only a few inches away from the broken bone, fascinated by the slow ebbing away of life.

"She is like me," Ona Mae whispered. "She is slowly dying."

Ona Mae eyed the tiny splinters and the tears in the flesh where the fox had tried to gnaw her own leg to free herself. As she leaned closer, the fox seemed to give itself over to her. The growl shifted to a deep panting, a lift and fall not only of the creature's chest but of her entire body.

She cupped the fox's head in her palm and in a slow and subtle floating in and out began to emulate the breath, to breathe in the rhythm of the fox.

An opaque glaze settled over the fox's eyes and she appeared to be staring at a distant predator, a predator larger and swifter than herself, a predator who had caught her scent and was now moving through the underbrush, brushing aside the sumac bushes and rattling the dried crimson leaves like the soft rattle now hissing from her throat, a razor-clawed, blood-hungry predator named Death.

Ona Mae trembled with the fox. She felt the pain coursing through her broken leg and gently touched her tongue to the dark blood dotted under the fox's skin. At that moment, as she suckled on the wounded fox like a child on its mother, the fox died.

With the sight that such a spirit moment gives, Ona Mae saw her own life as the fox—fearful, trapped, and crippled by her own dull teeth.

I will bear no children, she knew with all certainty. *This man is bitter and barren and will give me none.* She wept quietly as she buried the fox in the soft dirt beneath her bedroom window, where the knowledge of its being would comfort her for the better part of two decades.

She had resolved to leave that night. That was twenty years ago. She was still waiting for the right moment.

Now when she remembered the fox and her early years of breathless fear, she saw herself as a distant cousin in a photograph, a child she seldom thought about and, when she did, she wondered what had become of her.

One thought continued to haunt her like a cruel joke.

Though the fox would surely have died, *What if she were still living when I buried her? What if my troubles are caused by my own cold nature and not the bitter spirit of my husband?*

She shuddered to consider this and replayed every cruelty he had dealt her as a way of proving to herself *he* was the mean one, the crazed one. In reliving these scenes she became what she most despised, one whose very existence was sketched out and defined by the punishment she withstood. Without his mean fist and bullying arms, Ona Mae was nothing. Without her life of avoiding him, cringing before him, and maybe unconsciously taunting him to drunken meaness, she had no life.

These moments were her worst, when she doubted herself.

When she heard him slam the front door, she jumped to her feet. The marshal circled the house, never intending to come inside. His door slamming was what passed for a greeting. He strode to the backyard arbor, pushed aside the drying vines covering the doorway, and stepped into his refuge.

Robert Hardwicke sat on an oak chest that doubled as a bench and place to store his whiskey. A small stone fireplace occupied the center of the arbor. Constructed of river cane and green willow boughs, the structure was more a long-range campsite than part of a homestead. The vines and shrubs shading the arbor were wild and unkempt.

In truth, the marshal never fully gave himself to civilization, never committed to the rudiments of domesticity, neither to his home, his buggy, the kitchen table, or his marriage.

Perhaps no scene more accurately depicted their marriage than the picture drawn at this very moment. Ona Mae stood over her kitchen sink, scrubbing her hands, while her empty eyes stared at the upturned collar and scruffy neckline of her husband, sitting between his two hunting dogs. His back was turned to her. He sat hunched over, clutching his quart jar of whiskey with both hands and wishing he were beholden to no one.

Lifting her gaze at the sound of the night train, Ona Mae watched the strange and beautiful fireflies hovering over the grave markers near the tracks.

SAMUEL THE NIGHT WALKER

Samuel Willis sat leaning against the barn in a cane back chair, cleaning catfish and throwing the fish heads into his mother's garden. Three feral cats leapt from the shadows, hissing and clawing and fighting over the stinking remains of the day's catch. Samuel knew he was both fertilizing and feeding, but his manner was listless. He sensed a cool front blowing in, felt it in his skin.

An hour before sundown he heard the wind's first whistle bow the tops of the pine trees. Within a quarter hour, the whine was steady and loud. Samuel stepped indoors only long enough to pick up his coat and hat. He pulled the brimmed hat low over his ears. Circling the barn, he shooed the cats away, selected four fish heads, and slipped them into his coat pocket. Leaning into the wind, he eased into a quick and youthful pace.

He turned north toward the Nahullo farms, into the rising gray wall of the coming storm. He knew where the creek bed offered the shelter of overhanging rocks, in case the weather turned bad in a hurry. He walked with no focused intent, but to say he had no purpose would be wrong.

Samuel went seeking the eye of the storm, the real source of the trouble brewing between the Nahullos and the Choctaws. His steps, he knew, were guided, and he felt the time was nigh.

Samuel had rounded the bend in the railroad tracks five miles north of town when he heard the low moan. He knew this moan. It was a higher, deeper wind that moved the elms and oaks and splintered the brittle sycamores. He paused and turned to face the wind, to read the moisture in the gale. *No rain for several hours, no need to hurry,* he thought.

Retracing his steps in the direction of town, Samuel felt the tracks shake with the weight of an oncoming freight train. He slid on his backside down the embankment and had barely regained his footing when a small doe leapt from the undergrowth, almost knocking him off his feet. She darted up the slope as the train's headlights scorched the night. Frantic and fearing for her life, she wheeled and came at Samuel again. He flung himself into a clump of sumac bushes.

As he disentangled himself from the broken branches, Samuel saw the light of a farmhouse a half-mile in the distance. He turned away from the lights and spotted, some fifty feet in front of him, a sight he had heard his father speak about. Instantly he knew the reason his steps had followed this path. Many times before, on other walks, he had seen the slate stones lying almost flush with the ground, a dozen more or less.

He knew them to be grave markers of some forgotten family who had sold their land or had it stolen from them before they moved away or died. The graves were too near the tracks to be disturbed. The land they slept upon had little use.

But the graves were disturbed, the sleeping ones no longer sleeping. Like large fireflies, the spirits hovered over their graves, moving slowly, visiting, returning, a dozen spirits walking. Samuel was overcome with a reverence for the moment. He leaned against a tree trunk, took a deep breath, and closed his eyes.

When he opened them, the fireflies were tiny balls of golden flames, a whisper away from becoming the people they once were. For long minutes he barely moved, taking in the nimble beauty of the sight: flickering lights surrounded by a pulsating silhouette, almost taking the shape of the living, then turning into light, pure light.

They know I am here, he thought. He moved among the stones and found that he could read the names. He stopped before Estella Roe and lingered there, searching the dark cavern of his memory. *Estella Roe. Estella Roe.*

Dead by the hand of her husband.

He'd heard his father speak of it.

As suddenly as they appeared, the spirit lights vanished. Samuel looked to the farmhouse in the distance and realized he was on the back acres of the Hardwicke place. Staying in the shadows and keeping a careful ear for dogs, he crossed the back pasture and five-acre corn patch. Nearing the rear of the house, he crouched in a clump of brown and brittle stalks, the remains of last year's corn. He could see Mrs. Hardwicke in a yellow square of window light.

Samuel decided to ease himself into the still warm dirt of the new garden and learn what he could from this vantage point, when he felt sweat dripping down his ribs. His breath quickened and his eyes locked on a dark gathering of foliage fifty feet to his left. Coming into slow focus, he made out the flimsy frame of an arbor covered with grape vines. A quick glimpse of lightning split the sky. In the afterimage and thunder that followed, Samuel found himself staring at the brooding darkness of Marshal Robert Hardwicke.

The marshal was gripping the neck of a jar of whiskey. Samuel sat without moving for a quarter of an hour. When he heard the nervous whine of conversation between two hunting dogs, he reached in his pocket for the fish heads.

Both dogs leapt to their feet and dashed in his direction. The marshal lifted his chin and said, "Sic 'em, boys. Go get 'em."

Soon Samuel was scratching the ears of two bluetick hound dogs eating catfish heads. Hearing no barking, the marshal decided the intruder to be a snake or rodent too small to worry about.

He looked to the house, to the figure of his wife moving in and out of view in the kitchen window. Hardwicke rose to his feet. In a stumbling grip for balance, he kicked over his whiskey jar. He cursed and turned his anger and his footsteps to the quivering light in the kitchen. A strange look passed over his face. He struck his fist hard against the wall of the house and stomped his boots twice on the back porch. Mrs. Hardwicke looked to the door.

The marshal entered the house. With a crash and shattering of glass, the light vanished. Samuel scrambled to his feet and ran toward the house. He stood at the window and watched a shifting play of shadows, screams, and curses as the marshal raised his fist and gripped his wife by the back of her neck. He feinted with a quick thrust of his shoulders and Ona Mae flung her head aside and closed her eyes.

Samuel stood leaning against the window, ready to spring through the door. Only the fear of Ona Mae's death kept him immobile. The marshal moved his knuckles to Ona Mae's face and rubbed his balled-up fist across her nose, slowly, taunting her with what was to follow.

"No," Ona Mae said, over and over, "Noooo," but her lips clenched tight to her teeth and all that emerged was a strange and primal humming sound. Samuel shuddered to hear it.

When Hardwicke drew back his fist, she lifted her elbows and crossed her arms over her face. He grabbed her by the hair, and when she raised her hands, exposing her face, he hit her with his fist. Ona Mae's knees buckled and she fell against the wall.

Samuel felt his hands shaking and his breath burned in his chest. He clutched his own fists and held them tight against his belly to stop the shaking. Hardwicke loomed over his wife and hit her as she cowered in a corner of the kitchen. As her screams shrank into soft moans, he began hitting her at random moments. Just as she felt he might turn away, just as she relaxed, ever so slightly, he struck her again.

Samuel knew by the strange rhythm of her crying that he was witnessing the bleeding of a wound, the playing out of a ritual much older than he was. He slumped against the wall and listened for any change in the awful pattern. With every blow from Hardwicke, he jumped as if the blow had struck him.

Samuel Willis became a child again, covering his face and sobbing quietly, as helpless as the woman who clung to her life ten feet from him.

When Hardwicke finally turned from his wife and slouched his way to the arbor, he overlooked the young Choctaw boy hiding beneath his kitchen window. He would never know that Samuel entered the kitchen soon after he left, helped his wife to a chair, and bathed her face with his shirttail.

Ona Mae was unquestioning in her surrender. She looked into Samuel's face as if beholding a heaven-sent apparition. He stood by her side for half an hour. He moistened the cloth of his shirt with his tongue and touched her skin lightly, moving around the cuts on her face and lips. He continued until he was assured the wounds were not deep and the bleeding had stopped.

Samuel lifted her arms one at a time by the elbow. He knelt before her and took each foot with his hands, one behind the heel and the other beneath the sole. He slowly stretched and lifted each leg. Curious at first, Ona Mae soon realized the boy was making sure no bones were broken.

"I will be okay now."

"I want to help."

"You have. Bless you, my child, you have."

"Will he hurt you again?"

"No. Not now. You have to go."

Samuel stood slowly and quietly. He took her hands and waited for her eyes to join his.

"You have to go too."

Her eyes never wavered.

"You are Samuel, the preacher's oldest son."

"Yes."

"You have my solemn word, before God, that I will go." As he moved to the door, she said over his shoulder, "You pray for me, Samuel."

In a moment, Samuel was gone, racing the storm. A mile before he reached home, it struck. He was grateful to be caught in the blasts of wild wind and water. He slowed to a walk, lifted his face to the sky, and spread his arms aloft. The wind whipped the buttons of his shirt free and the rain stung his face. In the pounding noise, he screamed till his throat scorched.

"Where are you, God?" he cried with the full power of his lungs.

A lightning bolt slapped against the wall of rock fifty yards east of Samuel, and the clap of thunder that followed sent the boy to his knees in fear and wonder at the powers before him. Samuel Willis had never doubted either his courage or his strength, but on this night he felt the sting of guilt to see Mrs. Hardwicke lying helpless and alone. He covered his face with his hands and wept to think of her cowering on her own kitchen floor.

With Samuel gone, Ona Mae focused her attention on her big toe. In the dim light of the kitchen, she squinted and stared and sent her will into the toe. It throbbed in response. She moved her attention to her ankles, then her calves and thighs, her bruised and aching shoulders, her bleeding, swollen face, till inch by inch she felt again her body.

She straightened her knees and stood on uncertain legs. She leaned forward and gripped the kitchen table, feeling the blood rush to her prickling feet. Through the thin crack of light between the door and threshold, Ona Mae saw the fireflies in the bottoms.

"Please, Grandma, can I go see the fireflies?"

"Now, hon, you know it's too late for you to go off in the woods by yourself."

"Come with me, Grandma. Please!"

"Oh, child. I'm too old to go chasing fireflies."

"Pleeease."

"Mercy, Onie. You are a strong-headed one. Pity the man that marries you. No, you get along to bed now."

Ona Mae made her way to bed, slipping quietly beneath the covers, quietly so as not to wake her bruises. She arched her neck against the pillow, as she had learned to do so long ago, to peer through the open window and watch the fireflies flash and flicker their silent joy, beings from another world, a world of light and laughter.

"Dead by the hand of her own husband," Samuel thought. *"Dead by the hand."*

"Lord God in Heaven," he prayed, *"please look over Mrs. Hardwicke.*

Please look down tonight and cast your eye to her suffering. Surround her with your strength, if it be Thy will. Please, be the God I know you to be, the good God of my father. Please see her through this night that she may know a better life someday. Please God in Heaven Almighty, please help her to leave. Please God. Help her to see a light beyond these woods."

Ona Mae opened her droopy eyes one final time before drifting into the welcome warmth of sleep. Her eyes beheld a glow from the bottoms, as if all the fireflies floated together in a warm ball of yellow light. Through the pain of coming bruises, Ona Mae smiled and fell away.

ESCAPE IN BROAD DAYLIGHT

MAGGIE AND TERRANCE

With his newly-acquired pistol in hand, Terrance Lowell strolled boldly into the Spiro Bank. After waiting politely in the longest line and letting everybody in town get a good look at him, he demanded, "All the money in your drawer," from the terrified teller.

Once he was satisfied he had all the money from the teller's drawer—and forgetting about the safe, where the real money was kept—Terrance pointed his pistol to the ceiling and fired a warning shot, just to let everyone know he meant business. Folks cowered into small groups against the wall, crouching and covering their ears.

CLICK. That was it.

CLICK.

Not *boom* or *pow*.

Just CLICK. That's all they heard.

Terrance had cleaned his gun out the night before in preparation for his first day of becoming a full-fledged badman, a bank robber, but he had forgotten to reload it.

CLICK. At first everybody just looked at each other, dumbstruck. Had he taken advantage of their confusion and run and jumped on his horse, or even walked briskly and climbed aboard Old Paint, a more likely scenario, seeing as how he never was much of a horseman, Terrance could probably have escaped.

But how bad is a badman really with no bullets for his gun? Nobody would ever make wanted posters of a bank robber whose gun went CLICK. Nope, the next time he had occasion to use his gun, he wanted his victims flung into the throes of death to the auditory equivalent of exploding dynamite, less a CLICK and more a KA-BOOM, followed by a teeth-shattering recoil.

For one brief moment of enlightenment, the disjointed elements vying for control of his thinking came to a unanimous agreement. There was no way around it. Terrance Lowell needed bullets.

Quick as he could, he untied Old Paint and led her to the hitching post in front of the hardware store across the street. A dozen of his would-be victims, leaving their bank business behind them, came trailing after him. They didn't speak, but the incredulous looks on their faces were noted by dozens of sidewalk minglers, who soon joined the throng of Terrance's followers.

Terrance was so intent on finding the proper gauge bullets and leaving Spiro, he didn't notice people following him through the door of the Spiro Drygoods Store. But Hiram did.

"Oh, mercy," he said. "What has she gone and done now?" He was convinced that Maggie had advertised a sale without even telling him, a sale the magnitude of which Spiro had never seen, judging by the size of the crowd.

"Now see here, folks," he said, but nobody paid any attention to Hiram. "Stop!" he hollered, but the crowd continued flowing in. "Ok, now, listen closely. Nobody buys anything till I have a talk with Maggie."

This didn't set well with Terrance, who had by now located his box of bullets. He faced the swelling crowd and grew nervous, recalling how he had just done his best to rob the bank across the street.

Maggie was in the storeroom sorting through unwanted items she intended to put on sale beginning Monday—without telling Hiram. When she heard her name, she strapped her leg on and stump-walked around the counter.

"Just what is it," she said loudly, then finished in a whisper, "we… need…to…talk…about," as her eyes moved from the crowd to Hiram and back again.

Terrance pushed his way through the crowd and to the cash register.

"I need to pay for these," he said, slapping three boxes of cartridges on the counter.

"Over my dead body!" hollered Hiram. He grabbed the bullets and clutched them to his chest. "Maggie doesn't set the prices here, I do." Hiram stuck his lower lip out and his left eyebrow began to twitch. He glared a *dare ya* look at Terrance.

It could be said that Terrance Lowell lived a life of quiet confusion, but nothing in his muddled existence prepared him for his present dilemma, as Spiro's finest citizens crowded into the hardware store, pushing and shoving to get a better look.

From Terrance Lowell's point of view:

A chubby woman barely five feet tall with what appeared to be a wooden leg stood behind the cash register prepared to take his money for sorely needed bullets. A tall skinny man with a twitching face and bobbing Adam's apple stood stubbornly holding the bullets.

"Over my dead body," the Adam's apple man hissed again in a low whisper. The idea seemed a good one to Terrance, who lifted his pistol to

Hiram's head, sending his Adam's apple into a leaping frenzy.

The onlookers gasped and cowered, but those from the bank hooted and hollered.

"He ain't got no bullets!" someone shouted.

"That's what he's trying to buy," said another.

"His gun is EMPTY!" they called in unison.

Hiram dropped the bullets to the counter and said, "Full price, not a penny less."

The onlookers groaned. Everyone was understandably disappointed, hoping for a bit of blood to top off the most memorable day in the town's history.

As if in answer to their unspoken prayers, a tiny child's voice lifted above the mayhem and sang out in high-pitched beatific beauty, "He tried to rob the bank."

Everything froze. Hiram closed his eyes and shook his head. To come so close! He timidly slid a box of bullets across the counter in the faint hope of completing the transaction.

"Hiiiiii-Rummm!" Maggie bellowed. "He's a BANK ROBBER. Don't sell him bullets. He'll kill us all!"

"No, ma'am, I will not," said Terrance. "You have my word on that."

"Over my dead body," Hiram said for the third time.

It is a sign from above, thought Terrance, spinning his gaze around the room in search of a deadly weapon. His eyes settled on a tall cabinet at the end of the counter with shelf after shelf of kitchen utensils. Terrance plunged his fist into a box of knives, butcher knives, steak knives with serrated edges, all manner of cutlery. He grabbed a knife by the handle and leapt over the counter.

Maggie balled up her fist and swooped it at his head. Terrance ducked and kicked her wooden leg out from under her, sending her crashing against the wall, where she settled like a ball of wet laundry, whimpering and rubbing the skin where the hinge met her knee. Terrance turned his back to Maggie, an error he would soon regret, for all the while Maggie was whimpering, she was also loosening the hinge to her leg and recalling girlhood fantasies of her wooden leg as weaponry.

Terrance spun Hiram around to face the crowd, pinned his left forearm to the shopkeeper's chest, and gently touched the knifeblade to Hiram's throat. The spectators backed away from the embracing men, uncertain if being washed in Hiram's blood was after all a fine way to spend a Saturday.

Terrance had not a clue as to what to do next.

"May I say something? Please," said Hiram.

"Uh," grunted Terrance.

"Don't get me wrong. I am very afraid."

"Uh-huh," said Terrance.

"Please don't try to cut my throat with that knife," said Hiram.

"Huh?" said Terrance.

"It will never work," said Hiram. "It's a butter knife. You are holding a butter knife to my throat."

Terrance lifted the knife from Hiram's throat. He stood stupefied, staring at the dull blade as Maggie scooted backwards and eased herself to a standing position against the wall. She gripped the ankle of her wooden leg and clutched it like a bat. A voice from the crowd declared, "It's a butter knife. The bank robber has a butter knife."

Terrance's brain had barely absorbed the word *butter* when Maggie swung the fat calf of her maplewood leg at the back of his head. Terrance melted in a warm puddle at her feet.

"Step aside now," said Marshal Hardwicke, entering the store and pushing through the crowd. "The excitement is over. Go on home, now. Let the law handle it from here." Marshal Hardwicke rolled Terrance over, wrestled his arms behind his back, and handcuffed him.

"Give me a hand," he said, nodding to two stout Irish farmers in town with their Choctaw wives. The two took a leg apiece and dragged Terrance across the floor as Marshal Hardwicke cleared a path through the crowd. They paused at the door and Terrance floated into blurry-eyed consciousness. When he spotted Maggie, his face softened and he took a deep breath.

"Wait," said Maggie. She knelt to Terrance and lifted his head from the floor.

"I didn't mean to hurt you, ma'am," he said. "I feel real bad about that."

"I know," said Maggie. "I didn't mean to hurt you either, you sweet and tender man."

"My name is Terrance. Terrance Lowell."

"Pleased to meet you, Terrance. My name is Maggie. Maggie Hazel Johnston."

At the sound of the word *Hazel,* Terrance fell into a swoon from which he never recovered. He would remain a warm puddle at Maggie's feet for the rest of his life. He was much the better for it.

Or so the story went.

Hiram Blackstone had never seen so many potential customers in his store at one time. Seeing them now desert him to follow the marshal and his prisoner, he tried blocking the doorway and announcing, "Half off everything! Half off, aren't you listening to me!" He quickly came to his senses. "Uh, that's twenty percent off certain items." Hiram was pushed by the flow of the crowd onto the sidewalk.

"Ok, you pick the items. Ten percent off with purchase of…"
Hiram sat on the wooden sidewalk, dangling his legs over the edge as he watched the parade to the jailhouse.

"Never mind," he said to nobody. "Have a good day. Hurry back."

"Hush, Hiram," said Maggie. "Can't you see a man's been hurt?"

Charges were filed—bank robbery, attempted murder and kidnapping—and a trial date was set. "He'll hang, no doubt about it," said Marshal Hardwicke, recounting the arrest at the Salty Dog Saloon that evening.

"A drink for the marshal!" was the rallying cry as Hardwicke flung down one drink after another. By ten p.m., the entire story of the bank robbery was reduced to Hardwicke's slurred verdict, "No doubt… hang'em, gonna hang."

Just after midnight he tried to stand and instead sprawled across the table. He sat by himself for almost an hour before the same two Irishmen who had earlier carried Terrance to jail, much to the dismay of their wives, now carried Marshal Hardwicke to his front porch and woke his wife, who thanked the men as they carried him to bed.

In his younger days, when he carried his liquor better, Marshal Hardwicke had often been the last to leave the Salty Dog, buying the final drink of the day before the bartender closed the saloon. But this eventful day saw a most unlikely customer enter the saloon and make the final purchase. Maggie Johnston.

"Good evening, Maggie," said the bartender, lifting his brow and placing his hands on his hips. He was making his final towel swipe over the shiny cedar surface before retiring. "What brings you here?"

"I would like to purchase a bottle of whiskey."

"A bottle of whiskey?"

"Yes, a bottle of whiskey," said Maggie. The bartender didn't move. "You do sell whiskey by the bottle?"

"Yes, we do. What do you want with whiskey?"

"It's a gift for the marshal," said Maggie. "He saved my life, you know. What does he drink?"

"Well, Maggie. Why didn't you say so? I thought you'd gone to drinking," said the bartender. "The marshal likes rye whiskey. He carried a bottle of this very brand home tonight," he said, lifting a bottle for Maggie to see. "In his gut."

"I'll take it." Maggie said and paid for the purchase. "Let's keep this to ourselves."

The bartender had already turned his back to her, but she caught his blue eyes reflected in the sparkling glass of the full-length bar mirror. They flashed in silent acquiescence.

"My little surprise of gratitude," she said as she left, closing the door behind her and stepping into the sweet pregnancy of the morrow.

MAGGIE THE WOLF

The day following the arrest of Terrance Lowell, Maggie rose at four a.m., a full hour earlier than usual. She dressed quickly and packed an overnight bag with three days of clothing for herself, and a pair of white muslin britches and a shirt for Terrance, clothes she had spent the previous evening sewing while she waited for the Salty Dog to clear of customers. She filled the bag with a canteen, a bar of shaving cream, a mug, a straight razor, two towels, and six pieces of jewelry from her modest collection.

She paused at the doorway, then turned to take her last look at the house where she had lived for twenty-nine years. By the time she opened her front gate, Maggie's face sported a smile that stretched her skin to bursting. Maggie Johnston was about to undertake the adventure of her lifetime.

She made her way to the hardware store for a tin box filled with four hundred and twenty dollars, enough to make her feel secretly wealthy. Hidden in the back of her desk drawer, the dollar bills represented money saved once a month for the duration of her employment under Hiram. Depending on how honest she felt she'd been, Maggie slipped herself an extra fifty cents or a quarter every month.

"Honesty is not always rewarded," she had often told Hiram. "But it should be." And every month it was, as Maggie watched her pile of honestly earned dollars grow.

Before leaving the hardware store, Maggie peered through a small opening in the window curtains. The streets were clear. She saw the marshal's horse tied to the rail in front of the jail. Maggie crossed the street and paused for a brief moment at the door to the marshal's office.

Through four small squares of windowpane she saw Marshal Hardwicke, or at least the top of his hatless head. His hair was disheveled and he sat facing her, but sound asleep and slumped over his desk. A cup of coffee, filled to the brim and still steaming, stood by his balled-up fist. She turned the knob carefully, pushed open the door, and entered the office.

The room smelled of strong tobacco and her eyes fell upon tin ashtrays scattered randomly about, ashtrays overflowing with cigar stubs like piles of bodies in various stages of decomposition, chewed at the feet and burned at the scalp. A dark-stained oaken chair, square cut and serious, faced the desk. Maggie eased herself into it without a sound.

For several minutes she listened to the wall clock's ticking. So rhythmic did the cadence of the clock blend with the quiet breaths and snores of the marshal that for a moment even Maggie was softened by the irony of innocence slumbering before her. Here lay a man so loathed by his enemies, so ridiculed and feared by those closest to him, yet his door was open and his throat lay bare.

And I the wolf, she whispered.

Years later, at the quiet hour of her awakening, Maggie sometimes replayed this scene for reassurance that her senses did not lie. At the precise moment she whispered, "And I the wolf," the right eye of Marshal Hardwicke popped open, only the right one, and not another muscle moved or even twitched. Of this also she was certain—his snoring never ceased.

The eye stayed glued to Maggie. When she gasped and fell back into the chair, it neither blinked nor gave any indication of human emotion. In fact, Maggie Johnston later recalled that the lone eye soaking up her form was anything but human. It seemed a beastly eye—callous and calculating.

Or so the story went.

Maggie stood and placed the bag containing the whiskey bottle on the desk, hoping to slip out unnoticed and into a more recognizable world. Hardwicke's arm shot out with such speed, the speed of a striking snake, that Maggie stumbled backwards. The marshal sat upright and held the bag aloft.

"What did you bring me, Maggie?"

"A gift," said Maggie, surprised at the unwavering sound of her own voice.

His mouth curled into a sneer. "What gift?" He lifted the bottle from the bag by the neck and puckered his lips. "Why, Maggie, you've gone and brought me whiskey."

"You were there when I needed you," she said.

"There when you needed me. I was there when you needed me, is that how it was, Maggie?" Hardwicke pulled open a desk drawer and placed two short, thick glasses in front of Maggie.

"Now you are here when I need you," he said. "I hate to drink alone, especially when I have company. Have a seat." He poured the sparkling whiskey, filling the glasses an inch from the rim.

"Let's get a good start on the day," he said, lifting his glass and downing the contents in a single gulp. Maggie took a small sip and shivered visibly, partly for effect and partly in response to the burning liquid coursing over her tongue. Hardwicke's eyes came alive and a red glow rose in his cheeks. He refilled his glass and lifted his gaze to Maggie.

"Not your cup of tea?"

Maggie replied with a tight smile and took another sip.

Half a bottle later, after twice lifting the marshal's glass to his mouth for him, Maggie found the jail keys in the desk drawer. She left the slumbering lawman with a full glass of whiskey within easy reach and the curtains drawn over the door. Her confidence returned as she moved down the narrow hallway and past one empty cell after another. Just as she had hoped, the jail was empty except for Terrance.

"Wake up, Terrance," she said. Terrance was huddled against the wall on a far corner of the bed. From where she stood, Maggie could smell the grime and stale sweat on his dirt-layered skin and clothes.

"Terrr-unce!"

"Huh," he said, opening his bloodshot eyes.

"I'm coming in," said Maggie. "Get your clothes off and don't be long about it. We are getting out of here, but we have work to do first."

"Lady," Terrance said, rubbing his eyes and sitting up, "I shure do wanna git outta this jail. I smushed bugs last night even I ain't never seen before. But I ain't taking my clothes off fer you or nobody."

"Don't get your dander up," said Maggie. "Just slip down to your longjohns and roll your sleeves up to your elbows."

Some tone in Maggie's voice, as if she spoke to a child, a silly misbehaving child, bade Terrance to comply. He soon stood before

Maggie in the most foul-smelling men's underwear she had ever laid nostrils on. Maggie only smiled.

You will hate my bossiness, many people do, she thought, *but you will love being clean and well-fed. I'll see to it.*

"Fine. Now sit," she said, and Terrance warily settled himself on the cot. Maggie rummaged in her bag before placing the shaving mug and brush, soap, and razor on the cot beside him. She poured water over the soap and whisked around the mug till it was filled with foamy lather. When she turned to face Terrance, her right hand held a straight razor.

"What's that for?"

"Your beard, to begin with," said Maggie. "Then your head…your arms…your eyebrows."

"You musta lost your mind, lady," but even as he said it, Terrance closed his eyes and leaned back to enjoy his first clean shave in three years.

Maggie alternately flicked whiskers in the air and wiped cream and curly facial hair from the blade to the bedsheet.

"Easy, now," she cooed. "Your skin is raw and sore, I know. I'll be nice as I can. Don't jump and we'll be fine." Her strong hand cupped his chin in her palm and she moved his face from side to side with gentle ease.

Terrance smelled the cloudy scent of Maggie's powdered cheeks. He soon fell asleep, remembering the flowery smell and warm lips of Miss Palmer when she kissed him on his fourteenth birthday.

Thirty minutes and a quick trip to refill Marshal Hardwicke's whiskey glass later, Maggie arched her back, placed her hands on her hips, and announced, "That does it. You are a new man forever after. Now get into these clothes. We've got to be going."

Maggie held up a pair of men's britches and a long-sleeved shirt with no collar or buttons. Both were loosely sewn from the same flimsy white cotton. Terrance lifted his eyebrows briefly, then his right leg, followed by his left, and after ducking into the shirt Maggie held out for him, he stood before her as shy and uncomfortable as a bug in a dress.

"Ma'am, you better git me some real clothes. If you think we're gitting outta here without nobody noticing, me dressed up like this and all, you crazier than I thought you wuz." Ignoring him, Maggie dashed down the hallway to the marshal's office.

"Okay," she called back. "Everybody's at church. Come on, Terrance."

Terrance tip-toed down the hall and soon appeared at the doorway.

"Take those boots off!" Maggie whisper-hollered. "Everything that once belonged to Terrance Lowell stays behind!"

When he didn't move, she said, "Somebody might recognize you by your boots." Terrance stared down at his boots and looked back at Maggie, cocking his head like a bewildered puppy dog.

"My dear Terrance, we are not intending to go unnoticed, just unrecognized, at least you. I want everybody to see my poor disease-ridden brother, who has lost all his bodily hair and is on his way to California to live out his few remaining days in an isolated colony of like-suffering souls."

"You talking 'bout me?"

"Yes, Terrance. You."

"What am I 'spossed to be stricken with?"

"Stricken with never-you-mind, Terrance Lowell. I haven't thought of everything yet. But we'll have a humdinger of a disease for you when we need one, don't you worry about that."

"You spectin' me to walk out in full light of day looking like this?"

"Not exactly," said Maggie. "More like this." She bowed her head, hunched her shoulders, folded her hands over her waist, and shuffled her feet like a chain gang convict. "Give it a try."

Terrance did not move.

"Terrrr-Unnnn-Suh. I will tolerate having to tell you everything twice on one condition. You must promise, for the entire train trip…"

"Train trip?"

"Yes, train trip. You must promise for the entire trip to speak to no one. Do nothing anybody asks or tells you to do. Except me, of course. Now, sit down and remove your boots."

Once Terrance's boots were safely tucked under the cot in his cell, Maggie opened the door to the outside world with a sweeping gesture, pinched Terrance on the left hindquarter, and said, "Let's move. I lead, you follow."

"That comes as no surprise," Terrance said.

"What's that?"

"I said it's durn sure good to be alive."

"That's what I thought you said," said Maggie.

Or so the story went.

SAM ANATUBBY

Not until they were on the sidewalk did Maggie realize the boldness of her plan. She had not anticipated, on an otherwise normal Sunday, their shocking appearance. Sam Anatubby, a Chickasaw horsetrader from Ada, was about to receive a first impression he would never forget.

Sam was looking to negotiate a deal on a dozen mares he'd already located a buyer for. After receiving directions and coffee from John Burleson at the train station, Sam mounted his horse and started the slow ride through town before turning northwest to pasture country.

"I know it was a long ride just to come back empty-handed," he told his wife two days later over breakfast. "But after what I saw coming out the marshal's office, I wadn't 'bout to buy no kind of livestock from that sickly spot on the map."

Melvina Anatubby scrunched up her nose and lips in her favorite and most often-used expression, resulting in a face so remindful of a bullfrog that Sam had to count off her good qualities at least a dozen times a day just to live in the same house with her.

She is one funny woman. She cooks real good. Lord knows, just look at my fatbelly self. She's no slouch about kissin', neither, he often told himself, though

Melvina had come close to spoiling a long, wet kiss one lazy Saturday morning when Sam made the mistake of opening his eyes and discovering she scrunched her face when she kissed. He never did that again.

"Honey," Sam said. "I wished you coulda seen it. Here come a short squatty-bodied little white woman walking on a wooden leg. Well, I seen wooden-legged people before. 'Member my granddaddy's Cherokee cousin by his marriage to that Creek woman over in Seminole? He had a wooden leg and I liked him just fine. He used to take me fishing. He would run sometimes six trot lines at a time.

"He'd roll his britches up, drive six nails into his leg, tie a line to each and every one of 'em, and go to fishing. I 'member one morning he caught three fish all at once't. He just unhitched his leg, throwed it up on the shore, and them fish flew right over our heads. One of 'em, I promise you, landed right in the frying pan.

"But best I can recall, that was a bass and once we fried it and cut it open, it had worms, little maggoty critters, so we couldn't eat it, at least not the part where they was crawling.

"But Granddaddy's cousin's wooden leg never did bother me is the point of it. Have a sip of coffee, sweetheart." A week after their honeymoon, Sam made a discovery that saved their marriage. Melvina couldn't sip her coffee and scrunch her face at the same time.

"Nope," he continued, after stirring two heaping tablespoonfuls of sugar into his own coffee. Melvina scrunched her face in disapproval. "It wadn't her wooden leg that bothered me, though you got to admit you don't see one every day, that is unless you work over at that hospital in Talahina, you know, the one where all them veterans do the best they can."

Melvina Anatubby was a patient woman. She often told herself,

Anybody with less patience would have left Sam long ago, the way he circles and strays before he gets to the point of what he's trying to say. He just won't stop talking!

Not long after they were married, Melvina discovered something that made even Sam's rambling tolerable. She found that if she twitched her nose and puckered her lips in that cute way her daddy just loved, Sam would say what he meant and get on with it. It was her only weapon short of rudely interrupting him *like any other woman on the face of God's good earth would do—that or scream.*

"Nope," said Sam. "It wadn't that leg that bothered me. But trailing after her was the most pitiful excuse fer a man I ever in my life see'd, and, hon, I see'd some messed up folks. 'Member that fellow what used to hang around the saloon losing ever penny he had whilst all the time cheating at cards? You 'member, hon, that white man what smelled so bad you almost didn't want his money 'cause you had to sit and smell him just to git it.

"Well, as bad as that fellow wuz, with bugs crawling outta his hair and all, this yer fellow I'm tellin' you 'bout, he was wurst. His skin was pale and ghost white, like he'd been living underground, that ugly pink color of a possum belly. He wuz all over colored like that. And he didn't have no hair, not on his head, I mean not even no eyebrows."

Melvina took another sip of coffee and Sam leaned over the table, closed his eyes, and kissed her. When he settled back in his chair and started talking again, he saw that Melvina's eyes were beaming bright and her cheeks were rolled into a puffy bisquit dough grin.

"I asked that woman that seemed to be leading him around like he wuz some kind of a white slave or something, you heard 'bout white slaves, aintcha, darlin? 'What is it he got?' I ast her. 'He got a real bad disease, mister, and it's catching. You better don't ride over so close,' that's what she told me. I turned around and rode right home to you, Sweet Dimples."

Other than Sam Anatubby, no one saw Maggie and Terrance leave the marshal's office. Three doors from the jailhouse, Terrance caught sight of his own reflection in the millinery shop window. He paused for a moment, cocking his head like a puppy dog seeing himself in the mirror for the first time.

Once assured it *was* himself he was beholding, Terrance jumped back and grabbed his head. He leaned forward, peering at himself in the glass and patting his naked forehead where his eyebrows had been. His eyes bugged out and he spun around and ran full speed to the jail, hissing over his shoulder at Maggie, "You crazy women. I'm gonna be arrested, looking like this."

"Terrance," said Maggie, lifting her skirt and thump-walking after him, "you already were arrested, remember…kidnapping, bank robbery, attempted murder."

"I didn't murder nobody. And that bank got all their money back."

"You are right, Terrance. I am certain a jury would be glad to turn you back out on the streets of Spiro. You look innocent to me."

"I did before you did this to me," he said, gesturing at his shaved head.

"No, Terrance, you did not. You have never looked innocent. But you will someday. You have to kill the weeds before you grow a garden."

"I am not your dirt garden, Maggie."

"No, you are more like the dying weeds. The garden will come later."

Terrance had by now reached the jail. He touched the doorknob and froze, whirling about and pressing his back against the wall.

"The marshal is awake. He saw me."

"Do not move a muscle," said Maggie. She strode through the door and into the office, where a thin column of smoke billowed up from the wooden desktop. A lit cigar had rolled from the lip of the ashtray. In a bleary-eyed stupor, the marshal sat watching the snaking smoke.

"I thought you were a ghost, Maggie."

"That calls for a drink," said Maggie, filling his glass.

"Ummm. Good day for whiskey," Hardwicke said as he downed the drink and reached for the bottle. Maggie drowned the cigar fire with water from her pouch and poured him another drink. Four whiskey shots later, Maggie stepped out to the sidewalk. Hardwicke never opened his eyes.

"Does he know I ain't in the cell?" asked Terrance.

"No, he does not," Maggie said. "But the whole town will know it when church is over and his friends stop by for their Sunday social club. We do not have time for this."

"Sorry. Mother knows best."

"What did you say?"

"I said a Norther snows best."

"That's what I thought you said. But if you want to see another winter, get out on the sidewalk. You look suspicious lurking in the shadows."

So on they went, Terrance hunched over and clinging to the building shadows and stouthearted Maggie dragging him back to the sidewalk. Nearing the station, Maggie heard church bells pealing and the soft murmur of conversation working its way down Main Street as first the Presbyterians and then the Methodists and finally the Baptists filled the street. Terrance glanced back and began to walk faster.

They climbed the steps to the railroad platform and were met by

John Burleson, who dropped the rag he'd been cleaning tables with and stared at Terrance like he was an overgrown monkey in men's clothing.

"John," said Maggie, "when does the next train leave for Oklahoma City?"

"One o'clock, Maggie," said Burleson, never taking his eyes off Terrance, who slid behind Maggie. "How are things at the store?"

"Fine, John. Mind getting me one round-trip ticket and one one-way ticket to Oklahoma City?"

Turning to Terrance, she said, "Now, Daniel, I'll take care of the tickets. Don't you worry about a thing, you just have a seat out here and don't talk to any strangers."

Burleson said nothing as he entered the stationhouse with Maggie a step behind. He unlocked the door to his office, slid open the frosty glass ticket window and placed two tickets on the counter.

"One dollar and fifty cents," he said. "You did say one round-trip ticket and one one-way ticket to Oklahoma City, Maggie?"

"Yes, that's right, John. I am taking my poor brother to Oklahoma City. We'll spend a few days together before he continues on to California."

"Your brother?"

"Yes. We have not seen each other in years, not since he returned from Panama. He worked on that canal, you know."

"Oh."

"Yes," said Maggie, "they dug that canal right through the jungle." She paid with the exact change, all the while displaying a tight grin.

"Maggie?"

"Yes."

"Why would you think I could let you get away with this?"

Maggie dropped her grin and met John Burleson's gaze for a long moment. "Because you of all people understand about living alone. You don't like it any more than I do, John. You will not, for this reason, deny me my chance at happiness."

"You plan on marrying him?"

"He is a good and misguided man and that is my intention."

"What did you do to him?"

"To Daniel, my brother?"

"To Terrance Lowell," said Burleson.

"You must mean Daniel. I merely made him a suit of clothes. If you are referring to his appearance, he contracted a terrible disease in Panama."

"A disease?"

"Yes. He can't seem to kick it, even after all these years. He helped dig that canal."

"Yes, I know. Through the jungle. Your brother, I am guessing, has lost all his hair to this disease."

"His appearance, you must agree, is a fate worse than death," said Maggie.

"You shaved him," said Burleson, shaking his head in soft laughter. "Where was Marshal Hardwicke?"

"Funny you should ask. We did stop by to visit, but the marshal was passed out on his desk."

"Maggie Johnston, you are either the most brilliant woman I have ever met or the craziest."

"Possibly both," said Maggie.

"You do realize I cannot allow a man with a terrible disease to associate with my healthy passengers."

"I have already paid you for the tickets," said Maggie.

"And you may use them. But I will insist on a quarantine. You will have an entire car to yourself and you may not leave it."

"And no one else may enter the car?" asked Maggie.

"Absolutely no one. You and your brother must avoid all contact with other passengers. You must travel in total privacy."

Maggie felt her chest heave in a sigh of relief. She leaned through the window and kissed John Burleson on the cheek.

"How can I repay you?"

"Make this work, Maggie. And let me know how you are. That will be enough."

Maggie nodded, took the tickets, and was turning away when Burleson said, "I have always cared for you, Maggie."

"Thank you, John," Maggie said. "I have always respected you, the way you work, how kind you are." She slowly turned to face him. At that moment the shrill whistle of the Oklahoma City train cut the air.

"He'll die without you, Maggie. Especially now, with what's happened this morning. The marshal will drag him to the woods and gun him down like a coyote. You couldn't live with that."

"We'll be fine. We can make a good life together. It's what I have been waiting for, somebody to take care of."

"Somebody to raise," said Burleson.

"You know me, John Burleson." A bittersweet pause hung in the air, broken only by the hissing screech of the steam engine braking

"Is this my train?"

"It is the one you have chosen, Maggie." She saw the train reflected in the gradual slumping of his shoulders. The softness left her face and was replaced by a more familiar look of determination.

"One thing you should know," she said. "Now that I've opened the cage, the beast is out."

"I wouldn't go calling him a beast, Maggie. He's to be your husband, you know."

"I am not talking about Terrance. I am talking about Marshal Hardwicke," Maggie said, turning quickly and stepping onto the platform, where Terrance rose to meet her. Maggie and Terrance seated themselves in the final car of the train while Burleson spoke to the conductor. As they entered the car, a handful of passengers cast bold looks at the strange pink-skinned man in their midst. They huddled in whispering clusters till the conductor stepped to the front of the car and loudly cleared his throat.

"This car is being quarantined," he announced. "Bring your belongings and exit through the door behind you. You may sit wherever you like in any of the forward cars."

When their car was empty, the conductor eased the door shut and hung a CLOSED sign over it. Strong-willed Maggie and misbegotten Terrance Lowell thus began their life together, a long and happy life that earned them the respect and admiration of all who knew them.

Or so the story went.

WAKE-UP CALL FOR HARDWICKE

Hardwicke was dreaming. He was chasing a strange and elusive someone or something through the river bottom. With every step he sank deeper into a boggy wetness of mud and stagnant water, so thick with life the odor clung to his clothes, his hair, even his breath. He scraped his tongue against his upper teeth and spat.

Stung by the bitter taste, Hardwicke jerked himself awake. He gripped the edge of his desk and tried to stand, but his legs wobbled and he rocked back and forth. He felt a hard rippling of stomach muscles. He lurched to the back door, flinging it open as a thick rope of chewed steak and whiskey flew from his jaws and across the dirt path winding to the outhouse. Hardwicke grabbed his knees and steadied himself against the pine planks of the building, wiping his mouth with his sleeve.

He was still leaning against the wall ten minutes later, tilting his head in wonderment at the dizzying shifts of the earth, as four well-dressed Methodists, led by Agent Taylor, entered his office.

"Smells like a saloon in here," Taylor said, spotting the overturned whiskey bottle. "Looks like the marshal started a little early today."

A door slammed at the rear of the building. All eyes turned to the ragged sounds of Marshal Hardwicke weaving his uncertain way down the hallway. When he appeared in the door, his body tilted forward and his head and face, down to the fat skin of his lips, drooped to the floor. The agent and his companions stared at Hardwicke for a long moment before the marshal realized he was not alone.

They watched him waver in his private stupor, gripping the threshold with both hands to keep from falling forward. When he shook his head and spat on the floor in front of him, the four men locked eyes in stone-clad judgment. Their eyes returned to the marshal at the precise moment Hardwicke discovered the open cell door twenty feet to his right.

"Ahhh oooh," he said, kicking the wall and staggering to his desk.

"Marshal Hardwicke," said Taylor, stepping forward and clasping one hand on the marshal's shoulder, the other on his forearm. "Let me help you." Hardwicke stiffened, but Taylor pushed him around his desk and into his chair.

"Prisoner's gone," Hardwicke mumbled, his head bobbing against his chest.

"What? What are you saying?"

Hardwicke waved his arm in the direction of the cells.

"See for yourself."

In less than an hour, the events of the morning fell into place.

"Of course, it was unusual," said the bartender, when questioned by Agent Taylor. "Till last night, I don't recall ever seeing Maggie Johnston step a foot through that door," he continued, pointing to the swinging double doors of the Salty Dog Saloon. "But she wasn't trying to hide a thing. Even told me who the whiskey was for. 'Marshal Hardwicke,' she said. 'For being there when I needed him.' Who duh ever think she was planning on breaking that bank robber outta jail?"

"No sir, I didn't notice anything different about Maggie," Hiram lied, when his turn for questioning came. "Same old Maggie. Bossy, hard-headed. Now, she didn't care much for the marshal, not since he took after that Indian with a board. But she never liked him much before that, either. No, same old Maggie, most I could tell."

Agent Taylor was inclined to believe everyone he spoke to regarding Maggie, Marshal Hardwicke, and the prisoner, till he shared a table and coffee with John Burleson on the railroad platform. Even before the usually talkative stationmaster met his inquiries with cool detachment, Taylor sensed compliance with Maggie's actions.

How could he not know what was going on? Taylor asked himself as he stepped onto the platform. A slow Sunday morning, Maggie and the prisoner the only two passengers. John Burleson is neither a fool nor a drunk. He had to know. Then why?

"Morning, John."

"Morning."

"Quite a mess."

"So I hear."

"Several people say Maggie Johnston and a strange-looking fellow were seen heading your way."

"I saw Maggie."

"You saw her. Was she by herself?"

"Seemed that way at first."

"You want to tell me more?"

Burleson stirred two heaping spoonfuls of sugar into his cup. He took a long, deep breath and looked from one end of the tracks to the other before replying.

"Your honor, I never saw who she was with. Had no desire to see him. Maggie claimed he was her brother, come in yesterday on horseback from Fort Smith. She said he was dying, and he sure looked like walking death to me. I wanted to stay as far away from him as possible."

"Thought you never saw him."

"I saw the back of his head. He sat on that bench while Maggie bought two tickets."

"You never suspected he might be the same man who robbed the bank and held Hiram at knifepoint yesterday?"

"Now why in dickens would I think that? That fellow was in jail, last I heard."

"You sold Maggie two train tickets?"

"Yessir, to Oklahoma City."

"You didn't see any danger to the other passengers?"

"Oh yes, your honor. I did. I made certain the car was quarantined and all other passengers seated in other accommodations."

"Other accommodations."

"Yes, Agent Taylor. Other accommodations. That's pretty much how a quarantine works."

"That must have been difficult."

"No, your honor, not once they got a look at Maggie's brother. That prisoner, I mean," he said with a wave of his hand.

"Had you ever seen him before?"

"Never. And I would have remembered. He was pale as death, and he sat all hunched over. Even from behind he looked strange. Sickly."

Agent Taylor looked away and Burleson continued. "I was here at the station all day yesterday, the day of the robbery. No way I could know what the bank robber looked like."

"Of course. Did Maggie say when she might be returning?"

"Returning?"

"Yes."

"Well, she did buy a round-trip ticket. But no, she didn't say when exactly."

"John," the agent said, leaning over the table and lowering his voice. "Listen closely. I am going to ask you a very important question."

Burleson gripped his knees and lifted his brow in a look of slight surprise. "I am forthright with you, Agent Taylor."

"I am not here to assign responsibility. I am here in an effort to understand the most bizarre jail breakout I have ever encountered. So relax." John sipped his coffee and stared into his mug. "Did Maggie ever appear to be in any danger?"

Burleson's response was simple and immediate and swept away any doubts Agent Taylor might have carried regarding the stationmaster's complicity in the escape.

"Never. No danger. Not a smidgen." His beaming smile took Taylor by surprise.

"They will both be captured. Maggie will go to jail."

"That might come to pass," said Burleson. He placed both hands on the table, pushed back his chair, and with a ceremonious bow rose and turned to the door. "I pity the poor jailer," he said over his shoulder.

One week later, after assuring herself that Terrance was as softhearted as a new puppy, Maggie composed the following letter to the agent.

> Dear Agent Taylor,
>   I know you to be, from the numerous times you have made purchases at the hardware store, a fair and even-minded gentleman. I know also you have borne witness

to the cruel excesses of our current marshal. This previous Sunday I prevented said marshal from exercising his meanness. His intent was to hang the man who now sits beside me, wishing he could read.

I have committed a crime, probably several. I helped Terrance Lowell escape from jail. You will, of course, question how an otherwise logical and clear-headed woman could involve herself in an endeavor so foolish as to be doomed to failure from the start. I will deal with the latter assumption first.

Terrance Lowell and myself have not failed. We have escaped. We are free and will forever remain so. Terrance has escaped a lifelong attempt to gain attention and notoriety by outlandish behavior. I have escaped a life of mediocrity and loneliness.

Terrance Lowell is guilty of brandishing a bulletless gun at a bank teller, stuffing two hundred dollars in his pockets (all of which has since been returned) and threatening Hiram Blackstone with a butter knife, Hiram who has now reached the status he has longed for his entire life. He is one of the gang with a story to tell. Hiram has never been happier.

Regarding Terrance, he is a hardworking man and good to the very core. For the first time in his life, someone needs him. I understand that, other than a dozen or so arrests for being drunk and disorderly, Terrance has no criminal record or past criminal history.

Therefore, I am asking you to grant him a pardon for all crimes committed during the recent and unfortunate sequence of events in Spiro. Though we will never return to Indian Territory, I would like to someday inform Terrance he may hold his head high in the full understanding that he is a free man with all rights. If I have since been charged with any crimes related to helping Terrance escape, I request that the pardon extend to my crimes as well.

If your heart dictates that you follow my request, please

send a single notice to that effect within a month to the newspapers of Galveston, Texas; Santa Fe, New Mexico; St. Louis, Missouri; and New Orleans, Louisiana. You hold our lives in your hands.

May God bless you,
    Maggie Johnston

P.S. Please allow Mrs. Taylor to read my letter.

Three weeks later the following notice appeared in the *Galveston Daily News:*

Be it known that effective July 24, 1897, Terrance Lowell, formerly of Texas, and Maggie Johnston, formerly of Spiro, Indian Territory, are hereby pardoned for any and all crimes committed in Spiro on July 2 and July 3, 1897. This pardon is granted by the Honorable Indian Agent Roy Taylor. Mrs. Taylor sends her regards.

From their balcony overlooking the Gulf of Mexico, as the seagulls yelped in the evening sky and the gentle wash of the waves soothed their troubles, Maggie read the notice to Terrance. Upon hearing the news, he wept like a child. Terrance slept in a blanket on the balcony that night, and the next day he and Maggie were married.

Eleven years later, on September 13, 1908, Maggie again made the *Galveston Daily News*. Five days after the Galveston Storm—a hurricane which killed close to ten thousand people—struck the Gulf Coast of Texas, an article appeared under the following headline:

WOODEN LEG OR GOD'S ALTAR?

Mr. and Mrs. Terrance Lowell lost their home and belongings to the winds and high waters of the Galveston Storm, but they managed to escape with their most precious possession, their lives. As the waters rose on the evening of September 8, Mr. and Mrs. Lowell climbed to the roof of their single story home on Grand Avenue, a block from the bay. Winds battered the east wall of the building, finally toppling the entire structure into the churning waters.

While sliding from the roof, Mrs. Lowell, known affectionately to Islanders as Maggie, unhinged her wooden leg. Using the leg as a flotation device, the Lowells clung to the miraculous appendage, like grateful supplicants before the altar, till their rescue the following morning.

Before their rescue, as Maggie and Terrance clung to Maggie's leg and bobbed up and down in the crashing waves of the Gulf of Mexico, the following conversation took place:

"Maggie."

"Yes, Terrance."

"I'm not sure we're gonna make it."

"Just hold on tight, Terrance. We'll be fine."

"Maggie."

"Yes."

"If my fingers slip and I sink away, what will you do?"

"I will sink away too, Terrance. To be with you, I will sink away too."

POKONI AND AMAFO

SLOW LIKE THE RIVER

Rose • Winter of 1967

My grandfather was slow and deep, like the nearby Arkansas River, while Pokoni, my grandmother, was sharp and quick, like a crackling winter fire. That is how I remember them.

Amafo was so soft-spoken he could enter a room and go unnoticed for hours at a time. He preferred this, for Amafo was the greatest watcher of people I ever knew. He was also the best judge of character I ever knew and tried to teach me everything he could in that regard.

Even as I write this, I am laughing at the irony of Amafo being such a great watcher, for my grandfather had the worst eyesight of anyone in the family. His eyeglasses were thick and the right lens was broken. Till the day he died he refused to have it repaired. But seeing, in my grandfather's case, had very little to do with eyesight. Seeing had more to do with insight.

My grandfather *saw* people, he saw them as they truly were. He quickly spotted an individual's faults, then just as quickly forgave them. He also saw the goodness of people and was never surprised when heroes emerged from unlikely places. I once heard him say of Maggie

Johnston, "She's been a hero for years, a one-legged hero climbing ladders and working for that funny little bossy man. That convict didn't stand a chance."

When Maggie shocked everyone by breaking the convict out of jail and eloping with him, Amafo proclaimed, "Like I been telling you, that convict didn't stand a chance."

I still have in my possession Amafo's broken glasses—his spiderweb glasses, I have come to call them. Together with Pokoni's sipping mug, they are my most cherished possessions.

Now that I am old, I have to be careful how I hold Pokoni's mug. I cannot stand and hold it as I once did. My grip is weak and unsteady. I sometimes wrap my fingers around its blue porcelain roundness and place it on my windowsill, as if it was a place of honor.

I have been known to settle in front of my upstairs bedroom window, once my grandmother's window, and stare at nothing for hours. Pokoni would never do that. I can still see her dashing about the house. Only late in the evenings did she ever sit still. She would lean her skinny spine against the caneback chair in front of the fireplace and take one long, deep breath. The entire household, the very house, would slip into a blue sea of sleep.

This was her signal to Amafo that her day was done and she was ready for her hot chocolate. It was his way of loving her, when they were older, his making chocolate and serving it to her, always in her special mug. Once Amafo forgot and left the kitchen while the milk was boiling, scalding the chocolate.

"Look what you've done now," my mother said, clucking her tongue. "Here, let me make her another cup."

"I like it that way, a little burnt," said Pokoni, stretching her neck backwards from the living room. And that's how she got it, for the next ten years, a little burnt, all to save Amafo from even a moment of embarrassment. Till the day she died, my Pokoni always enjoyed her hot chocolate a little burnt.

Yes, Amafo was slow and deep like a river, while Pokoni was sharp and quick like a crackling winter fire. Reflecting on my grandparents, I realize now what should have been obvious to us all. A river flows on forever, while a winter fire is gone before you know it.

THE DAY MY POKONI ALMOST DIED
Rose • September 1897

The day my Pokoni almost died began as a very unspecial day. No threatening weather, no visitors coming, no visits to make. I was gathering sticks and kindling and helping Momma stoke the laundry fire by the back porch. Pokoni was in the garden filling a basket with ripe tomatoes.

She lugged that basket around everywhere. It was like Pokoni's skin, old and sagging. She had woven it from river cane long before I was born, she once told me. It was the color of exposed wood, soaked of color by the sun to a soft brown, but splotches of red and purple told the story of its use. Thousands of pounds of grapes, strawberries, and tomatoes had found their way to scores of hungry stomachs, carried by this basket, gathered by Pokoni.

If Pokoni loved this basket because she had made it and lived with it so long, I thought, then God must love Pokoni like she was his own child, loving her even more now that her skin was sagging from her skinny arms. God and everybody else found it real easy to love my grandmother. "Filled with the spirit," folks would say, shaking their heads and watching her go about her work at twice the speed of anybody else.

That morning especially, Pokoni dove into the thick green tomato foliage, her hands held together and her fingers pointed in front of her, like a man diving from a high rock into a river. After every dive, she emerged with a fat red tomato. Her strong fingers clutched it like a trophy and carefully nestled it into the basket.

Seeing her disappear into the leafy rise and fall of the garden, I imagined she was holding her breath, puffy-cheeked, while her eyes darted from tomato to tomato, mentally discarding the yellow and green ones, till, completely out of breath, she would settle on a pearl of a tomato and rise victorious from the salty sea. She knew I watched her and she sometimes smiled and held her prize high for me to admire, but only for an instant.

My grandmother burned with the hot breath of the spirit, the life fire.

Other grandmothers bent and knelt and gathered tomatoes in their aprons. Other grandmothers stood up slowly, mopping their faces and slapping horseflies from their necks and shoulders. Other grandmothers rubbed the small of their backs and made painful faces, brushing away mosquitoes or blowing hair out of their eyes. My grandmother, my Pokoni, leapt into the tomato vines and whirled and whistled when she found her treasure, a single ripe tomato.

I used to think that other grandmothers were made of brittle breakable bones and scratchable bleedable skin, while my grandmother was made of rubber—stretchable, bounceable rubber. I know now she was made of the same time-worn human hurtable stuff. She just refused to give in to it, to the pain, the aging, the dying.

On the morning my Pokoni almost died, she was at her best. Spreading her legs apart for balance, she rocked forward and, seemingly in the same motion, reappeared, sometimes with a tomato in each hand.

She had almost filled the half-bushel basket when I saw her stand straight up, sudden-like. She shook her head from side to side, slinging spit, then slumped forward. She grabbed ahold of the thick base of an old vine, hung on for a moment, then landed hard on her rear end. Her head fell to one side and her eyes seemed unaware, like the eyes of a trap-caught fox giving in to death.

"Momma!" I called, but she was on the other side of the house hanging laundry. I knew she couldn't hear me. I ran to Pokoni, but before I reached her, she stood up and straightened her clothes, removing a broken tomato stem from her apron pocket.

"Can you bring me some water?" she said.

"Are you *hoke?*"

"Fit as a fiddle. Could use a drink is all."

When I returned with her water, she had already filled the basket with tomatoes.

"This should do for today," she said. "Let's get some greens and start 'em a slow boil. I'll get the water going. You go find us some mustard greens that ain't gone to seed yet." She strode through the back door and into the kitchen, stepping strong as a pony headed home.

In the quarter hour it took me to gather a mess of mustard greens, my grandmother died. She died for real this time. Not in the garden sitting on her backside, but in the kitchen, staring up at the ceiling.

I think she tried it first in the garden and might very well have gone that way. But when she heard my frantic cry and nervous running feet, she thought, "Oh, this won't do. We'll just try it again later with a little less carrying on."

I got it right this time. I was slow and thoughtful, easing into the moment. I sat down on the floor beside her and picked up her hands. I held them on either side of my cheeks and tried to stop the tears from flowing down my face. I brushed her hair from her forehead. I closed her eyes. No one else was in the house and I was glad of that.

I left her for a moment. I walked to the east-facing side and picked a beautiful gardenia blossom, white and full of perfume. At first I placed her hands together at the waist, one hand on top of the other with the gardenia sticking up between her fingers. I right away decided this looked too much like a pose in a funeral parlor, so I stuck the flower behind her ear.

I stood over Pokoni for a long time, trying to be more grown-up than I was. I tried to understand how sometimes you loved so much you cried at how beautiful and brief it all was. Not just people, but everything—the basket, the flower, the knotty pine floor she laid on. I know I didn't understand any of it then, but for the first time I knew there was this understanding that some people came to. Pokoni would know how to make me see it rightly.

But she never would, not anymore. Pokoni now lay on the wide planks of that knotty pine floor in the last dress she would ever pick out for herself. It was a pale blue working dress, nothing special. Her apron was a faded yellow, only slightly darker than the color of the gardenia petals. But her dress, the blueness of her dress, was more in harmony with the gardenia, I thought. The fragrance of the flower seemed a soft summery blue, the blue of a clear sky, the sweet lingering blue of a robin's egg.

I knelt down, just this once more, this secret final time before everything exploded in motion. I felt the silky smoothness of her hair. I closed my eyes and drank deep gulps of gardenia. I kissed my grandmother on the lips, rose, and went to tell Momma.

She was hanging clothes, stooping and stretching. I walked to her like in a floating dreamwalk, watching myself move too slowly, too deliberately. My feet stirred up tiny clouds of dust. I was taking Pokoni's deathwalk for her. She couldn't do it.

She is alive until I tell somebody, I thought.

Momma stopped to stare at me, clutching the clothesline above her head. The closer I came, the slower I walked, the more her face grew worry lines and her mouth went tight.

"Say it," she said. "Please just say it."

But I could not say it, not until I touched her on the arm, her pink and brown forearm. She held her breath for a few moments, then started with a series of short, shallow breaths, breaths that became panting, panting that became singing, desperate hanging-on singing.

And He walks with me
And He talks with me
And He tells me I am his own.
And the joy we share
As we tarry there
None other has ever known.

We clung to each other and rocked as the heat of the morning and the warm smell of our mother-daughter sweat wrapped us in a quilt of comfort.

"Pokoni is dead," I said. She nodded and squeezed her closed eyes tighter shut. She pulled me against her hip and held me there, as if she expected me to cry. When she didn't hear any whimpers or sobs, she took my head in her hands, tilted my face to hers, and looked at me—into my eyes.

I was not numb to my Pokoni's death. Her death, I realized, would be a living presence for many years, maybe for the rest of my life. It would kiss my eyelids like a breeze, then vanish at my waking, leaving only the shivering window curtains—a ghost or a spirit or a thing born of sleep.

I am lying, of course, or forgetting. The years have eased my feelings. I hurt that day, a deep hurt, like a heavy stone was pushing on my chest. Pokoni's spirit was soft, but her death was quick and mean and I hated it.

The memory of her death now blends with moments of her life, like a slow-simmering stew of leftovers—potatoes, tomatoes, celery, chunks of roast beef, carrots, the broth thick as gravy—to be sipped and tasted one spoonful at a time. Today Pokoni's memory sends a warm and satisfying glow, just like that stew, down the inside of my chest and right to the pit of my stomach.

As days and months passed, I would forget about her death for an hour, then a few hours, finally almost an entire day. Then it would just be there, right in front of me, needing my full attention. I was only eleven years old, but somehow I knew it would be this way.

I was not numb to my Pokoni's death. I stood facing it. Momma smiled, a slight smile, but a smile.

"We have much to do," she said. She gripped my hand and together my mother and I walked to the kitchen to tend to Pokoni, my grandmother.

AMAFO ALONE

Rose

When Amafo was struck by the marshal, he retreated into himself, protected and encircled by his Choctaw friends of many years. Pokoni guarded Amafo from even those closest to him, for only Pokoni knew of the deep wound he had suffered.

Amafo had experienced a taste of his own death. New intrusions appeared, like strange unwelcome fish, in the clear river of his thinking. His mortality was now real to him, and so was the weakness of his aging body. He was forced to admit that he could no longer protect either himself or his family. His body was old and weak.

Pokoni allowed my grandfather to know this, to adapt himself to this new knowledge. Even his closest of friends would tell him well-meaning lies.

"You could have taken him when you were younger," they would say. "You would have made him eat that board!"

In the evenings Pokoni would sit alone with him for hours, bringing him coffee. I once sat with them on the back porch. My grandmother stroked his hand and said in a whisper that blended with the night music, the cicadas and the windy tree noises. "There are ways There are always ways."

Another time I heard her tell him, "Goodwill always has a place." Pokoni sang to Amafo in his troubled time. For hours she sang to him, sweet Choctaw hymns they both knew.

And so it was that, nurtured by Pokoni, Amafo grew in the strength of his own goodwill. The marshal had his muscle and his board. Amafo had his smile and his forgiving nature. And his Pokoni.

Pokoni and Amafo together had defeated the marshal, and now Amafo was alone.

At the funeral service, Amafo sat on the front pew with Daddy on one side and Momma, me, and Jamey on the other.

Pokoni looked powdery and very dead in a pink dress she would never have chosen. Amafo wore a navy blue suit with a dark brown tie, a suit that draped him like a flag and flapped and swayed with every step he took, a suit that fit him no tighter than the dark folds of skin hanging slack from the bones of his sagging face. I have never seen a body so devoid of happiness as that which carried Amafo's spirit to the burial service of the only woman he ever loved.

That evening, long after everyone retired, I heard Amafo moving in his room. *"I will bring him chocolate,"* I thought. *"I won't have to say a word. He'll know I am showing my love in a wordless way, like Pokoni would."*

Half an hour later I climbed the stairs with the chocolate. Amafo stood by the window when I entered the room. The room was fully lit, but he moved as if in total darkness, feeling his way with slow-moving hands and fingertips that softly patted the walls and furniture.

I stood watching him, holding the wooden tray and his blue

enamel cup, filled with steaming cocoa. Amafo knelt before his bedside table as if before an altar. He knew I was there. He lifted the back of his hand to me, both to acknowledge my presence and to ask me not to speak. This was a holy moment, a quiet and sacred time to my Amafo. As the scene unfolded, I realized I was witnessing not so much a worshipping as a new way, for my Amafo, of expressing his love.

Amafo began weeping. I saw him cry before I heard him. He rocked back and forth, bowing his head deeper with each motion and rocking the sobs from his chest and belly, sighing and crying.

I could not move. Why would I ever move again? Why would anyone ever move or need to move when we could rock instead, curled up and crying? But crying was only a door. It was the rocking, only the rocking that mattered.

Talking, working, eating, breathing, none of this was necessary. Only rocking. Pokoni would take care of everything else. All we had to do was rock. And when we tired of rocking, all we had to do was hold on tight and she would do the rocking for us—even the rocking. She did all of this, everything, even the rocking.

But Pokoni died. How could she die when all we knew to do was rock?

Amafo became an infant before my eyes, rocking and crying. And I began rocking. How could I not, seeing him so small and frail and beautiful. Even the wrinkles of his skin were beautiful, like sculpted leather waves that rolled and washed and tucked into each other. My grandfather was a newborn child, wet and wrinkled from the moist weeping of his birth.

As I watched, Amafo began wiping the tears from his cheeks with both palms and rubbing the moisture on Pokoni's face. He ran his wet palms across the glass of the picture frame holding my Pokoni's image. He was touching my grandmother, hoping somehow to reach her spirit.

I felt warm and strong and happy. I cried from deep inside myself at this beholding. Somehow my feet floated across the floor and my arms stretched to place the tray upon the table by the window. Standing over Amafo, I was engulfed in the fragrance of gardenias. I looked about the room, expecting to see a bowl of soft yellowing petals on the table, but the source of the fragrance remained unseen, at least to my eyes.

Moments later my back leaned against the closed door and I stood in the hallway, trying to form questions for my mind to ask, but I was mute in the presence of a power far beyond any I had ever known.

That night I lay as quiet as I could, out of my body limp, moving only by the ebb and flow of my breathing and the running of blood through my veins. I imagined I was Pokoni. I tried to smell the dried rose petals and cedar sprigs on the coffin floor beneath me, beneath her. I *was* Pokoni, dead to the world but still wanting to feel it, more intensely than when I was alive.

As I drew deeper and deeper into becoming my Pokoni, I realized that what I so desperately wanted—to be able to feel—would be forever denied me without a body. A body *is* the total of its senses, the fingertips of feeling, the ears like tiny hands that catch the breeze of sounds, the tiny circle doors for fragrance, all of it, the glassy eyes to blink in disbelief that what we see can *yes* be real.

Without a body I can never feel. I must find another.

I shivered and with a startling tremor, from my chest to my knees, I came to myself. My skin was cold. My breath formed clouds, illumined by a streak of moonlight through the muslin curtains on my bedroom wall.

I lay trembling in the knowledge of what was happening. Pokoni's *shilombish* was wandering, seeking a way to return.

I awoke the next morning unsure of what I had seen, thinking it might have been a sweet and mournful dream. When Amafo did not appear at breakfast the next morning I knew it had been real. Amafo wiping his tears on the picture of Pokoni, that had been real, as had the fragrance of gardenias.

Pokoni, I knew, was still with us.

SPINNING WHEEL OF SPIRO

One month later

Marshal Hardwicke leaned against the cedar post supporting his roof overhang, watching the gathering hordes of people. Several hundred town residents and outlying farm families crowded Main Street, Choctaws and Nahullos both. Some had risen as early as three in the morning to pile onto wagons for the long trek to town.

Saturday mornings in Spiro had the make-believe buoyancy of a carnival, courtesy of the local merchant association. Three aging Civil War Veterans—two trumpeters and a drummer—blared marching music at random intervals from a bench behind the day's real attraction, the famed Spinning Wheel of Spiro.

The wire spinning cage, circular and mounted on wheels, sat like a giant turtle in front of the Spiro Bank and half a block from the Spiro Drygoods Store. Every merchant, even Hiram, donated items to be given away. Red, white, and blue flutters of paper danced against the inside of the wire cage, each sporting the name of a hopeful *must-be-present-to-win* resident.

As town dignitaries announced the prizes, spun the wheel, and called the names of winners, the crowd broke out in scattered cheers and clapping.

Today was allotment day and hundreds of Choctaws made their way to Skullyville to collect their treaty-guaranteed monies. Many stopped at Spiro for the festivities and the crowd doubled in size.

Hardwicke always arrived at his office early on these once-a-month days—to *get ready for the heathens*, he told his friends at the saloon. He always bought an extra bottle of whiskey the night before and began his celebrating as the sun peeked over the railroad depot two blocks to the east.

Long lines of people waiting to sign their names to colored cards flanked the spinning wheel. When a name was called and a prize delivered, more people ran to join the line.

"Our next prize is a dress from Erlene's Millinery Shop. A dress made to fit from this beautiful green cloth," shouted Councilman Dilliard. The noise of the crowd swallowed his words, but he held aloft a ream of ladies' dress-making cotton, dyed a dark green. Dozens of women drew closer as Dilliard spun the giant wheel.

"Mrs. Meredith Blankenship!" he boomed.

"Oh!" squealed Meredith, and the crowd cheered. A breeze lifted the green-colored cloth, held at the skein by a young stockboy from Perkin's Grocery, and sent ten feet of it waving over the women.

"It'll take a cloth that long to wrap around that squaw!" hollered a young Nahullo farmer. Townsfolk within earshot laughed and looked his way, and when big-hipped Meredith stepped from a cluster of Choctaw women and ambled her way to collect her prize, a wave of laughter accompanied her every step.

From their perch beneath the awning of Hiram's store, Rose

glanced at Amafo. A friend and big brother to Meredith since their early childhood days, Amafo smiled and shrugged.

"She is one happy *ohoyo*. Little bit of laughing not gonna bother Meredith, I 'speck not now." A fat horsefly landed on Amafo's collar, humming and burrowing on the backside of his neck. Before he could lift his hand to slap at it, Rose brushed it away, kissing the spot and blowing behind his ear to tease him.

Amafo caught his breath and stood stiff and silent.

I know it's you, Hester, Amafo thought. *You gone and figured out a way to come through Rose. Yakoke, sweet lady. Come 'round whenever you want. I won't be sad no more. I promise. I just miss you is all.*

Nearing the wheel, Meredith broke into a sprint. She snatched the cloth in midair, flipped the loose end of it over one shoulder, and began a slow spin, wrapping herself in a cocoon of cedar green. Her friends giggled and covered their mouths before unleashing a babbling river of Choctaw.

"Mercy, mercy, mercy."

"Her momma is rising from the grave. I know it."

"Her daddy too."

"Her daddy! *Owww*, that man is coming to drag her to the grave with him."

"She always acts so shy. How come she carrying on so?"

"Yeah. She shy. But look at all these men. She not so shy now."

"They sure set Meredith to spinning."

"Mercy, mercy, mercy."

"Holy, holy, holy."

"She better be in church tomorrow."

"She better stay all day."

From across the street the marshal squinted his brow and settled a cold gaze across the crowd. He scanned the faces, noting the strangers, nodding and smirking at the parade of weak and worthless people.

Oscar Armstrong. Why you smiling? That daughter of yours chases every boy in town. Won't be long before she chases the wrong one and gets what she's after. You think all that money you give to the church gonna change that?

You keep on having those babies, Selma Conners. What happens when that old man you married cain't run the business anymore? You gonna do it?"

That's it, Tommy. Keep tugging on your daddy's sleeve. He'll knock your little ass to next Christmas and I'm gonna laugh when he does it."

Hardwicke felt the whiskey warm his belly now.

Nice fine little pony you got there till he breaks a leg crossing that stone pasture you too damn lazy to clean, Emmett Waterfield. Hardwicke spat. *That hired hand you so fond of will stick a gun to your pony's ear and blow his brains out. You won't even watch, you'll be off whimpering somewhere.*

A gnawing grew in his chest and sent him turning to the door, but his eye froze on the scene in front of Hiram's store. A young girl stood close to an elderly, stoop-shouldered Choctaw man. Even from the distance and across the crowd of townsfolks, Hardwicke recognized the man as the one with the broken glasses.

He watched as the young girl leaned to kiss the old man.

I know you. You were there. That morning. You kin. Yeah. You love that old man. That's good. He loves you, too. He'd hate to see you get hurt.

Rose felt his look burn her cheeks and her hand went to her face.

Yeah, I see you looking so strong. But I know something you don't. Yet. Some man's gonna beat that look out of you. Wonder how long it'll take. Long time, I hope.

A farmer snatched his hat from his head and slapped it against his thighs. The sudden sweeping motion of the hat caught Rose's attention, pulling her eyes from the spectacle of the wheel. She watched the skinny *Nahullo* stomp and swagger and when she realized he'd been drinking, her mind returned to the railroad depot and her first sight of morning drunkenness. Her eyes moved to the sign above the marshal's roof overhang before finally reaching their destined port.

The marshal stared hard and mean at her.

I know you, he seemed to say.

Gathering her strength and asking herself what Pokoni would do, Rose returned his look. She turned her mind to the words that flew between them, riding the hardness of the gaze.

I know you as well.

You belong to that old Indian.

You struck my grandfather.

You haven't learned?

You left him lying there.

Lucky I didn't kill him. I still can, you know.

You stay away from us.

Maybe I will let him stay alive.

Help me, Pokoni.

Maybe I'm the one—

I am not strong without you. Please, Pokoni.

—to beat that look out of you.

Hardwicke whirled and stepped into his office as Rose dropped her head and drew in gulps of air.

"Time we go," Amafo said. Rose nodded and nudged herself beneath his arm, a child in the still-firm grip of her grandfather.

An hour later they rested in the cool of Amafo's praying tree, watching the remaining people move to a slow and dusty rhythm. The noonday dance of blinding sun gave way to the long shadows of afternoon. Rose leaned against the tree and slept.

Sing me something, Hester. Anything. A breeze came up and Amafo heard the first verse of a sweet and simple hymn, one that always set the children to singing.

> *Hatak hush puta ma!*
> *Ho minti;*
> *Hatak hush puta ma!*
> *Ho minti;*
> *Hatak hush puta ma!*
> *Yakni achukma kut*
> *Uba talaiushke;*
> *Ho minti.*

Amafo sang the whole verse before he realized the words came from his own lips.

Ho, you never stop, do you, hon? Just like when you's living. Letting me know it's time to do things for myself. He leaned to touch Rose, then stopped so as not to wake her. He ran his hand instead against the flank of Whiteface. *But I am not lazy,* he continued. *I am just missing you is all. Don't ever leave me here alone.*

Two trees to the west, hidden by the foliage of a red maple, a panther stretched herself across a low-lying limb. Her tail twitched and her eyes followed every movement of the girl, the horse, and the man.

ROBERTA JEAN
Rose

That evening, barely a half hour till sunset, Roberta Jean Willis appeared at our front door, carrying a sharp digging tool and a drooping gardenia bush in a bucket.

"Come in, child," Momma told her.

"Thank you," said Roberta Jean, "but I didn't come to visit. I want to pay my respects to Grandma Pokoni. I'd like to plant this gardenia bush near her gravehouse. Would that be alright?"

"Of course," said Momma. "She'd be happy to see you plant it there. But it's getting on towards dark." I heard the whole conversation from the kitchen, where I was cutting potatoes and putting them on to boil. I dried and wiped my hands off, expecting to accompany Roberta Jean to the gravehouse. When she saw me peep through the kitchen door and hang my apron on the wall, she seemed a little embarrassed.

"I won't stay long," she said, looking from Momma to me and back again. "Besides, I know my way through those woods in the dark."

"I guess you do, hon," said Momma. "You purt near was raised there."

Roberta Jean turned to me, looked down, and said, "Don't let me keep you from your cooking, Rose. I'll come by tomorrow and we can go water it, maybe look in on it every few days, just to make sure the roots take."

I wanted more than anything to share this time with my best friend. But Roberta Jean wanted to be alone with a friend of hers, my Pokoni.

"Come see me early tomorrow," I said. She nodded and wrapped her thin arms around herself as she stepped into the cool of evening.

"Here," I said, "take my jacket. You'll need it by the time you get home." She draped my cotton jacket over her shoulders and went to be with my grandmother at her grave.

∽∾

Roberta Jean approached the cemetery with awe and reverence, stepping carefully among the gravehouses. She came to the newest, the one where Pokoni lay. Roberta lifted her face and closed her eyes, catching the sweet aroma of the fresh-cut pine shingles of the roof. The soft dirt circling the gravehouse was moist and easy to dig.

She removed Rose's jacket, set the bucket of gardenias near where she knew Pokoni's head lay and, kneeling, went about her work. When the hole was a foot deep, she brushed the dirt from her hands and dress and carried the bucket to the water pump, tucked away in a clump of blackjack oak trees on the east side of the church. The water was fresh and cool.

Roberta filled the bucket, lifting and dipping the gardenia bush to separate the fine-haired roots and give them a good drink before the planting. Returning to the gravehouse, she dug several scoopfuls of dirt from the hole and mixed it with the water in the bucket, thickening the mixture till a soft wet clump formed in the bucket bottom. She tilted the bucket over the hole and eased the gardenia bush, with its earth-rich root clump, into the hole near Pokoni's head.

"Just like you taught me," she said smiling as much to herself as to Pokoni. "The roots will live through the winter and rise again, so you can smell the gardenias in the spring." Her work complete, Roberta settled in for the real purpose of her coming. She had yet to have her own longing time with Pokoni, her best friend's grandmother. Roberta sat still and listening, leaning her back against the bucket. She closed her eyes and whispered.

"I 'member when you held me close the day I walked the aisle for Jesus. You told me you were proud to welcome me, how pretty I looked. I helped you plant your garden when I was ten years old. Rose and I both helped you. We cooked supper for our families that night. The grape dumplings, remember? You taught me how to make 'em."

Roberta cried soft tears. They trickled down her cheeks and she let them flow for long minutes before she wiped them away.

When the sun moved behind the treetops and the wind picked up, Roberta rolled to her feet, put on Rose's jacket, and turned towards home. She took the shortcut through the red oak woods beside the church, but soon the shadows of the thicket closed in around her. She wished she had stayed on the dirt path leading to the road.

She paused and considered retracing her steps. A soft sound, the thud of a heavy step, told her that the choice had been made and it was too late for her to return. With that sound a shift occurred, a shift in the wind of this day's final wording, a trembling move to fear and darkness. A strange shudder washed over her. She knew that something was wrong, horribly wrong.

She was not alone.

From the moment the sun sank behind the purple hills, she knew this with all certainty. Her senses were keen and told her she shared this small grove of oak trees with a drunken man. The wind was thick and carried the smell of slept-in clothes soaked by the odor of whiskey sweat.

She felt his eyes staring at her. She imagined his right hand holding a bottle, lifting it to his lips and sipping the burning liquid her father ranted about at least once in every Sunday sermon. At some point she felt his anger and impatience grow. She imagined he shifted his grip from the bottom of the bottle for drinking to a different grip, holding the neck of the bottle as if for striking.

The man's refusal to move sent shivers over her skin. Roberta thought of speaking, of calling out.

"Maybe he wants to be left alone," she thought. "If I walk away, he'll not come after me." She was lying to herself and she knew it. Tears welled up in her eyes and her breath left her. "Of course he will come after me. He *is* after me."

This man was mean, she could feel it, and he was watching her this very minute. And this also she knew. He wanted her dead.

He watched everything she did—every turn of her head, every shift of her weight—and he drew strength from her fear. An image flashed before her, a vivid picture of herself sprawled against a tree, her legs and arms broken at unnatural angles and blood trickling down her mouth.

Roberta stood rigid, tall and straight as the looming pines. Her arms hung at her sides and her fingernails dug into her skin. She shook in terror. When he finally moved, Roberta jumped and a low moan parted her lips. He was behind her, less than twenty feet, she guessed. He took only that single step, as if announcing himself a dancer in this dark and deathly reel.

Roberta's fingers crept to her purse, slowly so as not to attract his eye. Her hand moved to the dense ball of volcanic rock so feared by her brothers. She gripped the rock and eased her fingertips over the tiny pockmarks of its slick surface. She felt the sharp angles and knew that in a few short moments blood would soak these church grounds.

I must not cower before him.

His breathing suddenly stopped. Roberta heard the splintering pop of a glass bottle breaking, followed by a grunt and three quick shuffling steps. She turned and broke into a run in the direction of the church.

She ran straight into a clump of scrub oaks, holding one arm in front of her face to protect herself. As she neared the church, she heard his footsteps behind her. Her breath shot out in fire-hot puffs and she shook the tears from her face. He was almost upon her when she reached the front steps of the church building.

She reached for the doorknob, but her fingers slipped from the shiny brass knob. A heavy hand struck her in the ribs and sent her flying against the doorjamb. She kicked backwards at her assailant. He grabbed her ankles and jerked her legs out from under her. She fell against the top step, dropping the rock.

His hand gripped her shoulder and strong fingers seized her upper arm. He flung her on her back and a hot river of strength surged through her. He was massive and his figure blocked the sky. For a brief moment the moon shone behind him and Roberta looked up at a dark silhouette standing over her.

Marshal Hardwicke.

His hand held the broken remains of a bottle and his arm was raised and poised to strike. She smelled his breath, sweet and rancid with whiskey. His warm spit fell on her cheeks.

"You think you safe here, girl?" he said, slurring his words as he spoke. His jaws hung fat and loose and his eyes were bloodshot. His breath came short and heavy. He shook his head and reached out his hand to steady himself on the door, dropping the bottle.

When his head cleared he looked at her in confusion, squinting his eyes and saying, "You not that girl. Who you? Look at me." He put his palm to her chin and lifted her face. She trembled and drew herself into a crouch in the doorway.

"You the preacher's daughter. Oh, mercy Lord. What I goin' to do with you now? Look what I gone and done. Oh, Jesus, no." He buried his face in his hands and ran his fingers through his hair. "I don't want you. I want that old man's girl, his granddaughter. You got her jacket. Why you wearing her jacket?"

The marshal shook his head and stared hard at her. His voice grew deeper and Roberta sensed a new level of meanness.

"You stay right there. You got to unnerstand I never wanted you in this bidness. Now I got to kill you. Don't you go nowhere, you hear me? I don't want to chase you."

Roberta moaned. The marshal lurched down the steps. He squatted to pick up a large chunk of limestone, one of a dozen by the church entrance.

"No, they gonna find your body right here on the church steps tomorrow morning. Sunday morning."

Roberta lay still, calming herself as her fingers searched the ground for the lava rock. When he returned, his blood-red eyeballs seemed ready to burst from his head.

"You shouldn't ought to be here. Not my fault you here. But maybe it's best. The preacher's daughter. Dead on the steps of the church. They never gonna forgit that, hon. You be remembered. How you like that? Long as there are Choctaws living here, they gonna talk about how you died. And they gonna know who's in charge."

He lifted the stone with both hands, hoisting it high over his head and almost falling backwards from the weight of it. With a few stumbling steps he steadied himself. Roberta saw his face redden and his cheeks swell as he put all of his strength behind the stone, whirling it downward, aiming at her skull.

She rolled aside, and when the stone smashed through the thick wooden door, she struck him above the eye with her black lava rock. Hardwicke fell hard and blood gushed down his checks and neck, darkening the collar of his shirt. His hands flew to his face.

Roberta leapt to her feet and sped past the marshal. She took the worn dirt path to the road. With the moon now fully above the pines, she knew he could clearly see her, were his eyes not filled with blood. But hiding was not in her thinking—fleeing was, fleeing with all the speed her lithe young legs could gather.

She rounded the bend in the road and only then did she dare to look over her shoulder. An empty road greeted her, and above it a bright quarter moon tilting over pointed treetops, surrounded by a sky ablaze with stars.

She ran for half an hour, pausing to look behind her every few minutes. She neither saw nor heard any sign of the marshal. Rose's house was closer than her own and Roberta turned in that direction. She dipped into the woods to cross the creek at the back pasture of the Goode homestead.

She slowed to a fast walk, hearing nothing but the sound of her own breath, hot and stinging. These woods were thinned, kept clean by Rose's father to discourage wolves and predator cats from hiding so close to his best pastureland. Soon the creek came into view, its rippling waters flashing in the moonlight. Roberta stepped from the woods and knelt beside the creek, cupping her hands. She eased her fingers through the water and felt the coldness on her palms. She never tasted the water.

A strong hand grabbed her collar and dragged her into the woods.

KOI CHITTO COMES TO LIFE

Rose

It was eleven o'clock that evening and all but the night critters had found a place to curl up and sleep. Samuel was too shy to step on the porch without being asked, so he just stood in the front yard and hollered.

"Rose! Rose! Is Berta Jean here?"

Momma parted the window curtains and squinted her whole face.

"Samuel," she said, opening the door. "Come on in, son. What are you doing out this late at night?"

"Momma sent me to come get Berta Jean. She wadn't 'sposed ta be spending the night."

"Hon, we ain't seen her since late afternoon. She stopped by to visit is all. She was on her way to Pokoni's gravehouse. Had a gardenia bush she was meaning to plant."

"She ain't come home and Momma's all worried 'bout her," Samuel said. "I better run go tell her Berta Jean's not here."

"You ought to stay here," my father said, rising from his chair by the fireplace. "No sense two of you wandering 'round at night."

He pulled his boots on and told me, "Rose, light the lantern and go get Amafo up. Tell him Roberta Jean never made it home. We going looking for her. Tell him we 'bout ready to leave."

Momma boiled water for coffee while I was waking Amafo up. By the time he made all the necessary stoops and bends to get himself dressed and make his stiff walk down the stairs, she had a cup for everybody, myself included. The night air had turned chilly and the coffee cup felt warm and welcome. I tried sipping careful but the coffee still burned my tongue.

I hoped Roberta Jean was not still out. If she was, it meant trouble. She thought too much like a parent to be doing anything foolish.

"Daddy, I want to go." I couldn't see his face in the shadows, but I knew he was considering letting me, so I took the opening.

"She is my best friend. She was doing something for Pokoni. Let me go looking for her, please." Before he answered, Momma pulled a pair of Amafo's old britches from her sewing box.

"You can wear these," she said, holding them up for inspection. "Yes, I believe you big enough to get into these skinny britches."

"Let's go, hon. We not gonna wait on you," Daddy said. While I pulled the britches on and slid my dress over my shoulders he told me, "Stay with Amafo, back from the lantern light. We not 'specting no trouble, but it'll be safer if you cain't be seen."

He turned to Samuel and said, "You best stay here. If Roberta Jean comes here, don't go nowhere till we get back. We just going to the church. Won't be gone mor'n a hour."

When he headed out the back door, I knew we were cutting across the pasture and through the back woods where the underbrush was mostly cut or burned out. He took long strides and it was hard for us to keep up, but halfway across the pasture I saw Amafo come to life, like he was remembering—or his muscles were remembering—what it had been like to go hunting at night, like in his younger days. He was soon matching my father stride for stride.

Daddy was also in on this secret way of thinking and doing things nobody ever talks about. He had asked Amafo to come along so this manly way of going would maybe come back to him. It had happened and I was glad to see it.

Daddy held the lantern to his side and it swung an easy arc, casting a wide yellow circle on the ground. I covered my eyes from the lantern's full light and kept it in the corner of my seeing. We slowed down to a careful walk and crossed the creek bridge.

As we neared the trees, Daddy hollered loud, "Roberta Jean! Roberta Jean!" He paused to see if any sound would come echoing back. Hearing nothing, we entered the woods.

Daddy soon turned north towards the church. We had only gone a few steps in that direction when we heard a panther scream, high-pitched and long, an icy call that cut the night in half. Amafo put his hands on my shoulders and I thought I would faint from fright. I was panting and breathing hard.

"Didn't mean to scare you, hon," he said real soft. "No need to be scared now. This a holy time, a night like this," he said, and I thought of his rocking on the day of my grandmother's funeral, his sweet rocking. I turned and wrapped my arms around his waist.

"It's gonna be alright," he said. "Just hard to see sometimes."

Daddy hung the lantern on an overhanging branch and stepped back to join us. We crouched down for a long while, looking and listening. The panther's call seemed to silence everything else in the woods, save a small fluttering of leaves.

We waited for maybe twenty minutes, plenty of time for the panther to seek out the source of light. Twice Daddy moved us, when a shift in the wind put us upwind of the panther or at least upwind of the panther's call. I didn't hear any movement, just the sound of our own breathing.

Amafo whispered, "Let's go up yonder way. Back where she hollered. I hear something kicking. Sound to me like a animal in a trap. Not no panther."

Daddy nodded and picked up the lantern. We walked maybe a quarter hour when we saw a thick oak tree with layers of rope wrapped around it. The rope was clawed and torn, but still clung to the tree like an old woody vine.

When the light struck the tree, there was a flurry of motion. Daddy held up his hand, telling us to stay still. He moved closer to get a look.

"It's Roberta Jean," he said. "Come help get her loose."

A rope was strung across her mouth and pulled tight around the tree trunk so she couldn't call out. Daddy cut it quick as he could and Roberta Jean said, "He's coming back. He means to kill me." Her eye caught mine and she started sobbing. Her whole body shook. "Help me get away from him. Please help me," she said.

When the ropes were cut and hanging from the tree, Roberta Jean reached out her arms to me and I hugged her tight. She clung to me like I was keeping her from drowning.

"Who you talking 'bout?" asked Daddy.

"Marshal Hardwicke. He's drunk…he tried to kill me." Her voice trailed off into more cries and her eyes looked blurry, like she was looking at pictures none of us could see.

"Let's get her home," said Amafo. "If the marshal does come back, we don't want these girls anywhere around."

Amafo and my father lifted her to her feet.

"Can you walk *hoke*?" Amafo asked. Roberta Jean nodded. With Daddy leading and carrying the lantern and Amafo guarding us from the rear, the four of us hurried the short distance through the piney woods to the creek crossing. Daddy stepped easy-like across the plank bridge and hung the lantern on a fence post.

I walked sideways crossing the narrow single board, never letting go of Roberta Jean. The lantern flickered in the water two feet below us. I remembered falling off the plank and into the creek when I was seven. I could stand up in it even then, so I was not afraid of the water.

I was afraid for Roberta Jean. If she fell into the cold water, dragging me with her, I thought she might sink into her lonely nightmare and maybe never come back.

The plank was slick and rose and fell with our every step. As we eased from the plank to the ground, we heard a quick movement in a clump of sumac bushes near the water's edge. Daddy lifted the lantern and we caught sight of a dark shape leaping to the shadows.

"*Koi chitto*," Amafo said. "Panther."

Once we stood in the pasture and turned to the lights of our house, Roberta Jean seemed to realize she was safe. For this night, at least, she was safe.

Marshal Hardwicke had crossed a line in taking after Roberta Jean Willis, daughter to Preacher Willis and known and loved by every Choctaw in the territory. He had awakened the eye of the Lord, the vengeful eye, and I felt sure somebody would die for this—maybe and most surely the marshal, maybe others as well in the playing out of it all.

I cried myself to sleep that night, thinking how lonely and frightened Roberta Jean must feel. I lay looking at the yellow slice of moon, stubbornly clinging to my own sadness.

A grey cloud floated across the moon, leaving behind a world of blue, the blue of breath when all hope for warmth is gone, blue trees, blue earth, blue stars, a world cast in deep grey blue, a world as cold as moon flesh.

VENGEANCE IS MINE

Though his daughter lay safely wrapped in the quilts of her own bed, Reverend Willis never thought about retiring that night. He went through all the familiar motions. He tucked the children in and took his final walk of relief beneath the sycamore in the backyard. Afterwards he cracked the bedroom door open and whispered to his sleeping wife, "Just a little while and I'll be along," which always meant, "I am praying and might be a while."

Reverend Willis was not praying. In truth, he was avoiding prayer, for he knew the Lord would lead him to the usual path of turning the other cheek.

"Yes, Lord, I'll turn that other cheek. And then you watch while it gets slapped and kicked and stabbed and burned till finally it gets buried in a holy grave while we all sing your sweet praises. Yes, Lord, while my daughter fights off her attacker with a rock, right on the steps of your house. Oh, Lord, I am grateful, you know I am, that she is alive, but for how long, Lord? How long before they kill us all?"

Henry Willis spread his elbows apart on the table, grabbed his hair to the scalp, and whispered, "We are dead already, Lord. We are helpless and dead. You make us that way, helpless and dead." His eyes glowed like hot coals and his leg muscles flexed over and over.

"Helpless and dead," he said, gripping his fists and watching his forearms rise and fall to the rhythm of this new hymn. His body quivered.

"Helpless and dead." The wind picked up outside and he heard an owl call from deep in the woods. He hung his head and rose, feeling his full height. The kitchen seemed small and foreign.

"On your doorstep, Lord, if that's what you want, maybe on your doorstep. But not my daughter. You may be the Lord but you cain't have my daughter. No more helpless and dead," he whispered, his eyes mean with the mocking of the words.

As he was considering what course to take, the memory he was seeking finally came. He turned his hands over and over in the blue light of the kitchen, staring at the cracks in his skin till dark blood seemed to ooze from the pores. Stirred by the sight of blood on Roberta Jean's dress, Reverend Willis now sank into a deep den of memory, childhood memory, the kind best left behind.

He saw his uncle watch as Union soldiers took what cattle they could comfortably herd, then kill the rest. The family was ushered into the house and told to remain indoors. Unafraid and flaunting it, the soldiers camped within sight of the farm on the banks of a nearby creek. Huddled in the house and too scared to light a lantern or a cooking fire, the family sat in the dark and listened to the laughter of the soldiers. Their roasting fire threw sheets of blazing orange and yellow through the leaves of the cottonwoods lining the creek. The evening breeze carried the smell of cooked beef, his uncle's beef.

"Henry?" his wife called. Henry stood in reply and moved to close the bedroom door.

Returning to the kitchen, he stood over the sink. His eyes moved to the basin, where he discovered, hiding beneath a pile of plates, the long blue blade of the knife used to cut the meat for every meal. He moaned and sought the wooden handle of the knife.

He saw his uncle rise from the table and open the drawer by the kitchen sink. His hand disappeared into the drawer and emerged holding the carving knife aloft, turning the blade over and over in the light of the moon through the window. His uncle was a thin man and the blade of the knife seemed as wide as his arms. He sheathed the knife in his belt and moved through the house, exiting unseen through the front door.

Henry waited till he saw his uncle crawl through the rails of the back fence before he dashed through the door. His aunt rose to stop him, but Henry knew she would not call out for fear of endangering her husband. He crept in the shadows fifty feet behind his uncle.

He watched as his uncle found a safe spot in a cluster of sand plums. Resting on the root of a cottonwood, Henry began a three-hour vigil. He saw his uncle bite down on a chew of tobacco. He saw the soldiers slice hot chunks of beef from the turning spit and eat the dripping meat with their hands.

He watched as one by one the soldiers wrapped their blankets and rolled into a dozen tight cocoons of sleep. Henry wondered if his uncle had fallen asleep.

An hour later he watched a young soldier lift himself on his elbows and roll a cornhusk cigarette. His uncle stared intently at the soldier. The young man threw his blanket off and struggled into his boots. He stepped over his sleeping comrades and made his way to the creek.

Henry watched as his uncle rose to follow. When the soldier stood up from his drink, Henry's uncle buried the carving knife in the man's throat, flung him against the nearest cottonwood, and pinned him to the tree trunk with the blade.

Henry watched in fascination as the soldier flailed and flopped against the tree, the blood gushing from his neck. He felt a violent churning in his stomach and ran creekside to vomit. He tripped over a log hidden among the high grass at the creek's edge and stumbled into the creekbed.

The creek was dry.

Henry cried out. He fell to his knees and grabbed handfuls of dust. He leapt to his feet and turned around and around, stirring up clouds of dust. He choked and coughed on the powdery dust.

Over his shoulder Henry heard the rifle shot that killed his uncle. He fled to the safety of his house.

The next afternoon, with the soldiers several hours down the road, Henry returned to the creek. The water flowed cool and clean as always.

Henry pushed open the back door and approached the washtub where his wife had left Roberta Jean's dress to dry. He saw the dress hanging lifeless over the tub and saw his daughter lying on the steps of the church. He picked the dress up with the knife blade and saw once more the bloodstains in the folds of cotton.

The marshal lived north of town, a good five-mile walk. Henry knew if he kept a brisk pace he would arrive long before light of day. He re-entered his house and stepped lightly to the kitchen and sat once again at the table. A deep and distant wind carried the owl's call.

"He comes closer," the preacher thought. He dug his leather boot heels into the floor and scooted the chair backwards, away from the table. He sat in the middle of the kitchen floor, like a condemned man waiting for the call to die.

"Little David picked up a stone," he said, spitting on the floor and rising through the creaking soreness of his joints.

"Little David picked up a stone, Goliath for to kill." He held the knife aloft and watched the blade flash in the moonlight washing through the window.

"Little David picked up a stone, Goliath for to kill." He dragged his feet down the hallway, the knife hanging at his side. The words came faster now. "He walked unto the Philistine and flung his stone aloft. Earth trembled as the giant fell, the Philistine was dead."

He paused at his daughter's doorway, considered opening it, but turned away instead. This hour was not about Roberta Jean, not even about the Choctaws or the marshal. This hour was about the creeping darkness, the power of the creeping darkness.

"Little David picked up a stone, the giant for to kill." He sobbed now as he spoke. "God smiled to see the giant dead, at last dead, at last the people free, the giant dead. God's army won, the giant bleeding dead."

He paused and took a long, deep breath. "Little David picked up a stone," he said, "the giant for to kill."

A face appeared two feet from his, floating from a square of light against the wall. Henry froze and stared at this new apparition. It was a vision of his own face, staring back at him in the coppery glass of the grandfather clock. He saw the large fleshiness of his lips and nose. He lifted his palm to his cheek and saw the clumsy bigness of his hands. He was no David and he knew it.

"Poppa," came a small voice from his daughter's room.

Henry froze. He bent down and placed the knife at his feet and slid it behind the hall clock with the edge of his boot.

"Poppa?"

"Yes, it's me."

"Will you come be with me?"

Henry opened the door and moved to Roberta Jean's bedside, kneeling and easing his large frame over his daughter. Cupping her head in his palm, he lifted her from the pillow and kissed her cheek.

"Stay with me awhile."

"I am here with you," Henry said. He sat on the floor and pulled her to him. She nestled her head against his chest.

"I am so thankful you are my father," she said. The clock chimed the three o'clock hour and Henry knew he would stay by his daughter's bedside till dawn. *I must get the knife before anyone sees it*, he reminded himself.

"Anyone else would try to kill him," Roberta Jean said. "We could never be God's children again."

Henry clung to his daughter and sobbed till the tears washed all trace of the day's dust from his face. "You will always be one of God's children," he told her.

Father and daughter thus escaped the ravages of the day and gave way to the balm of sleep, in the blessed assurance that their lives, though scarred, would continue.

Henry never knew what happened to the carving knife, how it mysteriously returned to the kitchen drawer the next morning. When he unraveled himself from his sitting position on the bedroom floor that Sunday, he recalled placing it behind the hall clock. But when he went to retrieve it, the knife was gone.

Reverend Willis always considered himself to be the final guardian of his family, the last to bed and the first to arise. On the night his daughter was attacked, that duty was assumed by another family member. Young Samuel.

Having slipped quietly through his bedroom window, leaving a room he shared with his sleeping brothers, Samuel stood in the shadows and watched his father through the kitchen window. He was determined to follow his father wherever he went that night, determined to prevent a killing, with reason if he could, with force if he had to.

He was relieved to see his father hide the knife behind the clock and enter Roberta Jean's room. As soon as he heard snoring, Samuel scampered like a house rodent to the clock, grabbed the knife, and dashed to the back yard, where he buried it in his mother's rose bed.

While Roberta Jean slept in the arms of her father, Samuel spent the night leaning against her bedroom door, so his father could not leave the house without his knowing it.

Long before Reverend Henry Willis of the First Christian Church of Skullyville arose to preach the most difficult sermon of his life, his eldest son had already returned the family's meat carving knife to its rightful place in the kitchen drawer.

BROTHER WILLIS PREACHES

It was the shortest sermon anybody ever heard Reverend Henry Willis preach.

But one of the best, someone said.

No winding down a crooked road. Straight to the point, that sermon was.

Amen to that.

Willis knows how to get there when he wants to.

Amen.

I'm not even hungry yet.

Hush, now!

Well, sweetheart. You know how my stomach gets to growling sometimes.

I said Hush!

Straight to the point. One of the best.

"Little David picked up a stone, the giant for to kill." The deep familiar voice of Reverend Henry Willis eased itself over the lip of the pulpit, inspiring murmuring *Amens* from the congregation gathered at the First Christian Church of Skullyville. The words drifted to the back pew and hung in the stuffy air. An uneasy shifting of bodies responded to the scripture. Stones had never been Brother Willis' way.

"Little David picked up a stone, the giant for to kill," he continued. "But Jesus picked up the cross," he boomed, lifting his arms and widening his eyes. "And he carried that cross through streets of scorn and humiliation. He carried that cross. He bore that cross. He died on that cross. And he rose from the dead."

The congregation leaned forward now, as one.

"He rose from the dead as we will rise. We are God's children," he boomed. "We are God's children and we will be God's children, in word and in deed, and we will act as God's children. Forever and ever, till he returns and we rise from the dead. Let us pray."

EMPTY PRAYERS

Ona Mae prayed every night for the safety of her husband. They were her sweetest and deepest and darkest secret, these prayers. She prayed knowing the danger of his duties, him being the law in a town in Indian Territory, where so many arrived fleeing from the law.

With his bullying and drunken ways, she realized his life hung in the precarious balance of everyday fate. Any one of dozens of situations could already have resulted in his death. An ambush by angry Choctaws, a gunfight at the bar over a card game, a simple retaliation from someone weary of his relentless heaping of one abuse after another. Ona Mae prayed that Robert would survive the accumulation of evils he brought into play.

Empty prayers.

Ona Mae knelt every night and imagined the Lord protecting her husband from falling down dead-drunk on a sharp rock, or passing out too close to a prowling animal in the woods behind their house, or stumbling across train tracks at the wrong time, or dying beneath the hooves of a wagon pulled by stampeding horses.

The events were so clear and focused, her funeral dress so black, the veil so thin and lacy, the tears so deep within her chest, the condolences of friends so warm. She welcomed these prayers and knew the Lord would sift the gold from the limestone dust. Her faith was deep.

One night, when he fell asleep in the arbor and his heavy snoring woke her, she arose and made her way to the kitchen. She put water on to boil, intending to boil potatoes for her famed salad. She had peeled three potatoes before she realized that half the population of Spiro would not, after all, be arriving the next morning to help her in her time of sorrow.

Following the death of her husband.

John Burleson from the railroad depot would not hold her and say, "Be strong, Ona Mae," and she would not bury her face in his muscled and tender shoulder.

The roar of snores through the kitchen window brought her to her senses, but she boiled the water anyway and ate instead a boiled egg, for these times of fearless privacy, so close to the sleeping beast, were rare and precious.

At the very moment Roberta Jean struck the marshal with the black lava rock, Ona Mae was praying he would not stumble and die.

BILL GIBBONS TO THE TRAIN

Hardwicke took two lurching steps forward and fell face down in the muddy earth. Blood gushed from the top of his head, across his cheeks, and puddled against the porch steps. He sat up and spat a mouthful of blood. He wiped his lips and leaned against the wall of the church. Behind his eyelids he watched a dull and painfully slow replaying of events.

"Noooo," he moaned, dropping his head. Blood still streamed from the gash above his temple. He ripped the sleeve of his shirt and tied it around his head. The blood flow barely slowed. He grabbed a small handful of dirt, compressed it in his fist, and packed it tight against his skull. He retied the cloth and the blood thickened.

Seeing his own blood had a sobering effect. Hardwicke gradually felt the full weight of consequence, the consequence of attacking Reverend Willis' daughter on the steps of the church.

From the moment Marshal Hardwicke realized his life was at stake—not his reputation or his pride, but his very *life*—he moved with a swift purpose. Gathering an armful of thick rope and a five-foot length of cord from a shed behind the church, he hurried to the spot where he knew he would find Roberta Jean, the creek crossing to the Goode land.

Seeing her follow the path of the road, he cut through the piney woods and arrived at the creek soon after she did. He felt his breath quicken as she relaxed and crawled to the bank.

"She thinks she is safe," he whispered. Familiar feelings came over him.

His hand fell so hard across the back of her neck, she made no real struggle. He removed the bloody bandage from his head and tied it around her mouth. With the smaller rope, he bound her hands behind her back. Roberta Jean slumped over in helplessness and he dragged her far from the creek.

A thick oak offered a strong bonding place. He flung her against the tree trunk and tied a knot over her chest. He then stood and quickly walked six times around the trunk, pulling the slack and tightening the rope with every revolution. Roberta Jean stared in open-eyed horror, tasting the blood that slipped between her lips.

With his captive secured, the marshal sat down against the trunk of a sweet pine to watch and consider his next move.

"As I was saying back at the church," he said, "I got to kill you. You know that. I'm sober now, but that hasn't changed. You gonna die, so get on with whatever praying you need to do. This ain't my doings, you dying like this. Your friend, she was the one I was after."

Roberta Jean closed her eyes.

"Poppa. Help me, please," she whispered. She knew her father would send Samuel to look for her when she did not return. *They will never find me here alive. They will find me dead.*

Her thoughts were brought to a sudden halt by a high-pitched scream. The marshal stiffened in fear. A panther was nearby and the night air vibrated with her call. Hardwicke looked over his shoulder and his eyes and hands scrambled in panic to the ground around him. Realizing he had left his gun at the church, he leapt to his feet and vanished in the pines.

Roberta felt the presence of the cat. She knew the panther was approaching the tree. Soon the snug ropes moved as if tugged from behind. Roberta heard small ripping and clawing noises, together with low growls.

The panther is cutting through the ropes.

In a brief moment the rope ceased moving and Roberta saw a yellow light in the direction of the creek, a bobbing light, the sight of a lantern carried by someone walking.

"*Yakoke,* sweet Lord," she whispered and hung her head in waiting.

Marshal Hardwicke watched from the shadows as three figures crossed the creek bridge. Knowing the night had turned against him, he retraced his weary steps to the church. He retrieved his shotgun and followed the roan-colored road till it met the railroad tracks. Thinking of how best to leave Spiro, maybe forever, he knew the luxury of regret must come later. Tonight the task was staying alive and avoiding any Choctaws as he crossed their land.

His first thought was to hide in a clump of brush at the point where the track began a steep uphill climb. The morning train slowed to a crawl before topping the mountain and sped into a descent that carried it far away from Spiro, to the next stop fifty miles down track.

His plans changed when he saw the yellow glow of a campfire high above the tracks. Staying in the shadows, he crept in the direction of the fire, pausing often to listen. From the dark of a juniper thicket, he observed a lone figure holding a pan over an open fire, shaking it in an easy cooking motion. A horse was tied to a nearby tree and a blanket was unrolled near the fire.

A traveler planning on a quick meal and early sleep, he thought. *Appears to be about my height.*

When the man lifted his face, Hardwicke knew he was right. He was a few years younger than the marshal, slightly less than six feet, and stout of build. Hardwicke backed away for twenty paces and approached the campsite once again, this time with the natural noise of someone announcing their presence.

He saw the man rise and turn in his direction, then move to his blanket roll. He knelt and patted the blanket.

Yes, your gun is there. Hardwicke smiled. *You'll never get a chance to use it.*

"Hello," he said aloud, staying in the shadows. "I am Marshal Hardwicke, from over in Spiro."

"Oh, Marshal. Hello. I hope this not gonna be no problem, me spending a night here." Hardwicke said nothing and the man put his hands in his pockets and looked to his boots. "I didn't see no house or nothing. I'm just passing through, not looking for any trouble."

"No, no trouble, your being here," said Hardwicke. "We've had some problems with men along the tracks a few miles east of here. I'm just checking up on things around this bend in the tracks. Train has to slow down here, you know. You by yourself?"

"Yes, sir. Just me. On my way to Tulsa. Still got a good day's ride, I understand."

"Yeah, you maybe be there in a day." The man shuffled his feet as Hardwicke savored his discomfort.

"I was about to make some coffee."

"No, I don't have time for coffee," said Hardwicke, staring at the man, moving his eyes back and forth from the horse to the man's blanket.

"What's your name?"

"Bill Gibbons."

"Mind if I take a look in your saddle bag?"

"No, sir, you go right ahead. Nothing there but my belongings."

"Where is your gun?" The man pointed to his blanket and made a step to retrieve it. Hardwicke stepped into the light and held up his hand. "I'll take a look," he said. "You haven't fired it tonight, have you?"

"I shot these squirrels in my frying pan," he said, wincing his face when he saw the bloody bandage on Hardwicke's head. "Marshal, are you alright? You been hurt?"

The marshal tightened his mouth and picked up the rifle.

He assured himself the gun was loaded, then turned to the man and shot him in the chest. Gibbons looked at the marshal and moved his lips as if to speak. He staggered backwards while his eyes moved to his shaking hands, trying to cover the blood spreading across his midsection. His knees gave way and he twisted and fell forward into the fire.

Hardwicke slowly moved toward him, watching as the stranger struggled to roll out of the fire. His shirt caught the flames and one hand flew to his face. Hardwicke sat down and watched him for a few minutes, smelling the searing burn of hair and flesh.

He finally rose and stuck his boot under the man's chest. In a slow kicking motion, he rolled him over and out of the flames. The man's face was pink and his scalp was already bald well above his ears. As he lay on his back, still breathing, Hardwicke saw that his right cheek was covered with small scars and a searing brown liquid. He eased the gun barrel to the man's nose, pressing it hard till the man finally opened his eyes.

The train rounded the curve in the tracks and the whistle blew at the moment of this second blast, drowning out the sound and sending

Hardwicke into an eerie dream state of watching the flesh tear from the man's face for no apparent cause save the recoil of the rifle.

He found a change of clothes, a hunting knife and scabbard, and a few personal items in the man's saddlebag. He slipped the knife and scabbard in his belt and tossed the personal items into the fire. Seeing the color of the smoke darken, he peered closer. A red ribbon necklace curled and burned and released its grip on a milky white stone.

"A gift for Mrs. Bill Gibbons," he thought, watching the stone sink into the hot embers. He took a deep breath and felt a slow shiver move across his chest.

He then removed the man's boots and stripped him of his clothes. Blood still flowed freely from the wound in the man's chest.

The marshal unbuttoned his own bloody shirt and, lifting the man from behind, pulled the stranger's thin arms through his shirtsleeves. The belt and britches were more of a struggle, but in less than half an hour the dead man was dressed in clothes anyone in Spiro would recognize as belonging to Marshal Hardwicke. He dragged the body to the edge of the cliff overlooking the tracks and waited.

In two hours, the freight train from Little Rock to Oklahoma City reduced its speed as it approached the rising curve in the tracks. Once several cars had rattled past, Hardwicke tossed the body onto the tracks and knelt by the cliff to watch. The body was flung and torn as parts were scattered for half a mile on either side of the crossties.

"Those damn Indians," he said, anticipating the reaction of townspeople on finding his body. *"Well, after all that business with the preacher's daughter, cain't say I blame 'em all that much."*

"Might not even be Indians done this."

"No, could've been just about anybody."

"Hell, maybe he just fell on the tracks."

"Wouldn't surprise me none if that's what happened."

"Somebody gonna have to tell his wife."

"Yeah. She gonna be mighty torn up to hear it."

That is what they'll say, he thought.

"She'll be mighty torn up to hear it."

As the news of the marshal's demise swept through Spiro, the men in town did utter these sentiments.

"She'll be mighty torn up," the bartender said.

"Wonder what she gonna do now?" someone asked.

The women reacted differently, casting knowing glances at each other and saying nothing.

THE FRIENDLY COLOR

For the first ten years of her marriage to Robert Hardwicke, Ona Mae was afraid of her bruises, especially those that darkened her eyes and face. She sometimes delayed looking in the mirror for a week, at least until the tenderness grew less painful to the touch.

"Ona Mae. Ona Mae! Where are you sweetheart? Ona Mae, supper needs cooking. Come on in and help." Ona Mae's grandmother loved her probably more than anybody that ever lived. She would touch her hair while Ona Mae peeled and chopped the garden vegetables for the boiling pot.

"You my little girl, my little helper girl."

Ona Mae discovered that if she pretended to hear her grandmother call her in from those long-ago Arkansas woods, where she played with her little blonde-haired sister Emily, she would be more likely to laugh at how silly her face looked when she took her first glance after a beating.

"Wash your face up, hon."

Though the bruises would not wash off, a hot soapy face wash always felt good once the bruises turned yellow. Fresh blood bruises. Purple bruises. She hated those the most. They always brought the tears.

After a while you could tell the color of the bruise by the feel of it.
If you paid attention, you could tell. The later black and browning ones she
could tolerate, knowing they would soon fade into that greenish yellow color.
Green was a good color, the color of leaves on the redbud trees after that
early burst of spring. But green was too dark to hide. It meant more waiting.

Yellow, just yellow, that was the true friendly color. A dab of white
powder could easily hide the yellow bruises. They *were* friendly bruises, the
yellow ones. They meant she could go to town again. They meant she could
open her own front door and welcome someone, anyone, into her home,
without fear that they would peer too close and ask that awful question.

"What happened to you?"

She feared this question almost as much as she feared *him*.

"What happened to you?"

This question required a lie, a lie she would sometimes practice
even before she fell asleep.

After.

His sweat.

His breath.

His fist.

As she lowered herself into bed.

Carefully.

On the side he had not kicked.

On the side that had not caught the edge of the kitchen table as
she chose to cover her face with her hands rather than break her fall.

"What happened to you?"

The friendly yellow bruises meant the dialogue she feared most
would not occur, not this time at least.

"What happened to you?"

"Nothing."

"Why do you stay with him?"

"Where would I go?"

"Somewhere. To your folks."

"I am afraid to leave. He would find me."

When nobody answered, and nobody ever did after she told them she was too afraid to leave, she could always say, "I am not feeling well," and they would go. Mrs. Roundtree did. They all did.

One afternoon she parted the living room curtains and watched as Mrs. Roundtree paused on the front porch, considering knocking on the door again to insist on something. It was the consideration of what this something would be that sent her away, clutching her purse and *thanking the good Lord that my husband loves me.*

"It is my fault," Ona Mae told herself. "I am not a good wife. I cannot love him properly."

To her closest friends from church she sometimes said, "It is my duty. He is my husband. He will change. Besides, he is not himself. He doesn't mean to hurt me."

The real reason she stayed was a secret, a deep secret that *everybody knows* but never said. It was a secret that darkened even the friendly yellow color. Sometimes she stood before the sink and brushed away this hateful, this mean and hateful truth, waving and swatting her hands in front of her face, brushing the air thick with it, slapping her cheeks to drive the unseen biting gnats that whispered what only she and Grandma knew. Grandma who loved her so. Grandma who said it every day.

You are my sweet little helper, my angel, and your Grandma doesn't care if you're not pretty like your sister Emily. Pretty's not everything.

Now that she was grown, Ona Mae said it. "Pretty's not everything." Every day she said it. But why did these gnats keep humming and tormenting her, swimming before her like his breath, his stale breath, mean as his unfeeling eyes. Sometimes she said it out loud just to make the humming go away. She said the secret only she and Grandma knew.

"No one else will have me."

That was the darkest of all the secrets.

NEWS FOR ONA MAE

Mrs. Idabell Taylor, wife of the Indian agent, held her chin high and waited for her husband to step down from the carriage and help her descend. She was to deliver the news to Ona Mae Hardwicke of the death of her husband. When Agent Taylor offered her his hand, she nodded, clutched her dress in her fist, and took his hand in hers. He leaned back, lifting her hand as he did so, and took her elbow with his free hand. The entire ritual of her removal from the Taylor carriage was as practiced and rehearsed as a ballroom cotillion.

"Just a small part of your training," he had explained. "Being the wife of a federal agent has social obligations. You must rise to every occasion, even the most mundane."

In fact, Agent and Mrs. Taylor—a week before their wedding, when she was still Idabell McCurdy, the daughter of an Arkansas farmer and his mixed-blood Cherokee wife—had practiced the maneuver for the better part of an hour. Her mother peered through the living room window, wiping the tears from her cheeks with a towel dotted and puckered with flour from the bread she was kneading.

It was mid-morning and Mrs. McCurdy lifted and pounded

the thick slab of oat bread. When Agent Taylor's two dark horses and shining Memphis-made carriage neared the house, she moved to the front room window to watch. Her oldest daughter Idabell dashed from the house and into the arms of the man who would rescue her from a life of hot sweat and hard work and give her a life of leisure only seen in fairy tales.

From her mother's perch on the windowsill, the scene was idyllic; her daughter stepping from carriage to the ground, her hand held high and gripped softly by the man who had so properly asked for it in marriage. Idabell felt the first hint of impatience in the tightness of his grip. Unaccustomed to the new shoes he had insisted she wear for this rehearsal, she slipped clumsily from the top step.

"Look where you are putting your feet. You must pay attention," he said, squeezing her fingers in a painful balling of his fist.

Now, thirty years later, as she approached the modest Hardwicke home, Idabell smiled to remember her awkward efforts at becoming his wife, his perfect complement. When she spotted Ona Mae's face at the window, Mrs. Taylor stiffened her lips in judgment. Ona Mae's look was quick and furtive, like a small animal in the woods, much as her own mother's had been. It was the face of an uncultured woman.

"Who is it?" Ona Mae asked, pulling her hair from her face as she stepped through the door. Still clutching her dress, Mrs. Taylor watched her own feet in her black boots ascend the two steps before she replied.

"Mrs. Taylor," she said. "Mrs. Idabell Taylor."

Ona Mae said nothing. She tilted her head and furrowed her eyebrows as if her mind were sorting through sounds of a foreign tongue.

Mrs. Taylor gestured to the carriage and said, "I am the agent's wife, Agent Taylor."

"The agent," Ona Mae repeated. "You are the agent's wife."

"Yes." A long and awkward pause ensued. "May I come in?"

"Yes. Of course. You may come in. The marshal is not at home."

"I know," Mrs. Taylor said, lowering her voice to a barely audible hush and looking to the floor.

"What? What do you know?" said Ona Mae.

"Please, let us go inside." Mrs. Taylor stepped to the door and Ona Mae followed, reaching around the matronly woman to hold the door ajar for her.

"Sit down, please," said Ona Mae, nodding to the sofa by the window. "May I make some tea for you?" Her hands began to shake and her first impulse was to swat the gnats now buzzing about her face.

The gnats are not real, she told herself, *and I am not alone.* She clutched her trembling right hand with the other and felt the muscles of her face tighten into a smile.

"Tea, would you like tea?" she asked again in too loud a voice, she realized, for Mrs. Taylor, the agent's wife, leaned back in surprise and looked away.

"In a moment, Mrs. Hardwicke."

"Ona Mae. Please call me Ona Mae."

"Yes. Ona Mae. Will you sit down beside me?"

"Yes. My name is Ona Mae. You are Mrs. Taylor, the agent's wife, and you will have your tea in a moment."

"This is hard for me as well."

"Why are you here?"

"Please sit down."

"I will not sit down. I would rather stand, at least until you tell me what you came here to say. Please give me this respect in my own home. Our home. What do you know about my husband?"

"I am sorry." Mrs. Taylor stood and took Ona Mae's hands in her own. "Your husband has been killed. Accidentally."

Ona Mae squinted her face in an expression of bewilderment and wonder. Her chest heaved and her breath shortened to a series of quick pants. Mrs. Taylor wrapped her arms around Ona Mae's waist and eased her onto the sofa.

"It must be someone else," said Ona Mae. "My husband is Marshal Hardwicke."

"You sweet, dear woman. Marshal Hardwicke, Robert, was found dead this morning on the railroad tracks. He apparently fell from the boulders on Gilliam's Hill."

"Take me to him. I want to see him," said Ona Mae, rising to her feet and smoothing her dress. "Please, will your husband the agent take me to see him? Where is he?"

"Mrs. Hardwicke. Ona Mae. There is no doubt it is your husband. Before you see him you should know how he was found."

Ona Mae stared at Mrs. Taylor as tears coursed down her cheeks and sobs shook her entire body.

"How...was...he...found?"

"He fell across the tracks and a train hit him. Without his clothing and belongings, it would be difficult to know who he was."

"You must take me to him."

"You poor, poor dear," said Mrs. Taylor, embracing her as a mother consoling a daughter. Ona Mae instinctively reached for the baby blue scarf encircling Mrs. Taylor's neck, touching the silk to her wet cheeks.

The scarf came untied and Ona Mae clutched it in her hands and raised it to her face, taking in the soft powdery smell.

She closed her eyes and laid her head on Mrs. Taylor's shoulder.

"Thank you for coming."

"I know how hard things are for you. I wanted to be the one to tell you."

"How hard things are?" Ona Mae heard herself saying.

"Yes." Mrs. Taylor unbuttoned the top button of her dress and leaned her neck far to the right. She touched the loose flesh of her neck with two fingers, gently rubbing. She moved her fingers to the cloth of her blouse and pulled the cotton away from her skin.

A deep purple bruise extended across her collarbone.

When Ona Mae shook her head and stared at the bruise with round, incredulous eyes, Mrs. Idabell Taylor took a deep breath and sighed.

"You poor lonely child," she said. "Did you think you were the only one?"

Ona Mae accepted the helping hand of Agent Taylor as she ascended the steps of the carriage, settling herself onto the rear seat. The three rode in silence to Hermann's Funeral Parlor. Ebert Hermann met the three and offered necessary but insincere condolences.

"I am so sorry for your tragic loss," he said, bowing and revealing his shiny balding head. A nervous assistant led Ona Mae and Mrs. Taylor to the back room. As soon as they were out of earshot, Ebert turned to the agent.

"He was as sorry a man as ever walked the earth," he said. "He got exactly what he deserved."

Entering the back room, which reeked of alcohol, Ona Mae felt a slight touch to her elbow. She jumped in surprise at the intimacy of the touch and turned to see the assistant, pointing to a darkened corner of the room.

Three empty tables lay white and ready to receive the dead. Walking between the tables, Ona Mae approached an open wooden box. The marshal lay face down and pieces of his legs and arms surrounded his torso in random stacks.

Ona Mae gasped and covered her mouth. She felt a tremor in the pit of her stomach. She slowly lifted her hands to the front of her face. They hovered there for a moment, then flicked the air in random thrusts, grabbing at unseen gnats.

Mrs. Taylor stepped before Ona Mae and gripped her wrists.

"No more of that," she said. "He is gone and you are alive. Consider how lucky you are. Life is offering you another chance." Ona Mae met her gaze with a confused look, and Idabell continued. "You have more friends than you know. You will see."

Early that evening a steady flow of people streamed into Ona Mae's living room. Just after sundown, as she made her way to the kitchen to put more water on to boil, she heard a faint knocking at the back door. In the dim light through the kitchen window, she saw three people huddled together on the porch, each holding a pot or basket.

She pushed open the door to find Samuel, the preacher's son, flanked by Rose and her mother. Samuel nodded in a respectful manner, and instantly she knew he had told no one of their evening together. She stood holding the door in the yellow dark of night, and, for the first time in years, Ona Mae Hardwicke moved into forever time. Her mouth filled with the sharp taste of ebbing life, the memory of a red fox buried beneath her bedroom window.

When Ona Mae returned to the present, she saw a swath of kitchen light slice across the heads of three Choctaws bowing before her.

"Come in. Please come in," she said, stepping outside and holding the door for them.

Samuel entered first, fighting the temptation to cast his eyes about the room and compare the fully lit kitchen with the dark memory of his initial visit. He glanced sideways, only once, and saw the corner where she cowered and cried while he tended to her wounds. He remembered how thin and weightless her bones felt when he lifted her legs.

The others shuffled in and placed their foodstuffs on the already-covered table, shifting in embarrassment to be standing in a *Nahullo* household. Ona Mae lingered for a moment on the porch, taking in the cool night air. A small noise caught her attention, followed by a brief and shy movement. Someone was standing in the shadows, leaning against the wall. She heard a trembling voice.

"I brought you something too."

Roberta Jean stepped into view, holding a bundle of white daisies in her outstretched hand. "I grow these daisies in my room," she said. "They sit by my windowsill."

"I know you, don't I?" Ona Mae asked. Roberta Jean nodded. Ona Mae took her in her arms and held her tight. Roberta stiffened and the daisies fell to the porch. Ona Mae held the embrace till the young girl wrapped her arms around her and, like leaves in a breeze, the two began to sway, a soft and imperceptible movement at first. Swaying led to sobbing, sweet sobs of shared pain and joy. A quarter hour passed before Ona Mae spoke.

"Will you come to visit me?"

"Yes," said Roberta Jean.

"Good." She stooped to pick up the flowers, but Roberta Jean touched her shoulder, saying, "Leave them be. I'll bring you a living daisy, roots and dirt, all in a Choctaw pot."

"I will hold you to that promise," she said. "Now, come into my home." Ona Mae opened the door and ushered the daughter of a Choctaw preacher into the light of her kitchen.

AMAFO COMES TO LIFE
Rose • Early November 1897

We were all convinced the marshal was gone, out of our lives forever, save for the ashes he left behind. Over the next several days I spent every afternoon with Roberta Jean. Some mornings I'd just show up at her door for breakfast, always offering to help cook. She was quieter than her usual self at first, but after her family and mine both spent a Saturday picnic day at the church and the graveyard, she once more was the Roberta Jean I knew and loved.

Reverend Willis changed too, in little ways. Years later Samuel told me about hiding the knife so his father wouldn't kill the marshal. Looking back, I am dead certain the reverend knew it was Samuel who hid it. Partly out of shame for what he almost did, and partly out of gratitude, Reverend Willis little by little gave Samuel more respect. He let Samuel drive the family wagon to church, and he even let Samuel say the prayer at our picnic.

I still remember that prayer! We sat at the long wooden table behind the church. It was piled high with food. All that stood between our hungry stomachs and the best Choctaw food in the country was the blessing of the food.

"Samuel, will you offer the blessing?" Reverend Willis said. Samuel dropped his head so sudden-like, I thought he'd bump it on the table. When he finally looked up, his eyes were swollen big and he clenched his jaw. I knew why. I knew what he wanted to say.

No, Father, please do not make me do this! But he was too smart to say it. We all waited patiently. Samuel finally stood up and we bowed our heads. But we didn't close our eyes. Nobody wanted to be the only one at the table, save of course the reverend, who couldn't later describe what Samuel looked like at his first family prayer offering.

Samuel stammered and stuttered and started off by God-blessing people at the table, like a go-to-bed prayer!

"God bless Blue Ned, God bless Roberta Jean, God bless my mother and fa…" And that's when he realized he was not giving his usual prayer at bedtime. And that is when I first loved Samuel in a grown-up way, for he did not apologize or sit down or make any excuses. Instead, he lifted his eyes and looked at all of us. He took a deep breath and nodded his head and started over.

We were ashamed to be caught looking, so we closed our eyes and bowed our heads, the rightful way.

"Dear Lord Jesus above," Samuel said, "look down on us at this special gathering of the Willis and the Goode families. We have seen many things this past year. We have suffered the loss of New Hope Academy for Girls and we have buried Choctaw children. We grieve also for Pokoni and we pray now near her grave. We have known too much death.

"But your will and your ways, though forever a mystery to us, we will never doubt. We trust in you. We come together now to share our happiness, not our grief. For all that you provide for us, we give our thanks.

Please accept our blessing of this food as it goes into our bodies. May it make us stronger. May we do thy will, for always and forever. Amen."

No one said a word for the longest time. Samuel sat down and gathered himself in a hush. Reverend Willis waited. When Samuel finally lifted his eyes, the reverend nodded his head in approval.

That night, when I brought Amafo his cocoa, he was sitting at the table by the window.

"Sit right cheer, my girl. You not gonna be seeing your best little boyfriend, me, for several days, you know. Me and your Poppa going on a hunting trip. You gonna be *hoke*?"

"I think so, Amafo," I told him. I almost cried to see him happy.

"Come here, girl," he said. I leaned over to him and he held me close. "I guess we all gonna make it *hoke*, best I can see." He sighed and I felt the hope wrestling with the sadness. "Go get yourself a cup and come back here with me, want to?"

"I thought you would never ask me," I teased him.

"Well," he said, "you being the prettiest girl and all, I didn't even know you'd be interested." I dashed down the steps and to the kitchen to put the water on to boil. My grandfather was coming back, I could feel it.

When I returned to his room, Amafo pulled the chair out for me, in that funny way-too-formal way he had. Once he was settled in his own chair, he sipped his cocoa quiet for a few minutes. I just waited, like I had seen him do.

"She was the sweetest woman that ever walked the earth," he said. "And the strongest too." He took another sip and almost laughed. "Lord knows, she was strong."

For the first time I knew about since the funeral, Amafo was talking about Pokoni. I listened to him for almost an hour, till Momma called from downstairs.

"Let your Amafo get some sleep, now. Get on to your own room, let him be." Amafo squeezed my hand and whispered, "Best do what Momma says."

I lay awake that night thinking about how happy Amafo and Pokoni were, how they touched each other when they thought nobody was looking. Just before I fell asleep, I realized something else. For the first time since the funeral, I was thinking about Pokoni without crying.

DARK RESURRECTION

HARDWICKE IN TEXAS

Hardwicke turned south. He spent two days in the caves overlooking Wilburton, a small settlement where the law had little sway. Deemed Robber's Cave, these mountainous hideouts were used by gangs who haunted the territory by night and day.

He built no fire, ate dried meat, and drank the remains of his whiskey till night and day blended into a head-shaking fury at those who had wronged him so. He awoke from his stupor at noon on the third day. Hardwicke knew his options were simple. He could join a gang and always be the outsider, the man most likely to be gunned down when money was divvied up. Or he could make his way across the Red River and wait.

Staying in the shadows and approaching every bend in the trail with caution, he eased his horse down the mountain path. A week after throwing the body of Bill Gibbons in front of an oncoming train, Marshal Robert Hardwicke of Spiro, Indian Territory, crossed the Red River and fled into Texas. He left behind his former life and disappeared into the wilds of the Big Thicket. For the first time in twenty years, he was a happy man.

For several weeks he sought work, appearing at the front doors of struggling homesteaders. With a smile and a strong handshake, he introduced himself as Bill Gibbons. He offered himself as a worker needing only a place to sleep and three meals a day. He chopped wood, fed livestock, carried water, and repaired rotted roofs and broken-down barns, then said his goodbyes and moved on.

And he waited.

He soon found what he was looking for. He knew it the moment the old man opened the door.

"Hello," he said. "I don't mean to be no bother. I'm just passing through. If you need a few days help around your place, I can give you good work. I don't need money, just meals is all."

The old man's face lit up. He grabbed Hardwicke and pulled him to his chest. "Tommy, I knew you would come home!" the man shouted. "I have missed you so bad. Come into this house!"

Hardwicke lifted a forearm and blocked the old man's embrace. An elderly woman appeared in the doorway. "Excuse my husband," she said. "He doesn't always get things right. He thinks you're our son."

"Marty," said the man, "look who's here. Tommy come home. I been tellin' you he was gonna. Oh mercy, son, we been missing you."

"That's alright, ma'am," said Hardwicke. "I'm just looking for a few days work is all. I'm Bill Gibbons, from over at Fort Smith. I'm on my way to San Antonio."

"Well, you have a long ride ahead of you. I'm Marty Jacobs and this is my husband George. Long as we can trust you, we could sure use the help."

"I won't be no trouble, Miss Marty. All I needs is a place to sleep and meals. Maybe a day's eatings when I take my leave. I'll work hard long as you need me and be on my way."

"I'll get your bedroom ready," George said, entering the house. "Tommy," he said over his shoulder, "you've made your old man proud! I knew you'd come home, I just knew it."

"You cain't stay in the house, Mr. Gibbons."

"Call me Bill, please."

"Fine, Bill. And you can call me Marty. Make yourself a place for you and your horse in the barn out back. I'll fix you some lunch and let you know when it's ready. You're welcome to eat on the back porch."

Hardwicke led his horse to the barn, tossed his blanket to the floor, and surveyed his temporary home. He found a tool chest and went right to work, repairing a broken-down stall. Soon Marty stepped from the back door, followed by a small fluffy-haired dog.

"Come and git it!" she called out.

Wish I had my dogs, thought Hardwicke. *They would eat you alive and fight over the bones.* "Who's your little friend?" he said with a smile.

"This is Bobby," Marty said. "He likes people. We don't get many visitors back in these woods, so you two will git along fine."

"I'm a dog-lover myself," Hardwicke said, kneeling down and rubbing Bobby behind the ears.

"My, you come ready to work all right," Marty said, seeing the stall.

"Thank you, ma'am."

Hardwicke spent the afternoon prying and ripping rotten boards from the barn walls. He spotted a rain puddle in a rear corner and by mid-afternoon he'd repaired the leaky roof. He ate his supper of biscuits and beans on the back porch steps. As he rose to go, the back door opened.

"Tommy," said the old man. "Your mother cain't know about this, but I been saving something for you."

"What?"

"Follow me. It's hid out in a corner, back yonder in a stall." He stumbled down the steps and walked limp-legged to the barn.

"George!" Marty called out from the kitchen. "Where are you going? Leave him alone now."

"It's okay, ma'am," Hardwicke said. "He wants to show me around the barn. I'll see he's safe and help him back inside."

"Alright," said Marty. "Just don't be long or he'll fall asleep on you."

George entered the barn and motioned for Hardwicke to follow.

"Come on, Tommy!" he said. "I ain't touched a drop since you been gone." He knelt in a rear corner of the barn and started digging, tossing dirt and hay aside. "Lookie here," he shouted, then cupped his hands over his mouth with a giggle. "Oh, I better be quiet. Momma cain't know."

George lifted a short plank and held up a gallon jug. "Whiskey, Tommy! I know you like it."

Hardwicke's eyes lit up and he fought the impulse to knock the old man to the ground.

"Thank you, George," he said, taking the jug and popping the cork.

"You call me Dad. Like in the old days, Tommy."

"Yeaah. Thank you, Dad," said Hardwicke. *At least you're good for something*, he thought. He lifted the jug and took a long, slow swallow. As the first drops stung his tongue, Hardwicke stumbled backwards. His throat burned and his whole body shivered.

"Old man, I been needing that."

"George!" Marty called from the back porch.

"You best be going. Dad. You gonna tell Momma 'bout the whiskey?"

"Oh no, Tommy, that's me and you's secret."

Hardwicke helped George to the house, where Marty stood in the back door waiting. "Did he cause you any trouble?" she asked. "You know he don't think right, like I told you."

"No, me and him just looked around the barn is all."

Hardwicke spent the remainder of the evening sipping whiskey and remembering his hideaway back home. "Wonder what the old lady is doing tonight? Bet she's cleaning house of me. Probly building a fire and burning my clothes, anything reminds her of me. Her husband. Won't be long before she's whoring around looking for a man."

His eyes took on a dark glare and he saw her cringing before him. He clenched his fist and swung it hard against the wall of the barn.

"I'll get you for that," he said. "You ain't free of me yet. Oh no. I'll pay you one last visit, and when I do you'll be wishing you were dead." He curled up on the dirt floor and fell into a dream-filled sleep.

Hardwicke stood over the fire staring at the wrinkled flesh of Bill Gibbons. The embers popped and the skin fell away. Ona Mae stared back at him. She met his gaze with a strong, defiant look. He gripped the neck of his old whiskey bottle and smashed her face. Her eyes burst into flames and fire shot from her mouth. He stomped it, again and again, till she cowered in the kitchen and he stood over her, yanking her hair and flailing his fist against her cheek.

The next morning he was jolted awake by a loud knocking.

"Bill, you up in there!" Marty hollered.

"Yes, ma'am. I'll be right out."

"Your breakfast is waiting on the porch. Get on up and we can talk about the day's work."

Hardwicke froze. He had taken orders for months now, but these orders came from men. He had never in his life done the bidding of a woman. He felt a twitching in his face and he gritted his teeth.

"You'll be sorry you ever talked to me like that," he whispered to himself. "You don't know who you're taking to. But you will. Oh yeah. Be too late to do anything about it, but you gonna regret the day I come into your life. You and that worthless old man, you both be sorry."

The barn door opened and Bobby leapt through, barking and yelping. Hardwicke picked him up by the collar and gave him a hard squeeze. When he dropped him to the floor, Bobby rolled over and ran from the barn.

His plate of beans and bread sat on the top step. Hardwicke had no appetite, but his throat burned with thirst. He downed his coffee in two quick gulps and slammed the cup to the porch.

"You sleep good?" Marty asked, standing over him.

"Fine," said Hardwicke without looking up. She noted his rudeness, then decided not to say what was on her mind.

"Good. We got plenty of work needs doing, if you're still up to it."

Hardwicke said nothing.

"You can start with the garden," she said. "We got tomatoes, some corn and squash, but they gitting eat up by every hungry critter in the thicket. Don't spend too much time with the grass and weeds. Just clean out the brush soes we can get to the food crops. Keep your gun handy and see if you can kill a coyote. Maybe seeing one of their own hanging dead'll send 'em somewhere else. That sound good for the first day's work, starting out easy?"

"Good enough, if that's what you want," Hardwicke replied.

The next few days followed the same pattern—a night of whiskey and dreams and a day of sweaty digging, cutting, and chopping. Two milk cows had settled in the far corner of the garden, and Hardwicke built a small milking stall in the barn. He found an old crate and fashioned a stool. By the third day he presented Marty with a pail of milk when she called him to breakfast. He had a plan now and gaining Marty's trust was part of it.

Every night George joined him in the barn. "Momma won't know, Dad. Here, have a glass of whiskey," he said one night, handing the old man a cup of milk.

"Ummm," said George. "That's durn good whiskey."

"Yeah," said Hardwicke, sipping from the jug. So every night George had his glass of milk and Hardwicke his whiskey.

And every night he dreamed. Night after night he watched Ona Mae burn. But his thoughts by day took on a different hue. He knew she had lady friends, and lady friends have husbands willing to help a widow make her place in the world. Soon his dreams changed as well. Ona Mae no longer cringed. With every passing night she grew stronger, almost daring him to hit her. The fear had left her eyes.

Hardwick felt his time in Texas drawing to a close.

"Old man," he said between whiskey gulps one evening, "Momma told me you had something in the house, something real nice you wanted to give to me."

George wrinkled his brow for a long while and Hardwicke waited.

"Yes, Tommy. I do. A special gift for our boy. Momma made me promise not to be giving stuff away so you cain't let her know."

"I always been good at keeping secrets, you know that."

"Yes, Tommy. You always was my favorite little boy. Momma's going to town soon. We can get your special gift then. That be alright?"

"Anytime you like, be fine with me." Hardwicke worked later than usual that day. His supper was cold by the time he ambled to the back porch. Marty was watching through the kitchen window and met him on the steps.

"Bill," she began, "I'll be headed to town before sunrise tomorrow.

Maybe you can stay close to the house and keep an eye on George for me. No telling what he's likely to do if he's left by hisself."

"I'll keep a good eye on him," Hardwicke said. He spent the evening packing his horse and readying for the long ride home. He was tempted to empty the whiskey jug, but knew he needed to be wide-awake and alert in the morning. He took two long sips and wrapped the jug in a blanket. *Be nice to have some whiskey for the trip*, he thought.

An hour before sunrise Marty knocked on the door. "You up yet, Bill? I'll be leaving soon."

Hardwicke opened the door, dressed and ready for the day.

"Oh, yes, ma'am," he said. "I've got plenty of work to do in the garden. I can keep a good eye on George from there."

"Good. I'll be home early evening. George is sitting on the porch, guarding over your breakfast. He's all excited about spending the day with you. He still calls you Tommy. Hope that don't bother you."

"No, ma'am, he means well. Don't bother me at all."

"All right then. When you get hungry later, go on in the kitchen and fix you two some lunch." Marty turned to go. While George and Hardwicke huddled over plates of beans and biscuits, she climbed aboard the wagon, snapped the reins, and left for the two-hour trip to town.

They ate without speaking, but after every bite George glanced at Hardwicke and rocked back and forth, grinning a secret he couldn't wait to tell his son. He downed his last drop of coffee and slapped his thighs.

"Tommy, you ready for that special gift I been waiting to give you?"

"I sure am. Any time you ready."

"Wait right here," George said, entering the house. Hardwicke followed him through the kitchen and into the bedroom.

"Your momma's been keeping it hid. She thinks I don't know

where it is." George reached under the bed and dragged out a foot-long pine box. He took a deep breath and turned to Hardwicke.

"Tommy, what's in this box goes way back. It belonged to my grandparents and your momma's grandparents. Some of this jewelry come over the ocean from England. Some of it from back East."

He opened the lid and Hardwicke knew he could live for years on the gold and sparkling stones that shone back at him.

"I want you to pick one for yourself," George said. "She won't miss it. And if she does, I'll tell her it was my gift to you."

Hardwicke weighed his options. If Marty returned and found the old man dead and the box gone, she'd send the law after him and he could be facing a hanging. As he gazed at the stones, a soft breeze parted the curtains and the morning sun peeked through. A reddish-yellow light sparkled from the chest and Hardwicke smiled.

Nothing like a fire to send a message, he thought.

"Go ahead, son. Don't be bashful," said George.

Hardwicke picked out a gold watch chain and held it dangling. "This be alright?" he asked. "I don't want anything too costly."

"Oh, son, I am so proud of you. You picked a good one. That chain belonged to my father." He flung his arms around Hardwicke and pulled him into a tight hug.

Hardwicke gave himself to the old man's embrace. No one had ever held him like this, not in this father-son way. For the briefest of moments he felt the warmth of the old man, felt sorrow at the slipping away of a good man's life.

"I ain't gonna hurt you, old man," he whispered, his head still buried in George's shoulder. "But that wife of yours, she not getting away with it, treating me like her hired hand."

"I always knew you'd come home, Tommy. I'm so proud knowing you gonna be carrying my father's watch chain." With a final pat on the back, George released Hardwicke. "I'll keep this a secret from your mother," he said, returning the box to its hiding place under the bed.

"I better get some work done," said Hardwicke. "You wanna help me?"

"I'll be glad to, son."

"I been chopping weeds and brush from the garden for several days now," Hardwicke said. "How's about we have ourselves a brush fire and get that garden ready for planting? What do you say, old man?"

"Sounds like a good idea to me."

Hardwicke found a wheelbarrow in the barn and tossed George a rake, saying, "You rake and I'll haul." An hour later they'd staked a pile of broken branches and dried grass against the barn, as big as a dozen hay bales.

"Let's take a break," said Hardwicke. He rolled a log facing the brush pile and slapped the sweat from his hat. "Have a seat."

With George settled by his side, Hardwicke continued. "You 'member when you used to take me hunting, back when I was a kid?"

"I sure do. The woods were fulla any kinda meat you wanted back in those days. We killed wolves, wildcats, even a bear that one time."

"And 'member how we sat around the campfire at night?"

"Yes, Tommy. That's when you had your first taste of whiskey. Your Uncle Edgar brought the jug and I let you have a sip."

"Dad, why don't you get us a fire going? You got any matches?"

"Sure do, son. I'll be right back," George said. He returned with two cups of water and a pocketful of matches. "Have a drink, Tommy. It's good creek water."

"Thank you," he said, tossing down the water with a single gulp. "Dad, why don't you start the fire, like in the old days?"

"I'll be glad to, son. Before long your old man is gonna be his old self again." George stacked a handful of dried leaves around the edge of the brush pile and struck a match. He held it over the leaves till they burst into flames.

"Never waste a match, my father always told me," he said, backing away as the branches caught fire and the flames rose with a crackling pop.

"You stay here and watch the fire. I'm gonna get Bobby. He likes fires, don't he?"

"Oh yes. He always sleeps next to the fireplace."

Hardwicke found Bobby asleep in the living room. He carried him inside the barn and tied his leash to the rear stall.

"I wish I was here to watch Momma find you," he said, spitting and kicking sawdust in Bobby's face. "Better yet, I wish I could stay and give her the beating she needs—her thinking she can tell me what to do."

With the smell of burning pine, Hardwicke felt a pounding in his chest. He exited the barn and found George rocking back and forth and saying in a whispering voice, "Momma's gonna be mad," over and over.

"Oh no, Momma's gonna be glad to see this rotten barn gone. I'm here to build us a new barn. You can tell her. I'll go get the lumber and we can start on the new barn before she gets back."

"Tommy! Me and you can build a new barn!"

"That's right, old man. Me and you got plenty of work to do. Momma's gonna be so proud when you tell her you lit the fire. Be sure to let her know."

"I will, Tommy, I will."

"This is a good fire, old man. Look at it. A good strong fire."

The flames lapped higher, dancing across the roof. A whoosh of air sent a curling tower of yellow flames to the sky, carrying burning bits of dried shingles and twisting hay.

"You did it," Hardwicke shouted. "Tell her! You burnt down the old barn so we could build a new one!" Hardwicke tied his horse to the back porch rail and hurried to the bedroom. He yanked the quilt from the bed and wrapped the box in it.

George never saw him leave. He waited, rocking and crying and clapping his hands, part of him knowing this was a tragedy beyond anything he had ever seen, part of him hoping Tommy could make a miracle happen. As the rear of the barn crumbled, he heard Bobby barking.

"Bobby! You in there?"

George ran to the barn door and saw flames breathing through the wall. He flung open the door, covered his face, and made his way to the yelping sounds, through waves of flames rising from the hay floor.

"Oh Bobby!" he cried. He knelt to the dog as the barn collapsed.

Hardwicke heard the crash of the barn walls. He pulled his horse to a stop and watched a cloud of dark smoke rise over the treetops. "Yeah, old man, you started one hell of a fire. Your woman ain't ever gonna forgive you for that. I wonder how long before she runs praying to the bedroom, hoping you never showed me the box." He laughed and jerked the reins, turning his anger to his own wife—and to the Choctaw girl with the hard look.

Marty never ran to the bedroom seeking the pine box of family heirlooms. She knew better. From the moment she first saw the smoke, still a mile from the house, she knew better. She snapped the reins and urged her pony into a gallop, talking to herself the remainder of the trip.

"From that first morning I shoulda known he couldn't be trusted. Some men just hate women and he was one of 'em. I could feel it. We just needed the help so bad. Why did I let him stay?"

She found George sitting on a log and staring at a pile of burning boards and popping hot embers, all that remained of the barn. He held Bobby tight to his chest with his left arm and slapped hot ashes from his hair and clothes with the other. He shook his head and cried to see her.

"We gonna build a new barn," he said. "Me and Tommy. I burnt this one down so we can build a new one."

She lifted George to his feet and lowered Bobby to the ground.

"Momma's gonna be mad," said George, over and over, as she led him to bed.

"Here, now, let me take your clothes off soes you can get some sleep."

George lay his head on the pillow and closed his eyes.

Marty waited till morning to look under the bed. She knew the box was gone. He took the quilt, so of course he took the box. But until she saw the empty space beneath her bed, the box still sat on the cedar floor, just as it had every day for the past forty years.

HOMECOMING

After crossing the Red River, Hardwicke made his first social call. "Cain't be blaming a dead man for settling an old score," he reasoned.

He rode for what remained of the night till he passed the First Christian Church of Skullyville. As the sky lightened to the east, he slipped off the road and into the woods. Tying his horse in a clump of scrub oaks, he crossed the narrow wooden bridge and stepped onto the back acres of the Goode spread. Lanterns shone and people were moving inside the house, so he crept to the garden and hid between two rows of dried okra stalks.

Amafo appeared in the kitchen window. Hardwicke's eyes narrowed and he whispered to himself, "I bet you was relieved to hear 'bout my death, you old fool." He ran across the yard and knelt beneath the window.

"How 'bout we leave Whiteface here in case the ladies need to use the wagon?" Rose's father asked. "You can ride your Choctaw pony. She's small and quick, won't be no trouble."

"Sounds good to me," Amafo said. "I'll saddle Slowboat and bring her 'round front."

"I couldn't ask for anything better," said Hardwicke. He slipped Bill Gibbons' hunting knife from his belt and ran his thumb across the razor-sharp blade. "You and your pony both. That ought to wake 'em up."

He hurried from the house and entered the barn. Moving from stall to stall, he picked the small and slender pony as Amafo's. "Easy now, girl," he said, patting her flank and moving to the rear of the stall.

Amafo stepped gingerly from the back porch and made his way to the barn. The soreness played on his knees and his back.

"I am moving like an old man," he said. He paused and lifted his gaze to the bright morning stars. "I miss you, my Hester. It was better being old with you around."

"*No reason to be lazy*," he heard Pokoni say.

"You are right, hon," he replied. "I'm getting outta my laziness, I promise." He smiled at the thought of her as he put his weight against the door and pushed it open. "You get heavier every year," he said.

Entering the barn, he called out, "*Halito*, Slowboat. Good morning." Slowboat whinnied in response.

"Yes, it has been a long time," he said. "Thanks for not giving up on me. I guess I sorta gave up on myself. But you understand, don'cha? You 'bout old as I am."

Amafo took a single step into the barn and stopped. A feeling as sudden as a slap to the face came over him. A bitter chill crackled the air. He staggered backwards and shook his head to clear the dizziness. Slowboat stomped the floor and when Amafo paused at the door, she kicked against the gate of her stall.

Amafo felt his knees grow slack. He fell to the ground outside the barn. He tried calling for help, but his breath turned to fog as he slipped into unconsciousness.

When he came to his senses, Rose and her father stood over him. Rose bathed his face with a warm, wet cloth.

"You gonna be *hoke*, Amafo?" Rose asked.

"I think so," he said, rising to a sitting position.

"He better stay home today, Daddy," Rose said.

"She's right, Amafo. We can go hunting tomorrow or the next day. Looks like cold weather might be blowing up anyways."

"*Yakoke* for the thoughts," Amafo said. "But I done promised Pokoni I'd get out of my laziness. I don't want no *shilombish*, hers or anybody else's, getting after me. I better keep my promise."

"No need to rush it."

"I am better already," he said. "I had a dizzy spell is all."

Half an hour and two stiff cups of coffee later, Amafo returned to the barn. He smiled to see the growing spiderweb, now stretching from the rafter to the top board of the stall. "You've got it all to yourself for a few days, momma spider," he said, tipping his hat and stepping into Slowboat's stall.

She flicked her tail from side to side and twitched the muscles of her flanks. When he reached for her, Slowboat flung her head and knocked his hand away.

"What's the matter, gal?" Amafo asked, rubbing her ear and running a gentle hand along her spine. He lifted her legs to inspect her feet, walking slowly around her, talking and touching her softly as he moved.

"You're a purty gal, Slowboat," he said. "Everything's *hoke*. I been feeling low, but I'll be seeing you more often now."

As Amafo circled his horse, the marshal sank behind a haybale at the rear of the stall. His breathing slowed and his eyes focused on the spot where the teeth of his blade would sever the flesh—the blue vein running down the skin of Amafo's throat.

One cut and he is gone, he thought.

When Amafo moved to within three feet of him, Hardwicke slowly stood. His heart pounded in anticipation of the kill.

Your horse will be spotted with your blood, old man. Just like Bill Gibbons, I will look you in the eyes before I kill you.

He pressed the blade against his thumb and drew it slowly across the padding of his fingerprint. A bright red trail of liquid ran the length of the blade and dripped from the knifepoint to the hay on the stall floor. Hardwicke felt a small wet drop on the tip of his fingers. He flicked the blood at Amafo and it landed on his neck.

Thinking it was a horsefly, Amafo slapped at the spot. When he removed his hand and saw the blood, he muttered, "Mosquitoes!"

Hardwicke savored every moment, knowing he had the power to end the old man's life whenever he chose. He lifted the knife and reached for Amafo. As he did so, the upturned blade sliced the dangling spider web. The silky cluster drifted into his eyes and mouth. Instinctively, Hardwicke puckered his lips and blew, wiping his face with his free hand.

Feeling the sudden gust of air on her hindquarters, Slowboat went berserk, kicking her hind legs and sending the marshal crashing against the wall. She bolted from the stall and fled from the barn, bucking and kicking, with Amafo chasing after her.

Rose came running from the house and together she and Amafo caught Slowboat. They walked her around the yard before strapping her saddle tight. With all eyes on the horse, the marshal beat a shadowy path from the barn. He quickly crossed the back pasture to his waiting horse.

Once Slowboat was saddled, the family gathered in the backyard.

"Not a good start on the day," said Rose's father.

"She just hadn't been rode in a while," Amafo said. "She'll be *hoke*, and so will this old man."

Rose crept behind Amafo and gripped his hand as she had seen Pokoni do a hundred times. For the whisper of a moment, Amafo thought Pokoni stood with him once more.

"Gimme just one minute," said Amafo. "Somebody I need to check on." Without knowing exactly what he was looking for, Amafo moved through the barn to Slowboat's stall. Holding the lantern high, he spotted momma spider hard at work, whirling in quick, tiny circles to repair her broken nest. His voice took on a smile.

"Well, I guess it's not easy, rooming with a horse."

He lowered the lantern and his eyes followed the path of the spiderweb along the rear wall. "*Chi-pisalachiki*," he said. "See you in a few days."

Two fresh boot prints stared up at him from the stall floor, but he never saw them.

"I made my promise, Hester," he whispered as he exited the barn, "and I'm gonna keep it. I'll be counting on you to look after things 'round here while we be gone."

EMPTY HOUSE

Rose

With the men gone, Momma was nervous as a stray cat. "The house sure seems empty with nobody to take care of," she said. Daddy and Amafo had only been gone two hours, but Momma was right. I already did miss 'em.

"You can do these dishes by yourself," she said after we finished breakfast. "I got cleaning to do." She went to sweeping with a fury in the living room. Not two minutes went by and she said, "You finished with those dishes yet?"

"Won't be long, Momma." I had barely cleaned the table off and hadn't drawn the water yet. I was just soaping up the first plate when she dropped the broom and burst through the kitchen door.

"Get your brother and a change of clothes for you both," she said. "We're not lazying around this house with nothing to do. It's been half a year since we visited the McCurtains. Time she and I did some cooking and swapping canned goods. Get a move on!"

I knew better than to remind Momma I still hadn't done the dishes. I dipped 'em, rinsed 'em, and laid 'em on the counter to dry, then dried my hands and went looking for Jamey. Less than an hour later, with Whiteface hitched to the wagon, we were headed to the McCurtain place.

Whiteface was frisky and ready for the trip. She reminded me of Momma, how she shook her head and snorted impatiently as Jamey and I clambered on board. The McCurtains lived only five miles to the east, but the road was seldom traveled. Pine trees grew thick along the edge and scrub oaks and stubborn underbrush sprouted in the middle of the road, scarred as it was with rain-washed ruts.

Our visit—Momma had made it clear—was not a social call.

"We are going there to work." The plan was for Momma and Missus McCurtain to cook for the better part of two days. We had loaded dried corn and beans to trade for squash and pickles, a McCurtain specialty.

"Will Mister McCurtain be there?" I asked.

"No, just her boy Aaron," Momma said. "Mister McCurtain's off selling or buying horses or God knows what all."

Momma almost never talked about people like that, so I knew one reason we were going to visit Missus McCurtain. Momma had somehow heard Mister McCurtain was gone, and she wanted to see her friend without him around.

"Whatever reason she has for not liking him, it must be a good one," I 'member Pokoni saying. "Can't be the buying and selling of horses. Lots of folks do that. Must be the *God knows what all.*"

We'd been gone seemed like only half an hour when Whiteface started her whinnying, a nervous way she had of sniffing and pawing the ground, usually when she caught the scent of animals in the woods. It might be only a polecat, maybe a raccoon. Momma snapped the reins and urged her on.

"Giddap, girl. Get on along." Daddy always kept the road cleared close to our house. Once a month at least he rode his horse up and down that road looking for lost livestock. As we neared the noon hour, the brush grew thicker and the trees met overhead, forming a dark roof over the road. Once Jamey and I had to climb down and dig up a small oak seedling blocking our path.

We were only a mile or so from the McCurtain place when the first hint of trouble came, nestled in a clump of bull nettle too far out in the road to ignore.

"Rose, take the shovel and dig it up. Whiteface don't seem to want to go 'round it," Momma said. I climbed over the side and Jamey handed me the shovel. As I neared the bull nettle, Whiteface reared up and flailed her legs out in front. Momma did her best to settle her down, saying, "*Hoke*, girl, it's *hoke* now."

I once again approached the bull nettle. The yellow and white blooms stood tall on the spikes of the poisonous flower. I stepped slow, careful to avoid the prickly stalks. Something moved at the dark green base of the plant. It seemed almost part of the ground, like the brown dirt was moving. I was so curious. I knelt down close before I heard the rattler's dry hissing.

"Momma," I said, "it's a rattlesnake. I think it's a big one."

"Jesus Lord," Momma said. "Don't move sudden. Just back up easy, hon." I saw the flower stalks sway and the head of the rattlesnake appeared, leaping at me. I flung the shovelhead at the snake and ran towards the wagon. Whiteface saved my life. She pounded the snake with her hooves till he was dead. Momma came down from the wagon and picked up the shovel.

"Get in the wagon with your brother," she told me. She picked up the dead snake and threw him into the woods. I saw him turn over and over before settling in a pile of dried red leaves at the base of a maple tree.

With the distance and knowledge of half a century plus, I now think the events of our stay at the McCurtain place were contrived by the dead to prepare us for even stronger trials to come. The rattlesnake was our warning.

As we pulled up to the McCurtain place, Missus McCurtain stepped to the porch to greet us. Aaron came from around the back of the house, but you could hardly call what he did a *greeting*. He slouched across the yard and his skinny body squinted, him watching everybody else but never letting himself be seen. Pokoni once said, "That Aaron boy slithers 'round like a snake—in higher grass every time I see him. Hard to git a hold on that one."

Pokoni was right. Aaron started up not ten minutes after we arrived, tensing his lips at his momma and tossing his hand over his shoulder like he wanted to whisper something at her. Next time I looked up, Aaron was gone.

I didn't care. He could slither all he wanted to with his sweaty black hair and his skinny arm muscles that weren't any bigger than a rope. I knew he would hang around and not do a lick of work, so I'd just as soon he be gone. His mother must have known it too. That's why she let him go.

"Did you say *halito* to Aaron?" my mother said. When I didn't answer, I could feel Momma and Missus McCurtain looking at each other behind my back. That was *hoke* too. Momma was just making sure we were polite.

"I forgot, Momma," I said.

"That's alright, hon," she said. "Maybe later."

That first afternoon we spent mostly picking the last yellow squash of the season. Missus McCurtain had a bunch planted on the sunny side of the house. She covered 'em with a blanket when a frost threatened, so she had squash later than anybody.

The coming north breeze felt cool on my neck. The chiggers must have felt it too. They went jumping for skin, my skin, but I knew better than to itch. I knew come evening time Momma would have a cure and it would be *hoke* by morning.

After squash picking, I carried a bushel of white onions up from the root cellar on the south side of the house. Momma said Missus McCurtain could make squash pickles with onions and bread-and-butter spices better than anybody. For the next hour the three of us sliced and washed onions and squash.

Just after suppertime, Missus McCurtain put the vinegar and spice mixture to boiling, cloves and brown sugar mostly. The fuming vinegar burned inside my nose. My head swelled and I felt like I had to throw up. Missus McCurtain saw me growing wobble-kneed.

"Go sit for a while, Rose," she said, looking to the back porch. "Go get some fresh air. You feel better if you do." I saw her eyes tearing up as she said it and I knew why. Missus McCurtain was thinking about her babies.

The babies, two girls and a boy, had each died a few hours after they were born. They were buried in a corner of cedar woods a short walk from the back porch. All three babies were buried in the same gravehouse. The roof stood no taller than a small dog, surrounded by piles of dried yellowing flowers nobody was allowed to move.

Her children still lived in Missus McCurtain, in her sad eyes, her sloping shoulders, the way she would pat your hand and talk in her soft cracking voice when she told you to do something, like you might cry if she was too harsh. It was Missus McCurtain who might cry, anybody who knew her knew that.

Pokoni once told me, "It don't matter if her eyes cry or not. Her spirit cries most of the time. Death falls heavier on people like Missus McCurtain. She is your momma's best friend, you know."

"How come?"

"Your momma is the only person who can make the children laugh. She makes Missus McCurtain forget about them, so they can go off playing. Children will laugh if you leave them alone. *Shilombish* children are the same way."

Pokoni and I were picking green beans in our garden when she told me this. At the mention of *shilombish* children—spirit children in Nahullo talk—she lowered her voice and looked all around to make sure we were alone.

"Your Amafo can see the McCurtain children," she almost whispered. "I can sometimes hear them laughing, but I never seen 'em." Pokoni looked around again before she continued. "He says they look like glowing yellow children."

"Are they babies, like when they died?" I asked, feeling a little guilty about pretending not to know.

"No, they grow every year, just like you. 'Spec maybe they keep growing till they reach the age they 'sposed to die."

I tried to look surprised.

"If you take after Amafo," Pokoni said, "you'll be seeing the McCurtain children, all kinds of Walking People. That's what I call 'em, 'cause their spirits are still walking."

Pokoni crouched down among the bean bushes and took my hands in hers. "Rose, if you be real quiet and learn to see people, you can know the ones weighed down by death. Find out what makes them happy, what they like to do or talk about. Making Walking People laugh is a very good thing to do too, sweetheart. When the spirits laugh, everybody is happy."

Soon we went back to picking beans, at least our fingers went to picking, but our minds went other places. Thinking back, I'm sure Pokoni knew that I would someday see the McCurtain children.

THE MCCURTAIN CHILDREN

Rose • Four years earlier

He will gather, he will gather,
The gems for his kingdom.
Oh the pure ones, oh the bright ones,
His loved and His own.

Like the stars of the morning,
His bright crown adorning,
They will shine in their beauty,
Bright gems for his crown.

Mister McCurtain had half a dozen good plow mules for selling and we were spending a day and a night with them. Jamey was just barely walking so most of my morning was taken up seeing to him.

Let him run some on his own, now, hon, I 'member Momma saying. *If he don't fall, he'll never learn to walk.*

Momma was out back tending to a basket of mending. Daddy was in the barn talking to Mister McCurtain, patting mule rumps and pulling back teeth gums. When Jamey finally fell asleep between two pillows in the front room and I saw Missus McCurtain leave out the back door, I slipped out the front door to follow her. Something about the way she pulled a dark shawl up tight around her shoulders, even though it was a warm September day, told me where she was going.

I had heard talk about the little gravehouse on the McCurtain place. Missus McCurtain kept three dead babies in that tiny wooden house and would not let anybody else down there. The Willis boys, all excepting Samuel, had smart-talked about digging the babies up and burying them in the flowerbeds at church, but I knew they were lying.

The gravehouse sat quiet as a boulder in a small clump of stunted cedar trees, just east of the barn. Missus McCurtain kept the underbrush clear, *trying her best to keep rattlesnakes from nesting with her babies,* was how Pokoni put it. I hid behind the barn till Missus McCurtain entered the grove. The sun was streaking bright yellow through the cedars and I could see real clear. She knelt down facing the gravehouse with her back to me.

Except for the size, the gravehouse was like all others, a shingled roof over a hole in the ground. One end had a tiny opening, a door for the spirits to come and go by. Missus McCurtain knelt in front of this spirit door.

She had stuffed the pockets of her gingham dress with dozens of little cookies, her special butter cookies coated with sparkling sugar. Her pockets were large and puffy and I imagined she had sewn them so for this purpose. Using her fingers like a rake, she stooped and cleared a space on the leafy floor in front of the gravehouse opening. She then pulled three lace-edged handkerchiefs from her pockets, two pink and one blue, and topped each with a pile of cookies, much as you would divide cookies for children at a birthday party.

A large mound of dried flowers, over six feet tall, leaned against a squat cedar bush by the gravehouse. While Missus McCurtain spread out the cookies, I slipped from my hiding place and tucked myself behind the bush. Flower smells filled the clearing. I knew that a pile of brush this high would be a good breeding ground for snakes.

Why would Missus McCurtain keep the grounds cleared out so snakes wouldn't come 'round, them provide 'em a home of dead flowers?

Just as the thought entered my mind I heard a rustling and shifting of leaves. Something was crawling toward me from its home of stalks and stems. In an instant it leapt, landing on my lap. I muffled a scream.

A tiger-striped cat arched her back and flipped her tail in my face. *So you are the guardian of snakes,* I thought. *Clever Missus McCurtain, to have a cat mother her children when she cannot.*

Then Missus McCurtain began to sing. I closed my eyes and gave way to the magic.

> *When He cometh, when He cometh*
> *To make up his home,*
> *All the good ones, all the bright ones*

As she sang, Missus McCurtain rose and circled the cedar bush, approaching me in a steady-step walk that told me she had known I was there all along. She moved behind me as I knelt and I heard her airy laughter. She lifted the long strands of hair from my neck and spread them evenly over my shoulders. Her tiny fingertips rested easily on my back and neck.

Still she sang, her voice floating over the clearing sweet and high, from the now living gravehouse, to the cedars, to the ebbing afternoon sky.

Like the stars of the morning,
His bright crown adorning,
They will shine in the heavens,
Bright gems for his crown.

So large was the feeling, the sun through the cedars, the hum of the flower's fragrance, I didn't notice when the song was over, but some sweet unmeasured minute later I opened my eyes and beheld the true magic. Missus McCurtain knelt by the gravehouse as before.

She had never moved.

The tiny fingers still rested on my shoulders, three pairs of children's fingers, I now realized. The children laughed at my surprise. I felt the breath of their laughter on my neck. I was terrified, but they moved to relieve my fears. They emerged from the empty air in front of me, three children melted together.

Light surrounded their faces and sifted through their hair, red auburn like their mother's. Their eyes were large, as if they felt my wonder, and they laughed and laughed in the joy of my new knowing.

And what a new knowing it was. I saw for the first time what I had only felt to be true—the beyond and beyond of it. I saw it in the smiling faces of the children, two girls barely younger than myself and their glowing little brother.

With musical laughter, the children turned to their mother. When Missus McCurtain lifted her face, I knew she could hear her children but could not see them. I watched the girls surround their mother, like a sweet see-through cloud, moving in and out and through her. I saw her cheeks flush and her eyes grow wide in wonder as the girls caressed her, even embraced each other through her. The boy, meanwhile, tried to pick up sugar cookies, giggling and staring as his shimmering fingers flew through the cookies without moving them.

I heard Missus McCurtain whisper her children's names.

Esther, Evadelle, and Adam. Come to your mother, Sarah.

If ever anyone wondered how she could cling forever to her babies, *Cold and dead all these years and she still cain't let 'em go*, as I had heard all my childhood, I now waxed warm and confident in the abode of my new knowing. Like Missus McCurtain, I wanted to stay in the clearing forever. I missed the children and longed for their joy when they turned from me.

I soon realized I had been blessed by this seeing, but the children needed time alone with their mother. I rose, lifted my palm in an unseen wave, and crossed the open pasture to the back porch to be with my own mother.

Momma saw me coming. She patted the wooden porch beside her chair for me to sit and join her. She held up a green and yellow quilted coat for my approval.

"Come try this on, hon."

"It's Pokoni's quilt," I said.

"Not anymore," she replied, and smiled and helped me slip first one arm and then the other into the loose-fitting coat sleeves. Four brown buttons fastened the coat at the front.

"These have been in your button basket as long as I can remember," I said, fingering the buttons and examining the maroon thread tying them to the coat.

"Since long before you were born, sweetheart. Just waiting for you."

Like the McCurtain children, I thought. *They lie in that gravehouse, waiting for their mother.* Every time I buttoned that coat, till I finally outgrew it sometime before my fifteenth birthday, I counted the buttons by naming the children, just as Missus McCurtain had done in calling them to her.

Esther, Evadelle, and Adam. Come to your mother, Sarah.

I counted as I buttoned from the bottom to the top.

Esther. I button the first button, the bottom button.

Evadelle. I button the second.

And Adam. I feel the growing snugness and I fasten the next to last button.

I always pause and say the next line just as Missus McCurtain did.

Come to your mother, Sarah. I slip the final button through its slot.

Sometimes, if everything felt too ordinary, I would close my eyes and imagine I *was* Missus McCurtain, slowly tasting the ripple of her children's names across her tongue. Sometimes I said the names again, like in a God-bless bedtime prayer when all the names are said aloud. Maybe I was calling the McCurtain children. Maybe I was calling my own yet unborn children.

Esther.

Evadelle.

And Adam.

Come to your mother, Rose.

RENDERING THE SOW

Just like at home, we got up long before sunrise at the McCurtains. Soon the chores were sorted out, with Momma and Missus McCurtain doing the sorting. Most everybody went outside to work, but I ended up at the stove, stirring a boiling kettle of scoopanong grape juice, on its way to becoming jelly.

Jamey was supposed to be helping me, but I knew that wouldn't last. He soon grew tired of scooping sugar, wiping up spills, and spooning grape skins floating to the top of the boiling juice.

"Goin' to hep Momma," he hollered, running out the back door. Before I could say anything, the door slammed shut and Jamey was gone. Through the kitchen window I saw him scoot around the barn.

I went to stirring slow, thinking on the events of the past year, spooning up memories like the bubbles rising from the purple juice. I thought about Amafo and his broken pride, and what a good man he was to take the path he took. I thought about Pokoni.

I drooped over sad to think about Pokoni. I thought about Roberta Jean and how lonely she must be, surrounded by all those boys. I thought about the marshal too, and his mean ways.

Pokoni would read my thoughts, if she were here, and she'd have something to say to make it all seem bigger and still in the hands of the Lord.

"You just let that man go on ahead," Pokoni would tell me. "He's got to meet His Maker, same as we all do. I just wouldn't want to be him at that meeting." I smiled and squeezed my eyes tight shut.

Jamey's scream brought me back to life.

He had spotted piglets in the cedars behind the barn and made a beeline to them. He didn't see the momma sow, not at first. She raised from the brush, snorted, and went after Jamey, her sharp tusks lowered and ready to strike. The pow of a shotgun blast ripped the air. I froze and felt the breath whoosh out of me.

"Nooo," Momma called.

We all of us ran to the scene. Jamey sat on the ground, his whole body shaking and shivering. A bloody sow lay a few feet from her squirming piglets. She had rolled on her back and died from the gunshot wound to her head. Momma hugged Jamey tight.

"You *hoke*, son?" she said, doing her best to hide back the tears, but they came through her trembling voice. "You doing *hoke*?"

Jamey nodded and started sputtering and talking faster than anybody could make sense of.

"A panther, a huge, big panther, with sharp claws, her teeth were big…she jumped at the hog and the man shot her…she blew up and the hog died."

We tried to piece together what had happened from what we could see. There was no sign of any panther. Jamey crouched by a scrubby cedar bush near the piglets. The dead momma sow lay a few feet away. But what gave us pause to worry was the left-behind sign of the gunman.

Fresh boot prints tracked to and from the woods.

Jamey's cries were brief and of small concern once it was determined he was uninjured. The major concern—what with the absence of grown men—was the question: *Who had come onto the McCurtain spread and killed one of the sows?*

Why the man was on the McCurtain property to begin with, and why he fled after shooting the sow, we could not know. Later, while we packed for the trip home, I did slip away, unknown to the others. I studied the sight of the killing on the slim chance that Jamey had seen a panther. He had. The tracks were unmistakable, and by the size of the paw prints the panther was huge, just as Jamey had said.

I told no one what I saw, but these events, as it turned out, served as a prelude to the coming night. Drawn by the drama unfolding around the panther and the shooter, we were about to enter a tunnel of vision and deep mystery. It was as if God chose to split the veil guarding us from things we should not know.

He chose to let us see.

The storm had been blowing up all day. I remember feeling a chill and looking to see the clouds gathering overhead, promising hard rain. It was the kind of cloud cover you long for when corn is in the ground, those billowing gray blue clouds that swagger low over the hills. I feared more than rain was in the offing. But there was so much to do with the sow, lest we break that unpardonable sin of wasting livestock and, worse yet, wasting food. The threatening weather only added to the urgency.

Missus McCurtain took one look at the sow and told Aaron, "Get me the butchering knife." Aaron made no protest. Even he could see the need to hurry. When he returned with the knife, Missus McCurtain stuck it hard into the main artery of the sow's neck. Blood squirted out all over her hands, her arms, all over the front of her.

She turned to me and said, "Bring me something to dry off with, hon, quick." I found a worn-out cloth in the kitchen, tore it in half, and ran back to where she waited.

She nodded *thanks* and dried off her arms. She then jabbed the point of the knife into the side of the sow's head. She wiggled it to get a good hold and began to cut the thick skin of the sow across the throat. When the knife blade slid into the sow's windpipe, I heard a deep *whisssing* sound.

Missus McCurtain looked to a clump of elm trees on the edge of the cornfield, some distance away. Momma read her thoughts.

"Rose, go get Whiteface. Bridle her up and bring her 'round here," she told me. By the time I returned with Whiteface, Aaron had tied the sow's legs together, two and two, and worked a thick rope around her middle. He took Whiteface by the bridle and fastened a loop of rope around her neck.

"We gonna have to help roll the sow over to get Whiteface started," Momma said. "Jamey, come on, boy, you can help too."

Jamey ran from the porch, eager to get a better look at all the blood. We, all of us but Aaron, got behind the sow and pushed with all our might, driving our shoulders into the side of the sow and struggling to turn her over so Whiteface could drag her to the trees. Our feet kept slipping in the mud, made slicker by the blood still pouring from the sow's neck.

"Come on, girl. Attagirl, good girl, pull," Aaron urged Whiteface on, tugging on the bridle.

After an hour of struggling, we managed to pull the sow beneath the grove. A hoist and heavy rope hung from the only oak tree standing among the elms. Leaning up against the tree trunk was the biggest kettle I had ever seen in my life.

"There's some brushes up on the porch. Get 'em quick," said Missus McCurtain to anybody who was listening. Jamey was well into the spirit of doing now, and he made a mad dash to the porch. Aaron fitted a leather sling around the hindquarters of the sow and began lifting her off the ground, while Momma and Missus McCurtain dragged the kettle under the oak limb.

"Rose, you'll find some gloves up yonder with the brushes. And scrappers. They've got a thin blade and are real sharp on one edge, so be careful. Bring several pairs of gloves. We gonna need 'em. Those sow bristles can cut your hands to pieces," Missus McCurtain said. Her voice seemed to lose some of its edge when she spoke to me, almost like she was treating me like a lady instead of a young 'un.

"Yes, ma'am," I said. When I returned, Aaaon had lowered the sow into the kettle and Missus McCurtain already had a good fire going under it. The boiling water loosened the skin enough for us to clean the sharp bristles off, but it was hard going without the men. Aaron did his best to roll the sow over easy, but she was just too heavy.

"Get on away from here," Aaron had yelled at Jamey when the kettle tilted and hot water eased over the kettle's lip, blistering Jamey's hand. Jamey grabbed his hand and ran behind the tree. Neither Momma nor Missus McCurtain said a word to comfort him. There was just too much work to do to tend to a skin wound.

A few minutes later I looked up from scrubbing the hog bristles and saw that Jamey had discovered something even more interesting than the fat sow sitting dead in boiling water. The sow's head was lying up by the tree trunk, her mouth wide open, and Jamey was poking at her eyes with a tree branch.

When the scrubbing was done, Aaron lowered the sow on to the ground and went to butchering her. He had helped the men with the butchering enough to know how to go about it.

"Hon, find us some more knives in the kitchen, will you?" Missus McCurtain asked me. When I returned with the knives, she and Momma were rendering the hog fat. They were boiling the skins and scooping the hog lard as it floated to the top.

"Where is Jamey?" Momma asked. Jamey raised his guilty eyes. The hog was now dead and blind both, thanks to him. He hid his latest treasure behind his back, a two-pronged stick with the sow's eyes dangling from it.

"Come here, son." Missus McCurtain took some warm hog fat and rubbed it on Jamey's burn. "That'll make it feel better. You go on back to your playing, now. It's *hoke*. But leave that sow's head to your sister, hear me."

She turned to me and said, "Rose, there ought to be some pliers in the tool box on the porch. Aaron can show you what to do."

When I came back with the pliers, Aaron said, "We need to get the skin off the head. Here, let me show you." He took the pliers with one hand and gripped the tough skin while he held the head down with his boot. With his other hand he pulled on the skin, trying to pry it loose.

"There's good meat inside if you can get to it," he said. Aaron nodded and turned back to his butchering. While Missus McCurtain might consider me grown, it was clear to me I was still just one of the children to Aaron, who at fourteen was every bit of three years older than myself.

I tried to do what Aaron had done, tried pinning the sow's head to the ground with my shoe, tried prying the hard skin loose with the pliers and my free hand. My foot slipped on the bloody sow's head and I stumbled backwards. My back hit hard against the tree trunk and I sat on my bottom in the soft mud.

"Careful now, hon," said Missus McCurtain.

I sat for a moment to let the dizziness clear. I saw the hills turn from green to gray as sheet rain moved across the valley. With a sharp electric crackle, followed by a cannon's boom, lightning struck a red oak on the edge of the cornfield, splitting the trunk in a burst of flames. The fire soon sizzled and died in the path of the onrushing rain.

Momma and Missus McCurtain looked anxiously to the sky, then to each other. Though they said nothing, I heard their conversation.

"Storm looks to be only rain and lightning, no tornado."

"Might last all day."

"Hog got to be butchered, rain or no rain."

"Too heavy to carry to the barn."

"Just us to do it."

"Better get to work."

I struggled to stand, but the ground tilted and I fell backwards again.

"Stay right there, hon. You rest a minute."

A wet sycamore leaf, yellow and brown, slapped my cheek. As I peeled it from my face, I saw the sow's shiny blood on my hands. At that moment a gust of wind, freezing cold and hissing in my ears, seemed to suck my breath away. I gave in to the darkness and fainted.

When I lifted my head, the dark clouds were gone and the bluest sky I ever saw shone down on me. I smelled pine trees and saw their branches waving in the cooling breeze. I stood on the banks of the Kiamichi River.

It was the day of my baptism. The entire Choctaw community lined the banks of the river. Many held hymn books and everybody was singing. I strained to hear the song, but could not make out the words.

Preacher Willis stood waist deep in the river. His arms were lifted and he was beckoning to me.

"No need to cry, sweet child. This river's gonna wash you clean."

Only then did I realize I was crying. I was trying to smile, but tears streamed down my face. I lifted my hands to brush the tears away and saw the sow's blood covering my hands. I put my hands behind my back.

"No need to be 'shamed, child. We all got the stains. You 'bout to wash yours away," said Preacher Willis.

I stepped into the river and walked to meet Brother Willis. He took me by the hand and put his other hand behind my head.

"Fold your arms and close your eyes, Rose. Might help to take a breath now."

He dipped me slow and gentle into the water. As if I was floating above myself and watching, I saw the sow's blood wash from my hands. I saw it stain the river red, then pink, then wash away till only the light brown flesh of my palms remained.

When my head cleared and I came to, I was propped up against the tree trunk with a pillow. I looked up to see Aaron smiling at me, not like a slouching skinny boy or a snake in hiding. The smile didn't last long, but I saw it. He wanted me to. He nodded to my side, then flushed red and turned away. I saw a plate sitting next to me and knew that he had put it there. It held a thick slice of bread dipped in hog fat and beside it was a cup of water.

Even at the age of eleven, I knew that Aaron would not be the one I would marry. But something about his gentleness told me that he would find somebody to take care of, and that somebody would take care of him as well. I ate the bread and sipped the water as slowly as I dared, with so much work to do and the storm so close. The clouds had retreated to the distant hills, where they seemed to be darkening and

gathering strength for another run at us. The air was colder than when
I fell out. I struggled to my feet, wiped the blood from my hands, and
went to help.

Aaron and I were soon smoking the meat, cooking thick slabs of
pork steak on a spit by the porch. Momma and Missus McCurtain were
rolling out sausage, using the hog entrails as skin and stuffing it with
dried blood and innards.

About an hour before sundown, I saw Missus McCurtain pause
for a moment and look at Momma. Momma seemed not to see her, but
she did, and went to reading her mind again. Missus McCurtain was
asking if we'd be staying another night.

"See to your brother, Rose," Momma said. "Bad weather's coming.
Your father and Amafo cain't stay out in this. They'll be coming home.
We got to be there for 'em."

"Yes, ma'am."

"Jamey, help your sister. Do what she tells you."

"Yes, ma'am."

"You sure you want to be out in this?" Missus McCurtain said.
"It's getting near freezing. Might ice over."

"We'll make it fine. Whiteface knows the way. We'll likely be
home before dark."

We all knew better than that. Missus McCurtain just looked at
Momma. With the road slippery from the rain, we'd be lucky to be home
by midnight. Nobody wanted to mention the possibility of us getting
stuck in an ice storm, but we all thought of it.

Half an hour later—the wagon loaded with squash pickles and two
buckets of smoked pork and sausage—we set off for home. Momma drove
Whiteface and I curled up under a quilt with Jamey. We had been going

for about a mile when Whiteface went to whinnying again. I peeped from under the quilt and, sure as I suspected, we'd come upon the bull nettle.

"Easy, girl. Snake done dead and gone. Easy, now," Momma said, guiding her away from the bushes where she'd flung the snake. But Whiteface shied away from the roadside, shaking her head and coming to a halt. Momma climbed down from the wagon and took Whiteface by the reins to walk her past the bull nettle.

I saw it before Momma did, but the words caught in my throat. The rattlesnake was dangling from a tree limb. Backing up like she was, talking to Whiteface as she walked, Momma was almost on the snake before I could holler. The snake was writhing in the evening breeze and its mouth was open wide, its fangs just inches from Momma's neck.

"Momma!" I screamed. She saw me pointing over her shoulder and turned right into the snake. She flung her arm against it, but the snake curled back and slapped against her face. Momma fell to the ground. I leapt from the wagon and ran to her.

She was already on her feet and held the snake by the neck. Standing with her feet wide apart and staring above her, she ripped the rattlesnake from the tree.

"Somebody nailed that dead snake to the tree," she said. We looked up to see two nail heads on the tree limb. "Why would anybody want to hang a dead snake over this road?"

Something moved in the brush. The wind blew colder and the woods seemed to take on a darkness quicker than the hour of the day required. "We need to be home," Momma said.

PANTHER IN THE DARK

I knew by the way Momma acted that something was following us. I stayed under the quilt and pulled Jamey close. He made soft whining noises. I put my hand over his mouth, but he kicked back at me, scared and barely able to breath.

"No, you have to be still," I told him. "We'll be alright if we be still."

I felt him nod and I loosened my grip. I heard dried leaves rustling and slipped the quilt down to my nose so I could see. The moon was a thin slice peeping through the clouds. In the dim light I saw something slinking behind a tree trunk by the road.

The wind picked up and a hard gust sent leaves whirling around my face. I ducked beneath the quilt. When my breathing settled, Jamey slid close to me, till his lips were touching my ear.

"Did you see it?" he said.

"Un-uhh. Nothing to see. Shhh."

But I had seen something. I'd seen two burning green ovals peering down at me. They were the eyes of a panther, crouched and waiting on a thick tree branch overhanging the path.

"Hand me the meat!" Momma said.

"What?"

"The meat. Hand me a bucket of pork."

A tin bucket filled with pork steaks was tucked under the seat of the wagon. I was too scared to move. I drew my knees up to my waist, closed my eyes tight, and shivered to make it all go away. Surely Momma wasn't going to eat now.

"Get it! Hand it to me!" Momma said. I scooted Jamey away from me and rolled over to my knees. The wind was howling. I heard the slick whisper of sleet and felt the stinging ice on my arms and the back of my neck.

The bucket was wedged in tight and I had to yank hard. When I did, the quilt flew up and would have blown off the wagon if I hadn't grabbed it. I almost dropped the bucket. Jamey started crying.

"Hush, Jamey!" I pulled the quilt up over his face and tucked it tight around his shoulders. I felt like crying too. I struggled to lift the bucket over the seatback. It wasn't heavy but the wagon was rocking and jerking on the rutted road. The sleet fell harder now, making the wooden floor slick.

"You can do it," Momma said. "Careful and don't fall. Set the bucket right here beside me." It took all my strength, but I did it. Real careful, I eased it down next to her.

"Now git down under the quilt and don't you move no matter what," Momma said. I gripped the seatback with both hands and stood looking at her. Her face was drawn tight and her eyes squinted into the sleet. My face stung with the icy rain.

"Momma," I said.

"Get down!"

"Momma, what is it?"

"Get back with Jamey. Keep him still."

Momma's right hand held the reins tight. I saw her wrist quiver with the strain. Her left hand was cupped over her brow, protecting her eyes from the icy needles. In a frantic gesture—more like an angry man lashing out and whipping a horse than a women picking up a slab of meat—Momma grabbed the top piece from the metal bucket and flung it to the woods.

I now heard what Momma had no doubt heard, a quick and nervous rustling ten feet to the right of the wagon. I fell down to my knees.

"Help me," she said.

"Momma, what is it?" I lied in asking, for I already knew.

"Take the meat and be ready."

"No," I said. Her left hand made a stab in the darkness, brushing aside a small oak branch flying at her face.

"Do as I say and we have a chance. You must help. You are not a child."

No one had ever said that to me before. "No, I am not a child," I said too soft for her to hear. I had ridden in rocking wagons before. I had walked in colder, thicker sleet than this, through darker woods than these—and I had seen panthers before, big cats, *koi chitto*. I crouched and watched a mother panther lead her kittens to the river once. I saw a dead panther hanging in a neighbor's backyard, gutted and ready for skinning.

I stood up slow and easy, spreading my legs apart for balance. With one hand I gripped the seatback, with the other I picked up a piece of pork. "I understand," I said. "I throw a piece, wait a minute, then throw another."

"Yes," Momma said. "You are a strong girl. We will live through this."

Whiteface pulled steady, splashing through the shallow ruts now icing over. Momma held the reins and drove. Jamey curled into a fearful fetal rounding of himself and I hurled food into the underbrush to divert the killing that otherwise awaited. I knew that at any moment a cat half as big as Whiteface could drop from a tree limb onto the wagon and commence to tear into my skin with its teeth and claws.

I looked at Momma and for the first time understood the hard set of her jaw. Part of it was fear, but more of it was anger. I learned something about her too. If the danger fell upon us, if the killing came, Momma would die to protect us.

I touched her neck and she nodded, closing her eyes. Her left hand moved to grip mine.

When the bucket was near empty, our house came into view. Momma leaned into the reins, leading Whiteface close to the porch. When she drew to a stop, Momma leapt from the wagon and whirled to grab Jamey.

"Open the door. Hurry." I ran to the porch and flung the door open while Momma lifted Jamey from the wagon. I saw Momma, burdened down with Jamey's weight, splash though the mud and reach her long leg for the step. The single porch step was slick as pond's ice. Only the toe of her shoe landed on the step.

I opened my mouth but only squeals came out. I saw her slip and hit the porch hard with her cheekbone. Jamey fell from her arms and rolled beneath the wagon.

Now all motion ceased. Momma lay face down, her arms hanging limp at her sides. All of her weight rested on her already swelling face. Her eyes were closed and her body stretched half across the step and half across a brown puddle of ice and mud in the front yard.

There was an eerie beauty to the scene. For a brief moment I gave myself over to it. The wind came in strong gusts, swirling the sleet in icy threads. My bruised mother lay unconscious before me. Icicles were forming in her silverblack hair. My brother curled up in fear behind me.

Whether borne of fear or simple loss of breath at what I was beholding, whether I was lifted from my body and gently returned by a force more powerful than any I have ever known, I cannot say. I do know this had everything to do with my being a child no longer.

I closed my eyes and lifted my face to the stinging rain and I felt comforted. No more dark grief, no more deathwalk wandering, no more waiting for life to return. Life had descended upon us with a vengeance. This night was real. This daggered rain was real. I felt alive and within myself for the first time since Pokoni died.

I heard Reverend Willis boom out across the pulpit, "When I was a child!" Then in that way he had of whispering and talking straight to only me and making me shiver and cry, in that whispery voice he had that floated through the Sunday air and nestled in my ears, he said, "I saw through a glass darkly. But when I became a man…I saw him face to face."

When I opened my eyes I saw the panther crouching twenty feet in front of me.

KOI CHITTO ON THE PROWL

The panther was enormous. Her coat was shiny black, not dark—but more as if her velvet fur were wrapped around a cold white fire. Her fur seemed to move, every inch of it to move, though she sat still and stared at me.

I had seen larger animals—horses, mules, and cattle—though nothing quite this large stepping from the dark, wet trees; nothing suddenly appearing from the night air as this cat had appeared; nothing with this knowing sense of its own power; nothing—I realized with a shudder that hurled the breath from my lungs and left me panting— nothing that ate flesh.

I had never beheld a thing quite so big that had the teeth and claws to eat a human like myself, and I so frail to stand before it.

I heard myself whimper. Her face twitched and I was drawn to her eyes, to the green glaring of her eyes. I felt strength in their dark shining. A power surged through me and I began to move.

The panther's paws twitched and pulsed, as if she readied herself to leap.

I lifted Momma and carried her through the door. When I returned to the yard, the panther had dragged Jamey from beneath the wagon.

"No!" I screamed. The panther turned to face me and I flung myself upon her, pounding her with my fists. I felt her rippling muscles. She threw me to the ground with her paw and her full weight crushed my chest. She took my hair into her teeth and bit into my scalp. Her breath was hot upon my face.

Suddenly the door slammed shut and I knew Jamey was safe inside. I shook and cried with relief. I let my arms fall limp and I gave myself to this quick and cutting death.

Then the panther was gone.

The sleet still fell, but lighter now. I watched it floating, shimmering and beautiful in the lamplight streaming from the open door. I felt Momma's strong hands grip me beneath the armpits as she helped me to my feet.

"Careful. The step is slick," she said.

I felt her bony strength as she wrapped her right arm around my waist and led me to the front room. Her left arm held my father's shotgun.

"How can you be unhurt?" Momma asked. She had seen the panther draw her paw across my face. I brought my hand to my brow and touched the soft skin of my cheek, expecting cuts and scratches. I could still feel the cat's rough paw pad and knew that only shock was warding off the pain. But now I felt neither pain nor blood nor anything but soft, cold flesh—my own.

"Sit with your brother," Momma said. "You can keep each other warm." Jamey crouched beneath a blanket on Pokoni's chair.

I crawled into the chair and sank into its softness. The back and arms were padded, and soon I was a child once more, clinging to my brother.

What happened next convinced me I was dreaming. I heard a scream like nothing I'd ever heard before. I rose from the chair and went to join Momma. She stood by the front window staring at the sound. The panther pawed the ground once, then lifted her face to the dark sleet and screamed again. Past the short distance and through the thin pane of glass came the cry, piercing my eardrums and settling in a knot of fear at the pit of my stomach. The high-pitched cry was a mother's squeal, a birthing cry.

When the panther's scream stopped, I resumed my breathing and looked about the room. I expected broken glass, at least a shattered window. I looked for fresh blood and hurling winds, for death and destruction. I thought the sleet might turn to stones and splinter through the roof in a hail of falling rafters, followed by the panther in our living room, clawing her way through the order of our simple lives. I waited for a clap of thunder to announce the world's end.

Nothing happened.

The panther gazed through the window as she paced back and forth in full view of Momma and me. She began circling our house, flicking her tail as she walked. Momma ran frantically from room to room, tracing the path of the cat. The wind picked up again and blew so hard the sleet fell in long needles sideways to the ground.

"Tell me when you see her," Momma said, passing from her bedroom through the front room on the way to the kitchen. A few minutes later the panther halted once more in the front yard.

"Momma?" I tried saying, but the words stuck in my throat. In a brief moment, Momma stood beside me. She lifted the shotgun and the panther let fly another piercing cry.

For the next hour this pattern was repeated. The panther circled the house, pausing long enough to stop and cry. Momma moved from room to room and I moved from the window, watching, to the chair to settle Jamey. Once when he woke up and stretched, I whispered to him, "If you be very still, we can make peach fritters tomorrow. *Shhhh!* Don't let Momma know you're awake."

I think it was after midnight when Daddy and Amafo appeared on the porch. As soon as she spotted them, Momma ran to open the door. Their boots were covered in thick red mud and their hat brims drooped with ice. Momma spoke to them on the porch. I knew by the way they glanced to the woods she was telling them about the panther. Daddy squeezed Momma to his chest.

Amafo, I noticed, moved to the shadows and looked hard into the woods. He covered his eyes with one hand and squinted at the silver threads of sleet. As I watched, Amafo laid his gun on the icy ground, held his hands chest high as if he were showing somebody he was unarmed, and took several steps in the direction of the woods. Then he hesitated and turned back to the porch.

"He is *tashimbo*, crazy with grief," I whispered.

Momma and Daddy entered the house, followed by Amafo.

"Too cold to catch anything but frostbite," Amafo said when he saw me. He took off his hat and slapped it against his leg, knocking the ice to the porch before he came inside. Spotting logs by the fireplace, Amafo soon had a small fire going.

He rubbed his hands together, facing his palms to the fire. He then approached me in a slow and shuffling walk, as if he didn't want Momma and Daddy to know he had business with me. Leaning his shotgun against the chairback, he crouched beside me and waited, resting on the balls of his feet.

Momma and Daddy had retreated to the kitchen to talk. Every few minutes Momma looked through the kitchen door and glanced from the window and back at me, letting me know she was counting on me to alert them if the panther returned.

I could feel how hungry Amafo was to know about the panther. He sat next to me for the better part of half an hour, gazing into the fire and rocking so gentle-like. I had to pick a spot on the wall behind him and stare at it to make sure he was really moving. When he spoke I jumped like he'd grabbed me, but his voice was soft and laced with longing.

"You saw the panther?"

"Yes. She pinned me to the ground." Amafo nodded. His eyes had a glazed and faraway look. I knew he was imagining the scene, imagining the *koi chitto* on top of me.

A short while later, Amafo moved from his crouched position to sit on his behind and pull his knees to his chest.

"Did she hurt you?"

"She pulled my hair. She bit me on top of my head." Supporting himself on the arm of the chair, Amafo straightened his skinny legs and slowly stood. He rubbed his knees and took two steps to stand behind me. He ran his fingers across my head, feeling the small teeth marks and scabs forming on my scalp. I could feel the rough skin of his old fingers. He smelled like a cedarwood campfire. I closed my eyes and saw Daddy and Amafo crouching near a fire when the sleet came.

Amafo touched a tender spot and I winced.

"I'm sorry, hon." He took his hand away. "It's a miracle you are still alive."

"I was so afraid, Amafo. She had Jamey. I screamed at her and she let him go. That's when she knocked me to the ground." He opened his mouth to speak, but at that moment my parents strode to the front window. Daddy cupped his hands to his eyes to shield the fireplace light and stared at the darkness beyond the porch.

When he turned and looked about the room I could see the birthing of a plan.

"We going to build a bigger fire, heh," he said, looking at Amafo. "We'll see if we can draw her out. Rose, how about you keep the fire going? I'll get more logs from out back."

"Be careful," said Momma.

"Better take Jamey upstairs," he told her.

"What about the upstairs window?"

"We can hear her on the roof. She'd have to jump clear from the oak tree—that or climb up the side of the house. Either way we'd have time to get upstairs before she made it through the window."

As soon as Momma disappeared up the stairs with Jamey, Daddy nodded to Amafo. They picked up their shotguns and walked quickly to the kitchen. Amafo stood in the open doorway, gun in hand, while Daddy carried several loads of wood from the far end of the porch. He made a stack just inside the kitchen and I began carrying wood to the front room.

Soon we had the fire built and blazing, casting light and shadows on the walls in popping flashes of orange and blue and black. Daddy nailed a heavy quilt over the door to the kitchen to keep the rear of the house dark.

"If she does come through the kitchen window, this quilt should slow her down enough. We'll have our guns trained on her before she can get to us," he said.

We settled into a nervous and alert waiting. At least now, with two more adults and their guns, we could move about the room. Momma made coffee and even poured me a cup.

"It's better with a little sugar," she said. "I put a spoonful in for you."

"*Yakoke*," I said.

We did not have long to wait.

I thought I saw her first, but in looking back, I know Amafo saw her long before I did. Maybe he had seen her days before. Maybe he spotted her easing through the elm trees at the rear of the house as he sipped his evening cocoa. Maybe he saw her that very evening, watched her through the front room window as we sat and talked of how she pinned me to the ground. Maybe he eyed her from the back porch while Daddy gathered the firewood.

Of one thing I can now be certain. If he did see her, he hoped we would not. And something else I know as well—the panther saw my Amafo. I am certain of that.

The green flame of her eyes stepped from the woods, long before her body came into sight. I was hypnotized by her beauty. My mouth fell open and I drank my own breath in a dizzy swoon. I felt again the panther on top of me, her rippling muscles, her strength so much greater than mine.

A log fell in the fireplace in a crunching noise of brittle wood, startling me back to the present. My eyes flew to the shower of embers, and when they returned to the front yard, the panther's sleek black body had joined her eyes. There she stood, crouched ten feet from our front porch.

"I see her!" Momma called. Daddy now stood ready to open the front door. He turned to Amafo and said, "If I miss her, you got to be ready. She's big enough to come through this here window. Cain't let her do it." He nodded to Amafo and stepped onto the porch.

With his rifle shouldered, Daddy took aim at the panther. She kept her eyes on him and twitched her tail. I expected her to sink into a slow crouch as she readied to leap. Instead she rose up and looked to the window where I stood with Momma and Amafo. She looked back at Daddy, pushed off with her front paws, and turned and twirled to the woods, disappearing before Daddy fired even a single shot.

Momma moved quickly to the doorway.

"She's getting away," she said.

"Her work here is done," Daddy said.

"She'll be back."

"I don't think so."

"You should have killed her."

"No. I won't be the one to kill her," Daddy said, moving into the house and setting his rifle against the wall.

"She stalked us all the way from the McCurtains. She attacked us. You don't know." Daddy turned away, but Momma was mad and scared both. She grabbed his shoulders and twisted him round to face her. "She is still in those woods waiting for us."

"If she is," Daddy said, "you should be grateful. The panther followed you tonight, but she was not stalking you. She didn't want to hurt these children. She never would, nor you neither. She was protecting you. If she is still in the woods, she's doing it yet. But I don't think she's staying round here. She got other business this night to tend to. I think we safer here than we been in a long time."

"You talking crazy," said Momma.

"You probly right. But we in here safe and warm. Whatever took after you is still out there in the cold."

Amafo spoke up. "How 'bout I stay up, keep guard in case she come back. You all get some sleep. Been a long night for everybody."

"You sure?" Daddy said.

"I be fine," said Amafo. "I wake you up if I get sleepy."

Momma stared for a long minute at Daddy. With her eyes still on him, she motioned for me to climb the stairs to bed. From the top stair, I saw her slump on her way to the bedroom. The evening had taken its toll on us all.

When Momma closed her door, I crept back to the landing at the top of the stairs. Amafo and Daddy stood gazing at the fire.

"What did you see?" said Amafo.

"*Koi chitto*," said Daddy.

"What you know 'bout *koi chitto*?"

"I think you know, old man," Daddy said. "Maybe it'll all make better sense come morning."

AMAFO AND POKONI

I climbed beneath the pile of quilts on my bed and rightaway fell into a deep sleep, but the sleep was a short one. Maybe I heard a screaming again, maybe I was dreaming the scream, I don't know. My eyes popped open and I was wide awake.

By the yellow slice of light through the window I could tell only an hour had passed. A thin gathering of clouds passed over the moon and the room went to blue. My mind went racing backwards, through the sleet, the bloody gutting of the sow, the ghostly children. I snuggled in joy and cringed in fear as the pictures flew before my thinking eyes.

Amafo and his skinny grieving for Pokoni, my blessed Pokoni. I could not stop my tears thinking of Pokoni. I never want to think of her without crying, even knowing she would laugh out loud at this *silly way to be*. I can see her, hear her, saying it.

I felt like I was learning how to fly for the first time, like I was no longer a person—no longer just a person—with two legs to bind me to the earth. I was shrinking into nothing and learning that maybe nothing was the only road to everything—the trees, the river waters, the others, all the others, the slipping into it all.

My flying stopped sudden with the killings. I could not breathe. I saw the killings for the first time through my grandfather's eyes. The death of Lillie Chukma and the burning of New Hope, the killing of the sow, he knew who did these things.

Amafo knew.

At long last I saw through my Amafo's eyes and I knew as well. I knew who burned the school, who killed the sow, who chased us through the woods, who hung the snake. I saw Amafo now, over and over, touching his fingers to his cheek, long after the cuts had healed and the scars had blended with the lapping wrinkles of his skin. He was reminding himself never to forget the man who cut him down so. He could and would do it again. With every touching he was reminding himself.

I had to talk to Amafo. I flung the covers back and swung my bare feet to the cold wooden floor. My feet seemed guided and instead of walking across the landing to Amafo's room, I descended the stairs to the kitchen. I put milk on to boil, stoking the cedar embers in the woodstove. The cedar smell curled around my hair and filled the room. I broke a chunk of chocolate and dropped it in the bottom of the cup and stirred till the milk bubbled and boiled and stuck to the bottom. Gripping the pan with a towel, I poured the milk over the chocolate.

Chocolate steam rose to meet the cedar smoke. I placed the dark blue cup on the pine tray and stepped tiny, careful steps from the kitchen to the stairway, then climbed the steps two-footed, like a child, or like a grown-up unhinged to childhood by the day. I wrapped my left arm around the tray bottom and reached for the doorknob with my other hand.

"Amafo," I whispered, craning my neck and tossing the whisper across the darkened room. "Amafo. I brought you something. Chocolate."

The room was empty. I did not need to gaze across it to know this. In reply to my whisperings, the room spoke *empty*. I was at first confused. I moved to the window and set the tray on the table.

Maybe he fell asleep in front of the fire. Of course. He is keeping guard. He promised Daddy he would keep a watch out for the panther.

I would have seen him when I climbed down the stairs. I would surely have seen him when I came from the kitchen with the chocolate.

Amafo is outside. He has gone to the woods. He tried to earlier.

I took one quick and lunging step to the door and almost called out to wake Daddy. Then I remembered. The day Pokoni almost died. I remembered my frantic hollering and how she had to do it all over again. If I have learned anything, I have now learned to walk through sacred moments. My eyes told me I was in the midst of one.

I turned to the window.

My eyes moved to the edge of the woods east of the barn. Amafo crouched on the ground, facing the thick trunk of a red oak tree. A shaft of white moonlight pierced the clouds and etched deep into the bark. The beam slowly climbed down the trunk, illuminating gnarled and aging wooden knuckles on its descent.

My grandfather's hat cast a saucer-shaped shadow on the tree trunk. His arms were moving slow as a dream, first wrapping around the tree, then caressing his own cheeks. His head was bowed and he moved to kneeling.

Then the dance narrowed. Beyond Amafo and the tree, outside their circle, everything turned dark, midnight dark. This old man I knew only as Amafo now floated in a sphere of light before a living, breathing tree.

All froze—light, wind, even the pulsing fog—all but my Amafo. He tilted his head and I saw by the soft shimmer of his skin that he was crying.

He held the tilt. The light fell pure. Only his hands moved, slowly lifting to his face. His fingers unfurled as he wiped the moisture from his cheeks.

When he turned his palms to the tree, the tree was gone.

I saw now what my Amafo saw, maybe what he had always seen, the sacred life in all of it. I saw Amafo touching the tears from the tips of his fingers and spreading his moist longing on the face of the panther, my grandmother, *koi chitto*, my Pokoni. I stood in awe of what I saw and what I now knew, that Pokoni and the Walking Ones would be with us forever, till we join them in the Walk.

FINAL RECKONING

SOMEBODY LOOKING TO DIE

Rose • Remembrances 1968

I am old and dying and someone should know. I have long ago lost my best friend in the world, Roberta Jean Willis. I know she wants me to speak of that night, to reveal the mysteries.

The sight of Pokoni as the panther was startling, but in another sense it came as no surprise. I had always felt Pokoni would never leave us. I had always known she was nearby. During the long ride home, the panther's eyes sent the fear of death through me, but part of me always knew Pokoni would be there, helping us as best she could. When I saw Amafo smoothing his tears on her face, I knew the time had come for me to help my friend.

Since the night of her attack, Roberta Jean had taken to sitting next to me at church. I still occupied my place by the window, three rows back on the cedar bench. Now she sat beside me. We seldom spoke, but if the sermon should refer to an event that was likely to trigger a deep and fearful memory in her—*Yea though I walk through the valley of the shadow of death*—I would squeeze her hand and let her know I was there for her.

But part of knowing was this. Roberta Jean would never, could never, feel safe as long as he was alive. We both had tasted fear borne of his look and we knew that to speak of it was futile.

Standing at the window and staring at the two, the panther and my grandfather, I shook my head and turned away. I turned away from the sacred scene, from Pokoni and Amafo. I left the blue-starred mug on the windowsill and picked up my Amafo's dress hat, the one he always wore to town. I quickly crossed the hall to my bedroom, dressed in the warmest clothes I had, and slipped out the front door.

The dread of what I would say and how I could ever awaken Roberta Jean without Samuel knowing, these thoughts so occupied my mind that the distance and the cold were as nothing. Soon I stood before the home of Preacher Willis. The windows eyed me, asking why. The porch seemed to set her lips and bow in the knowing that my will was strong.

I crept to her window and stood tapping my fingertips on the glass, softly so I could barely myself hear the tapping. Only a moment passed and she appeared, wide-awake as if she had been lying on her bedcovers, sensing the night's beckoning. I waved a palm at myself, motioning for her to come outside. She pointed to the front door and placed her finger to her lips.

Five minutes later we stood by the road before the Willis place, in the shadows of a sycamore tree and far enough away from the house to speak.

"I think he is alive," I said. "The marshal."

"Where is he? What has he done?" she asked.

"I think he is after us. He tried to kill us tonight. He stalked us through the woods. We cannot live like this, waiting till he kills again. Lillie Chukma…"

"I know," she said, stopping me. "His home? Do you think he's at home?"

"I think so. Yes."

We walked in silence, neither of us knowing what we would do at Marshal Hardwicke's home. We followed the railroad tracks for what seemed like hours. Dark ice still clung to the trees, thick and groping. When we reached the curve on the tracks south of the Hardwicke place, we angled down the steep hill to keep from stumbling, finally landing in the old stone-covered graveyard.

I said a quiet prayer and picked up a gravestone big as the foot of a boot.

"Here," said Roberta Jean, reaching out her upturned palms. "This is for me to do." She took the stone from me and carried it beneath her arm as we approached the dark and lifeless house. We crossed the back pasture till we heard the whining and yelping of dogs, the marshal's hunting dogs. We began to run, not fearful running, but purposeful running, in the direction of the house.

We were crouching and catching our breath beside a run-down arbor when the dogs came at us. I grabbed a branch as long as I was tall and waved it at the dogs, slapping their faces. These were trained hunting dogs and knew how to circle their prey and attack from many sides at once. I knew we only had a moment till they flung themselves on us and we were on the ground fighting for our lives.

"Hey! 'Mon boys! Hey!" called Hardwicke, in a twangy, high-pitched voice, followed by a quick burst of whistles. The dogs stopped their lunging and backed away, only a few feet, growling deep-throated threats and still facing us. I threw Amafo's hat to the ground and the dogs leapt for it, tearing it with their teeth.

Marshal Hardwicke appeared on the back porch wearing britches and a coat pulled over his undershirt. In the dim light of the moon I could see scars running down the side of his face. Claw markings. The blood shone dark red and glistened on his cheek.

"*Yakoke*, Pokoni," I whispered.

We hid as best we could while the marshal leaned against a roof support and pulled on his boots, never taking his eyes off the arbor, squinting and calling softly, "What you got there, boys? Something coming round our house looking for trouble?"

He approached the dogs and wrestled Amafo's hat from them, grabbing the crown and ripping it from their frothing mouths. "Look like maybe somebody ready to die," he said, fingering the hat and eying the dark field behind us.

"You out there, old man?" he called out. "You think you gonna come for me? That it, old man? This is worth coming home for," he said, turning to the house. The dogs came at us again, circling and barking. "Hey doggies!" called Hardwicke. "Let him be for now."

Hardwicke walked to the house in a rush and climbed the three steps. He stomped on the back porch and took a hopping skip, then swung his leg sideways and kicked the door with such force we could hear the pine board crack and splinter, all the time hollering, "Git me my gun! Now! We got a prowler here."

Ona Mae Hardwicke came to his calling, but not in her usual manner. During the year of his leaving, a year of basking in the sun of life without questions, Ona Mae had changed. Hardwicke had not. Unable to feed his hatred with the blood of either the old man— Amafo—or the old man's family, Hardwicke had instead turned, that very night, to his most familiar victim, his wife.

As she stood in the doorway holding his shotgun, Ona Mae wore the bruises of the beating, her first in over a year.

When Robert Hardwicke reached for his gun, Ona Mae raised the barrel and shot him in the chest. The shotgun blast lifted him from his feet and he staggered for a moment, waving his arms to steady himself. When he regained his balance, he lowered his head to look at the blood pouring from his chest. He knew he was dying.

A final gust of anger swept across his face and his cheeks turned red. He glared at Ona Mae. I thought for certain she would drop the gun and flee into the house. She did not flee. Ona Mae stood her ground. Hardwicke lifted his doubled-up fist to strike one last unforgettable blow across his wife's face. For twenty years Ona Mae had longed for the strength to stand up to him. And now she did. When his fist fell like a heavy stone, her arm was there to block it.

His knees buckled and a soft *humff* came from his mouth. Hardwicke tried to raise his arms and grab her. Ona Mae never flinched. She stood staring at her husband till his last ounce of hatred oozed away and he lost his balance completely, falling backwards down the stairs. By the time he hit the ground, hard enough to bounce his head, his body was limp and lifeless.

The dogs ran to Hardwicke and began licking his chest. They lifted their faces and we could see their bloody tongues smacking as they swallowed. Ona Mae held the shotgun firm. No one could ever know for how many years she held her guard up, unable to fully bathe in the cleansing waters of his death. She stared at us as if we would try to take the gun away.

Roberta Jean held the heavy stone high as her chest, then reached her arms out in offering, as if to show our common intent. Ona Mae nodded, and gave us in return a slow and beautiful dance to see. Her feet and legs unmoving, she twisted her shoulders and torso and slowly knelt to lean the shotgun up against the door, her head and neck held tall, her eyes upon her husband lest he rise and once again return. Still moving in the thick fog of her deliberateness, her silent dancing liturgy, she took three steps and sat on the edge of the porch, smoothing her dress and gathering it tight around her knees.

We looked into each other's eyes and moved to join her, Roberta to her right and I to her left. The moment soon was broken as Samuel stepped from the shadows of the arbor. We joined Ona Mae in rising.

"You shouldn't touch him," he said, without so much as a glance at the marshal. Noting our surprise, he continued, "You know I couldn't let you come by yourselves." He approached the porch and laid Reverend Willis' pistol on the top step.

"Rose and 'Berta, you got to leave. Now. No telling who heard the shot. Come morning we'll have a good story to cover it. Prowlers. Ona Mae shooting over the heads of prowlers."

He slapped Amafo's hat against the side of his hip, saying, "Your grandpa's just gonna have to lose his hat and you can't tell nobody, not even him, where it got off to. No way of explaining the marshal's dog's chewing on his hat. I'll see it gets burned tonight."

When no one moved, he said, "Maybe be best if you girls went through the house, soes you won't leave no more tracks.

Samuel spoke to us as a big brother might, hardly as one two years junior to Roberta Jean, but his surprising arrival and the firm readiness of his logic gave no berth for hesitation. He gestured and we moved through the kitchen door, pausing only to watch his quiet doings with Ona Mae.

"Ma'am," he said to her, speaking more softly than he had to us. He bowed his head and climbed the back steps, then reached behind himself to help our people's newest member, our Choctaw family's newest adopted one, ascend the steps of her home. In vanquishing our common enemy she soon, we knew, would take her place among the most revered of elders, be she yet so young.

"I think it better if you stay inside," said Samuel, holding the door open for Ona Mae. "You never saw your husband, in case anybody asks. But if we do our job tonight, nobody will. We best carry this secret to our graves, all of us. All we know is the marshal died going on a year now."

Ona Mae nodded.

"It's a long way home," he said, turning to Roberta Jean and me. "Stay in the dark and don't be seen." He then slipped out the back door in the full expectation that his orders would be followed.

"He is right. You girls must leave now. Come see me in a day or two," Ona Mae said, trying to mask the pleading in her voice. As we left the kitchen, I heard another man talking. I turned just in time to see Colonel Tobias Mingo emerging from the darkness.

He lifted Hardwicke's shoulders from the ground, Samuel took his legs, and the two of them carried him past his sleepy, full-bellied dogs.

Best I could make out from later talkings—talkings I was not intended to hear—Tobias and Samuel dragged and carried the marshal all the way past Fort Coffee and to the river, a several miles distance. True to his word, Samuel burned Amafo's hat, digging out a hole between two thick roots of an old elm tree. Tobias tore off the marshal's shirt and stuffed his chest and belly with dark river mud to quell the blood flow, then they rolled him over so he lay face down, his body some six feet from the river. His back was a scrawling map of claw markings, swollen lines of glistening purple and red.

"Anybody wanting to know how he died not gonna have any trouble finding out," said Tobias. "Just have to roll him back over. That mud not gonna fool anybody don't want to be fooled."

"I cain't think of a soul gonna care," said Samuel, "Choctaw or Nahullo either one."

"That's what we got to count on," replied Tobias.

"Besides all that, he's already been buried, according to the law."

"Uh-huh, and grieved over besides."

"Some stranger to these parts saw the river, approached it, and missed seeing the panther watering nearby," said Samuel.

"Plain to see, claw marks of a panther," said Tobias.

"That's how I'd rule, if I was the law."

"You the only law I see."

"Wonder who's gonna find the body?" Samuel asked.

"Something tells me the Bobb brothers gonna stumble 'cross it."

"Sounds like a good idea to me. If the two of 'em happen to see it, they'd be strong enough to drag it to their wagon and get it to town."

Both men removed their hats and said a few private words in respect for the dead. By the time they pivoted away from Marshal Hardwicke and moved in a swift walk in the direction of their respective homes, all thoughts had turned to their own most beloved, Tobias to his wife Hannah and Samuel to his Rose.

CIRCLE OF BURIED SECRETS

Following the death of Marshal Hardwicke, later referred to in legal documents as "the animal mauling of an unknown intruder," the Bobb brothers discovered the body on an early morning hunting trip. They wrapped the body in an old blanket and removed it to the mortuary.

Agent Taylor supervised a private and lengthy inspection of the body, attended only by himself and undertaker Ebert Hermann. The true cause of death was quickly ascertained, as was the identity of both the deceased and the shooter in light of the obvious bruises to the face of Mrs. Hardwicke.

"Ebert?" Taylor asked.

"Yes."

"Do I need to tell you how the autopsy report will read?"

"No, Agent Taylor, you do not. I wish I had pulled the trigger myself."

"The body of this unknown intruder will be wrapped and buried within the hour, with no announcement of what has occurred save for a small notice in the obituary column," said Taylor.

"Of course, and no further mention will be made, not by myself."

"You are a good man, Ebert Hermann."

"Thank you, Agent Taylor." The two men shook hands, and minutes later, as Taylor snapped the reins and turned his wagon homeward, Hermann rolled the body, minus a coffin, onto his funeral wagon and took the back road to the pauper's grave. He was followed by a sleek black cat who sat in the shadows of a red oak tree till the final shoveful of dirt fell down upon the marshal.

As the body of Robert Hardwicke settled into the dark clay, Idabell Taylor prepared and served her husband a much-appreciated noon meal of fried pork and corn-on-the-cob. "Wonderful," Taylor said, leaning back in his chair and rubbing the full expanse of his ample mid-section. "Nothing like a Cherokee meal for a hungry white man," he laughed.

"I am glad you enjoyed it," Idabell said. Something about the manner in which his wife sat staring at him disturbed Mr. Taylor. Her usual habit, after thirty-five years of marriage, was to clear the table of dishes and bring him a glass of Scotch whiskey, along with the full bottle for him to partake of freely, depending on the afternoon's activities.

"What is it, dear?" he asked.

"You know of the upcoming sale of used and discarded clothing?"

"Yes," Taylor replied, wiping butter from his mouth and picking corn from between his teeth. "To benefit the displaced girls, I believe."

"Yes. To benefit the displaced girls. We will be selling mostly women's clothing."

"Well, I think it is a worthy cause."

"Yes, a worthy cause."

Mrs. Taylor paused till her husband eyed her curiously. "What?" he asked.

"There is another purpose. I have spoken to only a few women about it.

"Another purpose?"

"Yes. A personal purpose. I have donated all of my scarves."

"I don't understand. Why are you telling me this?"

Mrs. Taylor reached beneath the table and patted her husband on the knee before continuing. "For too many years my scarves and sleeves have served a need. They have hidden the bruises, dear. The bruises. The marshal is dead and gone. So are the bruises. *My* bruises. I will, from this day forward, wear my bruises, not my scarf. Do you understand now?"

The agent looked to his hands, folded across his belly, and moved them to his lap. For the briefest of moments, Idabell thought her threat had worked, a threat suggested by an elderly church friend, Mrs. Blakely, who had abandoned her own scarves ten years earlier following the death of her husband, a local purveyor of farming supplies.

Taylor lifted his eyes and saw his wife's strong and unflinching gaze. He reached for her hand and took it in his own.

"You would tell anyone, anyone who asked, the source of your bruises, if I understand what you are telling me?"

"Yes."

"From a fall, an accidental slipping in the kitchen?"

"No."

"You will stay inside and I will tell them you are feeling ill or not yourself. Like before, like always."

"No, I will no longer let you lie about me."

"Then how will you explain the cut across your lip, the swelling of your cheeks?" With every word, Taylor gripped her hand harder and his voice took on a vile and hateful tone. "How will you say you got them?"

"From the fist of my husband. That is what I will tell them."

Taylor twisted her wrist, and when Idabell struggled to wrench herself free of him, he squeezed it till the tears flowed down her face.

"I will kill you first," he said, clenching his teeth into a bitter meanness she had not witnessed since the early years of their marriage.

"You *will* have to kill me to keep me silent," Idabell said and spat into his face. In the fury of his surprise, Taylor released his grip and lunged across the table, his palms open and aiming for her throat. Idabell rose, very deliberately smoothed her dress, and turned to the front door, as if she were alone and answering a knock. In full view of Saturday morning travelers flocking to Spiro, she stepped to the porch a moment before he reached her.

Ona Mae was baking apples in the kitchen when she heard the knock. Whisked from the memory of her grandmother's cheerful banter and cinnamon-spotted apron, she wiped her hands on a dishtowel and stepped lightly to the door. She paused when she saw Idabell Taylor. Her hand went to her chest and short breaths pursed her lips. The darkness of the killing fell like a sodden fog.

I am a widow, she thought. *I defended myself. How much do they know? I will never tell them. No one keeps secrets like I keep secrets. I will take my secrets to the grave.*

She craned her neck to the window to see if Agent Taylor accompanied his wife as he had on the previous visit. Seeing only Idabell, she turned and panned the room with a slow gaze, seeking some safe place or object she could slip into and thus remain unseen.

Anyone watching, even God, she thought, *would never see me as alive. I am whitened dead and drained of blood, guiltless of everything below.* Ona Mae smoothed her hair with one slow stroke of her right hand, then slid her wrist across her neck. With the second louder knocking, her body jerked against her will. She wrapped her long fingers around her throat and took a deep breath.

I will take my secrets to the grave, she thought, and opened the door.

"Ona Mae. May I come in? May I please come in?"

"Yes. You may come in. I am by myself, you know."

"Not any more, you are not. I need to stay with you for a while."

As soon as he heard of the intruder, John Burleson let his workers know he would be "unavailable today, maybe for a few days," and drove to the Hardwicke homestead. He was relieved when Mrs. Taylor answered the door.

"How is Ona Mae?" he asked.

"I think she will recover. It may take a day or two, but she's doing well, considering."

"I don't want to be a bother," he said, removing his hat and looking over her shoulder, hoping to catch a glance of Ona Mae.

"Just a moment," said Idabell, closing the door behind her. After a brief pause, Ona Mae appeared.

"So good to see you," she said. "Thank you for coming. Please come in. We both would like to speak to you."

Thus John Burleson was welcomed into the circle of buried secrets. An hour later he found Samuel Willis feeding cane to the sorghum press behind the Willis' house. He relayed the message that Ona Mae needed him and Colonel Mingo to stay at the Hardwicke place for a few days.

"What is happening there?" asked Samuel.

"She is afraid," said Burleson. "Mrs. Taylor is with her, but they'd both feel better having you two look out for them. You'll do it, won't you, son?" Samuel noted a pleading look he had never seen on the face of the stationmaster.

"I'll tell my father and be on my way," he said.

The first night, Samuel and Tobias settled into a thicket of pines and undergrowth, allowing full view of the front door. When the women retired, Samuel slipped quietly through the back door, using the key Ona Mae had entrusted to their care. He spent the remainder of the night at the kitchen table, his father's rifle loaded and ready. By the second day, at Mrs. Taylor's suggestion, the two spent the morning seated at a table—moved from the dining room to the front porch—for any and all passers-by to see.

"If we have need of protection," she said, "people should know. They might even lend a hand. You never know the choices folks might make."

In a way she could never have expected, Idabell's speculation came to life before the women's awed and grateful eyes. Thinking the ladies were in seclusion and surrounded for protection from unknown intruders—possible gang members of the first night's now-dead assailant—a dozen men, urged by their wives, spent the second night playing cards in the kitchen and alternately patrolling the grounds of the Hardwicke place. Little did they suspect what their wives already knew, that by his very absence the feared assailant was Agent Taylor himself.

Four days later, with no disturbance by day or night, and life apparently returning to some semblance of normality, the men returned home, leaving only Samuel to guard the ladies. As soon as the last man, Matt Blankenship, had saddled his horse and returned to his own life, Mrs. Taylor returned to what was left of hers.

When she entered her house, she saw her husband seated where she left him, the empty whiskey bottle toppled over on the table in front of him. He lifted his eyes to her and asked, "Do you know anyone named Estella?"

"Estella?"

"Yes. Estella Roe? Is she a friend of yours? Was she ever?"

"Have you thought of what I said to you?" Idabell asked.

"Oh, yes," he said. "I have thought of nothing else for the last four days. Please tell me. Have you ever heard of Estella Roe?"

"No. I don't think I have."

"I have dreamed about her, seen her grave, every night since you left."

Idabell sighed and looked through the window to the distant limestone bluffs. The grandfather clock's ticking measured the moment and the room filled with the glow of settling evening. A sparrow flew across her vision and left behind the crimson stretch of clouds on sloping hills.

"I have seen her death," he said. "By the hand of her own husband. He beat her so until she died. I have seen this every night. A terrible vision."

"This is not about scarves, you know."

"No. Not about scarves. So much deeper. Can you ever find a way to forgive me?" he asked. He hung his head and reached for her, closing his eyes and lifting his palms.

"I hope we can get through this," she said, taking his hands in hers.

TRAIN COMES TO SPIRO
November 1897

On the slim chance that Maggie might receive the news, Agent Taylor placed a second notice in the newspapers of Galveston, Texas; Santa Fe, New Mexico; St. Louis, Missouri; and New Orleans, Louisiana.

> To Maggie & Terrance Lowell, be it known that a stranger, similar in build to Marshal Hardwicke, has been found dead and will be buried two days hence. You both are welcome in Spiro. Your safety and freedom from persecution I once again will guarantee. Mrs. Taylor says hello and urges you to come.

Two weeks later the following letter appeared, addressed to Agent Taylor.

> Agent and Mrs. Taylor:
> Terrance and I have decided to accept your invitation. We have been living in Galveston, Texas, since our departure from Spiro. We will be arriving by train next Saturday, November 24, in time for the holiday. Terrance says hello. He can read now, he wanted me to mention.

No one was more excited than Hiram to hear the news. A dozen times a day he told the story of Terrance holding a butter knife to his throat and threatening to *do me in! With a butter knife! But Maggie wouldn't hear of it. She bashed him in the head with her leg! The wooden one, you know.*

The two o'clock train was on time. Terrance was, of course, terrified. As the train rounded Gilliam's Hill and started breaking for its entry into Spiro, he read aloud the black-lettered sign facing the train a quarter mile from the depot.

"Spy-ro."

"How are you doing?" asked Maggie.

"Lemme just tell you this," Terrance said. "Did you see that cemetery we passed about a mile ago?"

"Yes."

"Well, Maggie, that's where I'd be right now, if it wasn't for you. The marshal would have hung me and buried me, and that's where I'd be."

The train jolted with the sharp sound of screeching brakes.

"Come to think of it," said Terrance, "resting nice and peaceful under those cemetery elm trees doesn't sound too bad."

Maggie squeezed his hand. "Don't talk like that, Terrance. I couldn't live without you." She leaned over him and peered out the window at the crowd gathered on the landing. "I wonder how Hiram is doing without *me?*"

Hiram was Hiram and he was doing fine, having hired two young Choctaw girls to take Maggie's place, one the granddaughter of *that friendly old fellow, the one the marshal beat up on, you know.* To the surprise of all, his business had actually increased since Maggie's departure. Choctaws by the dozens crowded the aisles on those ever-increasing occasions when Hiram himself proclaimed a sale.

"Wonder how Maggie is holding up without me?" he asked Dr. McGilleon, as the two stood shoulder to shoulder, craning their necks to get a look as the train made its approach. Dr. McGilleon started to speak, but the wispy thread of a spiderweb floated from the eave and settled on the tip of his nose. He brushed it away and glanced upward to see a long-legged spider nestled in the rafter. *No harm*, he thought. *Not a poisonous variety.*

The train pulled into Spiro with a long exhale of steaming breath and the gentle rocking back and forth of passengers and luggage. Hundreds of people stood on the platform, some holding signs reading "Welcome Home, Maggie."

"Would you look at that!" said Maggie, kissing Terrance on the cheek. He lifted his eyes in a wry smile and nodded his head.

"As long as you are with me, I'll get through this fine," he said.

Once most of the other passengers were disembarked, Terrance stepped down and dragged the luggage to a spot against the depot wall. Maggie waited and gathered her courage, realizing they would never know Terrance without her by his side. She stepped aside and allowed an elderly woman to pass.

Terrance offered his hand to the older woman, who took it gratefully. She eased herself down, halting for a moment on each step before reaching for the next one. When she stood on solid ground, she squeezed his hand and he lifted his eyes to meet hers.

"That was nice of you, young man," she said. At the sight of his hazel eyes, she caught her breath. Her mind soared through years of school sights and smells: pine benches, dusty books, and struggling children doing their best to please her. Her journey ended thirty years ago, staring at the face of a poor, sweet child.

"You have nice eyes," she once told him. "I call their color hazel. They are your eyes. Look at them some time." *What was that boy's name?* A moment later she had her answer.

"Terrance!" a voice called. "Are we ready for this?"

"Yes," said Terrance Lowell. Miss Palmer staggered to the lone empty bench as the crowd passed her by, attracted by Maggie's voice. Miss Palmer bowed her head, beaming at the man he had become. *Terrance Lowell*, she whispered. *Look at you now.*

Ona Mae stood inside the depot waiting room, apart from the crowd, watching as the train screeched and shook and pulled to a halt, the biggest engine she had ever seen. She clutched her ticket a little tighter. Two large suitcases sat beside her.

"Dallas?" John Burleson had asked an hour earlier when she purchased the ticket.

"Yes, please. One-way to Dallas. My brother and his family are there."

"One-way?"

"Yes. Please."

"When…how…will you be returning?"

"I do not plan on returning."

Burleson looked at her in a way she found disturbing. She slid three crisp bills across the counter. He handed her the ticket and stepped away from the counter. "Son," he said, addressing a young attendant. "Take over here for me, will you?"

"Yes sir, Mister Burleson," the man replied, stepping smartly to the counter and adjusting his bowtie.

Ona Mae watched as John Burleson appeared through a side door and reached for the suitcases. "Let me store them in the back room for you, out of the way, till the train comes," he said. Ona Mae nodded. He carried the suitcases down a short hallway and returned.

"Fine," he said. "Now, you can wait here or on the platform, though it is getting crowded out there, what with Maggie coming home today. Why don't you stay inside? There's an empty seat," he said, pointing to a tiny round table against a wall away from the windows. "Be nice and quiet for you. I'll have the waiter bring you tea. A piece of cake. My treat?"

When she hesitated, he said, "Please. Let me do this."

"That would be nice," Ona Mae said. "Thank you."

An hour later Ona Mae stood in a stupor by the window, hoping to move quickly through the crowd and board the train to the city without being seen and recognized—as she prepared to leave her home and the few adult friends she had ever known.

"Ona Mae?"

"Yes." She turned to see John Burleson.

"Would you please come with me? I would like to speak with you in private. For only a moment."

He turned and walked down the hallway without waiting to see if Ona Mae intended to follow. When she stepped through the door of the storeroom, he reached over her shoulder and closed it quietly.

"I cannot let you go," he said.

"I have purchased my ticket. What are you saying?"

"Ona Mae, I am so afraid at what I am about to do. Please be easy on me." He slipped an arm around her and pulled her to his chest. To his great relief, she did not resist.

Neither Ona Mae Hardwicke nor John Burleson were familiar enough with the nuances of love and touch to know what to do next, so they simply stood and held onto each other in the warmest embrace of their lives, till the noise of Maggie's stepping from the train, the cheers and clapping, awakened the two to the need for decisions.

"What can we do? What will we do?" she asked.

"I don't know what we will do. I only know what we won't do. I won't carry your luggage and you won't get on that train."

"I cannot live in his house. I will not live there."

"I can't live here at the station," John said. "Not now. Not anymore. I have land, a good piece of river bottom land. Good farming land, just a short walk from the river. The fireflies are so beautiful there in the summer. When I was younger I used to ride out to the bottoms just to watch them. Sometimes in the middle of the night. Especially after she died, my wife. The fireflies were so bright."

Ona Mae squeezed her eyes tight shut to hold onto the spell.

"I can build you a house, build us a house." John paused and looked at Ona Mae's bowed head. He touched her hair. "I know how it was with you. We all did. I banged my fists against the wall every time you came to town, to see you hiding yourself, lowering your eyes and… and being so afraid. No more of that, never again. I'll build a house for you. I have good timber on my land, a good stand of cedar lining the river. It's stout, straight cedar, good for planks."

"John?"

"Yes."

"Why would you do this?"

"Because you have been in my thoughts every day for years. You are the only thing left for me here. You never knew that?"

"I think I knew. I was afraid to think of it. I always thought…"

"What?"

"I always thought no one else would have me."

"Oh," he moaned. "What we do to hide from each other. How come we are so hard on ourselves?"

Ona Mae took his massive hands and looked John Burleson square in the eyes.

"Will you do something else for me?"

"Of course."

"Will you call me Mae? Not Ona Mae. Just Mae."

"Mae," he said, tilting his head. "Mae?" A smile curled at the edge of his lips. "Mae. Ahh. I like that. From now on you can be my Mae."

"You will build a house for me?"

"Oh, yes," he said, in full understanding of the vows they were exchanging. "I will build a house for you. A house of purple cedar."

POKINI'S WHISPERINGS

Rose • 1967

Death closes in on me now. I need no owl to tell me so—I've never put much stock in fearing owls. Staring at the cold unfertile egg upon my plate, I know the world was once a warm and sweeter place, full of runny yellow yolk and salt crystals perched on crunchy toast. I look backwards from the egg and my salt-free breakfast and my destiny is always the same—the white wooden Choctaw church in Skullyville.

Last night I had my dream again. I could simply say I saw a vision, but it was stronger than that. I had a vision—I birthed, I breathed to life, I lived a fleeting moment of vision. It was and is a vision for all the yet unborn ones, and it was thus.

We gathered in the church and sang, shape-note singing of a sweet old hymn, brought by the Methodists but now sung by two hundred Choctaws. Over and over we sang, till the Methodist skin flaked away and the dark red Choctaw clay hummed with sound. Every board of our little church vibrated with the music till our words filled the building and the sky as well.

Come all who love the Lord
And lift your voices high
We're marching to Immanuel's call,
We're marching to Immanuel's call,
So dance around the throne,
So dance around the throne.

We're marching to Zion,
Beautiful, beautiful Zion,
We're marching upward to Zion,
The beautiful city of God.

We stared at the man nailed to the wall behind the pulpit. Brother Willis sang. We all sang. The cross was painted on the wall. The man's clothes were nailed to the wall, and his eyes pleaded with us to relieve his pain. He writhed until we all knew his suffering, his tormented mind that would not set him free. Nailed to the cross of his own skin, of his own deeds, and longing to be free.

I squinted my eyes and tried so hard to see his face, but with every breath his cheeks rose and swelled.

I thought of all the suffering ones I had known. I thought of Mrs. Hardwicke and the cruelties she endured. I thought of Sarah McCurtain and the children she had lost. I remembered seeing my Amafo lying on the railroad platform, lifeless as a dried rabbit hide. Lillie Chukma held in the outstretched arms of her mother.

I stared into the face of the man nailed to the wall, but it was unrecognizable in the rising and sucking of the cheeks and nostrils.

We sang and stared, all of us, longing to see the face of the Suffering One. Then Pokoni came. The door to the church opened and my grandmother came, walking down the aisle. With one step she was the panther. With the next she was my Pokoni on the day she died.

She crept and walked and still we sang. With a nod to Reverend Willis, she circled the pulpit to kneel before the writhing one. The panther left forever and it was only my grandmother, my Pokoni, my tender Pokoni, my beautiful grandmother of my Amafo's eyes, younger and younger she grew, till I saw her as a little girl, fast and darting everywhere she went, running while others walked, her hands gripped a cat, stroked a dog, patted a birthing momma cow, touched my grandfather on the arm, kissed his lips, held her baby, my mother, older by the moment, till there she stood, surrounded by her grandchildren, finally lying sweet and blissful on the kitchen floor, covered in a quilt of yellowing gardenias, there she lay.

Now she stood before the one nailed to the cross.

The echoes of the hymn rang and shook the boards of the church, the ceiling, walls, and floor, before settling into a quiet and holy living moment. Only then, with the settling, did I know.

How could I not have known before the name of the one who suffered so before us? Now we all knew. My Pokoni returned to help us see. She touched his feet and he lifted his head to her. My Pokoni and the Suffering One, Robert Efram Hardwicke, staring at each other.

I trembled in disbelief at the blasphemy, the mockery, of his presence, that he should even be here on this most holy of all days. Knowing what he did, knowing how he lived his life, I can never forgive him. Pokoni turned to us and spoke.

"It is not for you to judge. That's for the Lord to do. He must face the Lord on Judgement Day and own up to the deeds that he has done. And if he wants the Lord's forgiveness, he must ask for it."

He stared at her as she spoke, and when she finished he lifted his face to look at us, the congregation of the church he so defiled. On these very steps he attacked the daughter of the preacher, Brother Willis. His eyes scanned the crowd.

He is looking for her, I thought. *She was the cause of his downfall.*

He closed his eyes and bowed his head in shame. I wrestled with forgiveness, knowing now the suffering of his dark life.

"No!" I shouted. "In the name of Lillie Chukma, no!"

I caught the scent of gardenias and Pokoni whispered in my ear.

"It is not for you to judge," she said. "Remember, he was a small one once, a weak and helpless one. To see him always as the standing over one, the mean-eyed one, the cruel-fisted one, is not to know. Knowing is different. Knowing is this.

"He threw the blows because he caught the blows. To think we put an end to him by slaying him is not to know, for we must kill the father and the father and the father yet before him, till wrapped in the blood-soaked cloth of all the killing, drowning in the blood of all the killing, we stand before the Tree, the first Tree, and wrapped around the Tree we find the father in us all, the unslayable one, the serpent. Nor gun, nor knife, nor stone can ever touch the living serpent.

"But something can, and it lies dormant too, within us all. It is the heaviest of all to wield, it falls so clumsily, so foreign to our thinking. Knowing is this. Forgiveness slays the serpent. It withers in the Light."

ACKNOWLEDGMENTS

One chilly winter night in 1998, I was driving through the Choctaw Nation seeking Helen Harris, a friend I'd met at a conference. The roads were icy and dangerous, but I finally found her home. Her husband graciously retired and left us sitting by the fire. She told me of a similar night, years past, when her mother drove a horse-drawn wagon through the icy dark, as she and her brother curled beneath a blanket. She whispered of the panther that followed them and suggested it was a protector. Thus began a fifteen-year journey that led to Skullyville.

I would like to thank my friend and fellow Choctaw, Greg Rodgers, who carried books, boards, and slung paint on the *Purple* walls through the final years of constructing this *Cedar House*. We drove thousands of miles and crossed so many graveyards we now have a large circle of friends who are residents—from Boggy Depot to Skullyville— and we both became writers in the process. *Yakoke* to Choctaws Helen Harris, Charley Jones, Reverend Bertram Bobb, Jay McAlvain, Judy Allen, Lisa Reed, Lee Francis, Leroy Sealey, Tony Byars, Buck Wade and Lizzie Carney, who all have left their footprints in this novel. A grateful bow to Mississippi Choctaws Estelline Tubby and Archie Mingo, and to members of the Choctaw Alliance of Oklahoma City—Stella Long, Catfish Bryant, and his brothers Kenny and Billy Bryant.

And to Choctaw Freedman Levester McKeeson, who lived near Skullyville and knew many of its secrets. To the library staff of Spiro and the many townspeople who shared their knowledge of the times, thank you.

Yakoke to writers LeAnne Howe, Louis Owens, Rilla Askew, poet Jim Barnes, researchers and writers H.B. Cushman, Angie Debo, Dan Littlefield, Clara Sue Kidwell, Dan Birchfield, Donna Akers, Tom Mould, Arthus DeRosier, Devon Mihesuah and—may they forever feel a glow of gratitude from Choctaws everywhere—John Swanton and Cyrus Byington. Doc Moore, my tri-book co-author, Lisa Eister, Susan Feller, Mary Gay Ducey and Dr. Michael Flanigan, my OU writing instructor, have shared valuable insights.

Respectful nods to fellow University of Oklahoma writers, Les Hanna and Phil Morgan. The support of Choctaw Councilmen, now and for the past twenty years, is gratefully appreciated. Chief Gregory Pyle and Assistant Chief Gary Batton provide the most powerful leadership the Choctaw people have ever known.

The folks at Cinco Puntos have earned a Choctaw name, *Okla Ahoshonti*—Cloud People—because they float above.

TIM TINGLE

Tim Tingle is an Oklahoma Choctaw and an award-winning author. His great-great grandfather, John Carnes, walked the Trail of Tears in 1835, and his paternal grandmother attended a series of rigorous Indian boarding schools in the early 1900s. Responding to a scarcity of Choctaw lore, Tingle initiated a search for historical and personal narrative accounts in the early 1990s.

In 1992, Tingle began mentoring with Choctaw storyteller Charley Jones. Tim retraced the Trail of Tears to Choctaw homelands in Mississippi and began recording stories of tribal elders. His family experiences and these interviews with fellow Choctaws in Texas, Alabama, Mississippi and Oklahoma—over two hundred hours and counting—are the basis of his most important writings.

Tingle received his master's degree in English Literature, with a focus on American Indian studies, at the University of Oklahoma in 2003. While teaching freshmen writing courses and completing his thesis, "Choctaw Oral Literature," Tingle wrote his first book, *Walking the Choctaw Road*. It was selected by both Oklahoma and Alaska as Book of the Year in the "One Book, One State" program, and is now studied at universities across the United States and abroad.

Every Labor Day, Tingle shares a Choctaw narrative before Chief Gregory Pyle's State of the Nation Address, a gathering that attracts over ninety thousand tribal members and friends. In June of 2011, Tingle spoke at the Library of Congress and presented his first performance at the Kennedy Center in Washington, D.C. From 2011 to the present, he has been a featured author at "Choctaw Days," a celebration honoring the Oklahoma Choctaws at the Smithsonian's National Museum of the American Indian.

Tingle is the author of ten books, including *Walking the Choctaw Road, Saltypie* (Cinco Puntos Press), *How I Became a Ghost* (Roadrunner Press), and *Danny Blackgoat, Navajo Prisoner* (7th Generation). His first children's book, *Crossing Bok Chitto* (Cinco Puntos Press), was an Editor's Choice in the *New York Times Book Review*. It garnered over twenty state and national awards, including Best Children's Book from the American Indian Library Association.

House of Purple Cedar was fifteen years in the crafting. Filled with hope in the most tragic of circumstances, *House of Purple Cedar* is Tingle's testament to Choctaw elders who continue to watch over the well-being of the Choctaw Nation and its people.

MORE GREAT FICTION FROM CINCO PUNTOS PRESS

Out of Their Minds by Luis Humberto Crosthwaite

Everything Begins & Ends at the Kentucky Club by Benjamin Alire Sáenz

Conquistador of the Useless by Joshua Isard

Make It, Take It by Rus Bradburd

Country of the Bad Wolfes by James Carlos Blake

Frontera Dreams by Paco Ignacio Taibo II